I0628381

Made by the Master's Hand

By

Joan Byrd

Deep Indigo Books
Published by Indigo Sea Press
Winston-Salem

Deep Indigo Books
Indigo Sea Press
302 Ricks Drive
Winston-Salem, NC 27103

First Deep Indigo Books edition published
May, 2022

For information regarding bulk purchases of this book, digital purchase and special discounts, please contact the publisher at indigoseapress@gmail.com

Manufactured in the United States of America
ISBN 978-1-63066-538-8

Dedication

Those who have been given the gift by God to become a carpenter, have been blessed to share the same profession as Jesus, our Lord. There are many devoted builders throughout the world and occasionally one is born among us who stands out. Their work is exceptional and these carpenters are sought after by many people. One such man, born January 19th, 1919, was one of God's gifted carpenters.

Lindsay "Tip" Bodsford and Ray Byrd

Lindsay "Tip" Bodsford had a special gift for carpentry and he was known for his expert skills. Like Joseph, Tip trained younger men in the skills of becoming fine carpenters, grandsons, sons-in-law, and others wanting to learn. One of Tip's famous quotes was, if you're about to hammer a finishing nail in the finished work, if you miss the nail, you better hit your thumb!"

One of his last projects was restoring our 1929 farmhouse, the actual home Tip grew up in with his three brothers, four sisters, and his parents. I am so blessed to have known this fine carpenter my entire life. He is my daddy. Daddy worked hard all his life at both carpentry and farming. Once his daddy asked him why he spent so much money on his family instead of spending it on himself. Daddy humbly replied, "I work so my wife and six little girls can have everything they need. They are the reason I work. They are my life. Now Daddy is in heaven, no doubt busy building mansions next to Joseph. Every time I look at my beautiful China cabinet or see my princess canopy bed, works of art made by my daddy, I can still see him happily hammering nails and recalling past memories while growing up in the old farmhouse. So, Daddy, I dedicate this beautiful book to you, not just because you're the best Carpenter I knew, but the most loving, giving Daddy to your beloved wife are mama and your six little girls, who hold you in our heart and will love you forever.

—Joan Byrd

Daddy and Mama

CHAPTER 1

There was a long-heavily traveled road that swept through the tranquil countryside between two large towns in North-Carolina. Many travelers learned about Grace Road and when they felt the need to avoid the busier highways or interstate, they chose the peaceful trip to either town by using it. There were no traffic lights to slow you down, no businesses or developments that brought out more traffic. The honest truth was, only one small driveway came off on Grace Road and just one center intersection where cars could reach the road if they lived outside the cities.

Although Grace had been placed there by an unknown source, no one seemed to wonder how it got there, they were just happy it was a pleasant change from the busy traffic and rude drivers, who always seem to be in a hurry. The small drive that swept down a tree-line vista and disappeared in the woods, never seem to draw anyone's attention, for not a single soul had ever seen a car either come out or go in, no matter how many times they used the peaceful country road. If anyone had chosen to slow down when they passed the sandstone driveway, they would have noticed the small sign just inside on the right of the drive. It was the name of the place that set hidden, deep inside the tranquil forest. Written in old script, both in Hebrew and English, on a very old piece of wood, the name, ZION.

Modern Day

Thirty-year-old James Jesu, sat at his desk working on his sermon for the following Sabbath, and as he read over it for the third time, he finally smiled, feeling his words were finally ready. The raven-hair pastor glanced up when his wife came in, drying her hands on a used dishtowel.

"James, I hope you're almost finished with that sermon darling because we have just gotten a visitor and he insists on seeing you."

"Of course, Sarah, the sermon has finally come together and speaks all that was in my heart." James stood up and stretched, then walked over to give his beautiful wife a kiss before following her to the living room where she had taken Simon Granger, a man who

1

helped his ninety-year-old uncle.

When James entered the room, Mr. Granger stood up, his old worn hat held steady in his hands. "Simon, I pray Uncle James is not ill and you are here for more pleasant reasons."

"I am happy to report Mister James is fit as a fiddle and planting twice as fast as I am, young James." The scruffy looking man gave them a cheerful smile. "Forgive my appearance ma'am, but I was busy digging in Mister James's garden when he stopped his planting abruptly, smiled up at the heavens and nodded. Yep, that is exactly what the boss man went and done. Then quick as a flash, the frisky old fellow told me to stop my hoeing that instant and come straight here to fetch his nephew James. So, here I am, following my orders!"

"So, Uncle James has asked to see me, right now?" James glanced over at his wife of two-years. "I wish my uncle would have gave me more notice in advance Simon. I have promised my beloved Sarah that I would take her out tonight for our two-year anniversary." James felt Sarah's hand rest up on his shoulder, a sign she used when she needed a word with him. "One moment dear. Simon, if you could tell Uncle James that I am free all day tomorrow, I'll be more than happy to come over and spend the day with him. I did promise Sarah and we both are looking forward to going to that little romantic café where we had our first date."

"But sir, your uncle was precise with his request that you come at once!" Simon Granger nervously rung his hat. "I cannot say for certain, young James, but I believe the request first came from heaven! Would you not come if you knew it was the Almighty God who called you to Zion?"

"James, darling please, if you will give me just a minute of your time." Sarah patted the disturbed man's back and motioned to the towel-covered chair. "Please Mr. Granger, have a seat while I speak briefly to my devoted husband." Seeing the man take the seat back before nodding, Sarah pulled her husband to the hallway. "James, your uncle has never asked you to drop everything and pay him a visit before, has he?" She waited for his head to shake a negative. "Exactly! If Uncle James has called for you now darling, there must be a darn-good reason and I want you to go with Mr. Granger right now! You have the entire day off tomorrow, remember? We can celebrate our beautiful anniversary all day together!" She reached up to kiss him and he pulled her into his arms.

"Sarah, my wonderful-understanding wife. Your caring and thoughtfulness is just one of the many reasons I fell in love with you." James held her tight. "I promise to show my beloved a spectacular time tomorrow!"

"Sounds perfect James!" She took his hand and went back inside the living room. "Mr. Granger, James is ready to visit his uncle."

The man practically jumped up laughing and thought, if he wasn't such a dirty mess he would have given that loving young woman a hug. "Thank you, ma'am and God bless you with that baby boy you want."

"Thank you, Simon. I feel sure one day soon I'll find myself expecting a son." Sarah gave James one last hug and kiss. "Give Uncle James my love darling."

"I will tell him sweetheart." James checked his watch, 2:00p.m. "I'm not sure when I will return so if you grow weary, go on to bed. I will slip in quietly."

"No doing James! I want to hear why Uncle James needed to see you so bad." She gave them a wave and watched them simply disappear. Sarah closed the door shaking her head, always amazed at how her husband just vanishes whenever he paid his Uncle James Jesu a visit. Sarah stopped by the full-length mirror and looked at her flat stomach as tears came to her eyes. "Dear Lord, I want so much to give my beloved husband the son he desires. Even before we got married, James told me that he had to have a son heir to name James, to keep some family tradition alive." The twenty-five-year old woman knew she was still young enough to get pregnant, but up until the present, she had not. Sarah glanced from the big window which faced Zion and wondered if James would learn something that day that would help him know why every generation needed a male child from the Jesu name to be called James.

CHAPTER 2

When James arrived at his uncle's small cottage, there was no sign of him. He turned to ask Simon Granger if he knew his uncle's whereabouts only to find the old handyman was no longer beside him. "What is going on around here? Uncle James is not inside his home waiting like usual in his oversize comfy chair and his trusted sidekick has disappeared as well!"

"Not so, young James." The scruffy man laughed when the young man twirled around to see his uncle's helper standing just inside the open door. "I was merely searching for Mister James for you since I noticed he had disappeared from the garden where I left him to fetch you here."

"Then, I hope you found Uncle James's location, Simon." The younger James walked past the helper and looked around. "I am aware there are lots of woods on my uncle's property, but I have never gone beyond his cottage and back garden."

"I dare say no one has ventured out in the forest that protects the sacred garden." Mr. Granger gave the confused man a cheerful smile. "You are confused over this garden's name or the fact that your uncle has never taken you there?"

"Then, you are not referring to Uncle James' garden behind his home?"

"No young James, I am not. Although, it does grow some perfect roses." Simon turned to point to what appeared to be a worn trail through the woods. "The sacred garden is just down that narrow path and through the hedge. That is where you will find your uncle waiting to reveal to you, old truths that will change your life forever."

James glanced down at Simon Granger who had gathered up his hoe and shovel. "You won't be coming with me Simon?"

"Oh no, young one, it will just be you and Mister James alone this day." The cheerful smile returned to the weather-beaten-face. "Oh, I have been there and seen it for myself!" the old bright eyes seemed to be in another place and time. "It is a memory I will hold inside my heart forever, until I can once again thank the blessed

4

Savior for my healing miracle the day I wandered inside, a lost soul and filled of hate and fell on the bench."

"Miracle? The Savior's healing? A bench?" James looked down at the man, unsure of what he was going to find beyond the narrow path, "Is there something inside that place that makes it called the sacred garden?" the helper was now lost in his happy memory as he walked away mumbling. "Simon?"

"Go on down the path young James. Your uncle is waiting for you." With that, Simon Granger disappeared behind the cottage.

James walked slowly down the shady narrow path and when he reached the thick hedge, it magically opened and the elder James was waiting just inside an open vista surrounded by very tall cedars, unlike any evergreen the younger man had ever seen. The second thing James noticed was the shape and size of the hidden garden. He estimated the length to be at lease ninety feet from end to end and the garden was laid out in a perfect arch with one straight end that had a visible path going out into the tense woods. There appeared to be only one object inside this hidden garden and it stood out on the far end, directly in the center of the perfect arch.

The elder James stood patiently as his nephew took in the sacred garden for the very first time. He had watched him look around at the open vista with its perfectly manicured grass, then saw his eyes rise up at the tall cedars, knowing his nephew would be surprised to learn their history as well as their great age. The old preacher smiled with joy as he watched the younger James catch a glimpse of the path of light before spotting the main feature setting inside the sacred garden. Filled with questions, James looked down into his uncle's smiling eyes.

"Uncles James, this is a most unusual secret garden. Is there a reason you have never brought me here before?"

"There is indeed, young James. I have not shown you inside the sacred garden until today because I have been waiting for the Lord to ask it of me." The elder James had been clutching a very large book in his hands and pulling it to his chest to hold secure with one hand, he reached for his nephew's hand and pulled him inside the vista to let the hedge close back up. Thirty-year-old James noticed the book for the first time as he watched his uncle juggling its weight to secure it with both hands.

"Good heavens Uncle James, what in the world are you doing

with such a large old book? That thing must weigh two-hundred pounds!"

"You are way off son!" Uncle James gave a cheerful chuckle, before lifting the extra-large book up and down, as though he were suddenly a human scale. "The last time we weighed the fine old record book, it balanced out at three-hundred and fifty pounds."

"You have got to be kidding uncle! There may be weightlifters out there capable of lifting that kind of weight, but anyone can see you can't weigh more than one-hundred and fifty pounds and that's only because you are tall." James had been eyeing the big book and could see it was heavy but common sense told him the man standing in front of him, elderly, thin bones and fail, could not pick up a three-hundred and fifty-pound book, much less hold on to it for as long as he had been there. "Give me the book Uncle James. Let me hold on to it for you. Why do you need it out here for in the first place?"

"It is part of your training James." Uncle James noticed his sudden confused face. "And, before you ask, this is the day the Lord has been waiting for to start your training into becoming the next caretaker of a very special inheritance, given long ago to the first James Jesu. This one-of-a-kind object is priceless, and it is a sacred keepsake for us to respect, love always and cherish."

"Uncle James, could this be the reason behind why every generation must supply a male heir and name him James?" the young preacher had always wondered why there had to be a male named James from the family of Jesu, but up until this visit, the young man was always left to wonder why his father named him James." The caring young man noticed his uncle once again juggling the big book, so he held out his arms. "Uncle James, give me the book to hold please!"

"I would James, but it's not time for you to manage it as yet." The younger James noticed the elder James size up his nephew before sadly shaking his head. "Nope! There is absolutely no way you can hold this heavy book at the present time. You must wait until the training is complete and you know all there is to know about the blessed inheritance."

"Please forgive my persistence over this matter uncle, but if you can hold that heavy book without giving way, I know I certainly can, without any problems." James stubbornly held out his hands, never expecting what was about to happen.

"James, do not say I didn't warn you!" the retired preacher merely shook his head. "Pride cometh before a fall! There are times like this a person can only live and learn." The uncle stood straight before laying the book in his nephew's outstretched hands and before he let it go he spoke softly. "At least the garden has a thick blanket of soft grass." Uncle James closed his eyes and pulled his hands free. James, eyes wide with disbelief, fell to the ground, the weight of the three-hundred and fifty-pound book pulling him down.

"What the heck just happened?" James could not move under the book's weight and started to push it away when his uncle smiled down and lifted it back up into his arms. The young man could not believe what just happened and how this ninety-year-old man could stand up straight and hold on to such a heavy large book.

"James, let me put your mind at rest son. You are confused to see me do the thing that is impossible for you to do, correct?"

"Of course, I am totally baffled over the fact that what seems easy for you is impossible for me!" James stood up, red faced from embarrassment. "How can you hold such a heavy book with no problem when I cannot?"

"Simple! I have been trained and past the Lord's test with perfect grades! The moment I succeeded, I received many different gifts, never before known to man. The gift to transport myself in a flash, the ability to hold heavy items with no problem, the photo memory to recall the past history as I watch it unfold back to a special time and place, the sacred job of keeping down each and every person's record whenever they are led to this sacred garden by the light and the most sacred honor of being the caregiver to our inheritance until I can pass it on to the next caregiver, you James."

"So, this is the reason for your visit today Uncle James. To learn about how and why we have to name a male heir James? To be trained to do what you obviously love doing." James stared out at the bench, obviously old and wondered if this could be the sacred inheritance his uncle was referring about?

"Yes James." Uncle James obviously had been given the gift for mindreading as well, and young James suddenly grew tense, realizing whatever he was to be taught that day would defiantly change his life forever. "I too was anxious the day I was summoned to come over by my father, your grandfather James. He too had heard the call from the Lord and ask me to come over at once. I had just gotten married to my Helen and we had big plans to moved out to Texas to be near her family. I had found a very large Methodist Church there in need of a young minister and we were overjoyed with our plans. But, things changed when father called me, put me through the training, then when we began to study the history behind our family's inheritance, my heart took on a different joy, one unlike any other family has ever been a part of. I fell right into the program and after working next to my father for five years, my training was completed, father past away in his sleep at ninety-eight, and I became James, the caretaker of the miracle bench!"

CHAPTER 3

"James, once you know the amazing history behind the bench you will soon inherit, the fire inside your heart will spark the thirst for knowing more about it." Uncle James had taken his nephew over to the beautiful old bench that had total domain inside the sacred garden. The young minister knew there had to be something special about the old bench that looked remarkably good. He could see it had been well built by a skilled carpenter but the truth he was about to learn would overwhelm the young man more than anything that had ever happen to him in his thirty-years on God's good earth. "Let me start with the reason everyone chose to be the caregiver had to be named James. The first man to inherit the miracle bench was named James. It was a gift made for the carpenter's brother, second eldest under him, so feeling blest with the remarkable workmanship and many hours of labor put in to build such a perfect bench, made with such rough tools for the time made, brother James was touched deeply. As time went on and the constant battle with his wondering just who and what his oldest brother really was, news came that the loving gifted carpenter had been crucified, leaving James filled with confused anxiety and deep depression. James had grown up with this remarkable brother who had always been different from his other brothers and sisters, but James knew in his heart, not a one of them could ever be loved by him more than he loved that one brother whose words to him throughout his childhood had made him a better person.

James had married young and had a child within a year and he worried over what to name the boy. Wise and knowing what lay ahead, his eldest brother simply smiled down at the happy infant and said, 'Welcome into my Father's world little James.' It was this carpenters' way of saying, to be the caregiver of my miracle bench, his name must be James."

"Carpenter? Saying: My Father's world, being the eldest? Being crucified?" Young James' heart was pounding, knowing all of this could not be coincidental. "Uncle James, are you saying this carpenter who built this bench setting in front of us, is Jesus, our Lord and Savior?"

Joan Byrd

"Dear boy, over two-thousand-years ago, while still working next to his Father Joseph in the small town of Nazareth, Jesus, the Christ, loving made this bench with his own loving hands, placed His healing blessing on it, and willed it to his brother James, second son of Mary, his beloved mother." Uncle James could remember his own tears at this revelation as he watched his nephew weeping from the realization of what set in front of him.

"Uncle James, this beautiful old bench was actually made by the master's hand? How on earth did it survive all those years?" James had noticed the smooth wood and the fine workmanship. There was not a single sign of decay or rot. The fact was, the bench looked as if it had just been made but the unusual hard wood, obviously cut out by crude tools, was thick and broad.

"As I said son, Jesus laid his hands on the bench to bless it before asking his mother to put it away and give it to his brother after his death." the elder James looked down at the bench with reverence, knowing by actual witnessing the many miracles that had accrued from the miracle bench, that the words he spoke to his nephew were accurate. "Son, soon in your training, you will see for yourself how the Lord built this very special, one of the kind, bench. Trust me James, when you witness these past happenings for yourself, there will be no doubt within that big heart of yours!"

James couldn't resist a chuckle. "My serious uncle, you make it sound like I will be watching an old film made over two-thousand-years ago, way before moving pictures, cameras, or television! How in the world does a person view anything that happened so long ago, unless it's through visions or dreams?"

"James, have you already forgotten about the three-hundred and fifty-pound book I could hold but you could not? Did or did not you and Simon get here in a flash, after becoming invisible? Then there's the gift of mind reading, not to mention all the other special gifts a caregiver receives once he dives into the program!" Uncle James checked his pocket watch. "Three o'clock! You have been here exactly one hour, so let's move on to the lessons for today."

"Lessons for today?" James suddenly remembered his promise to Sarah and he would not break this one. "Uncle James, you said you worked beside Grandfather for five years. Are you saying, I must drop my life as I know it and start training with you every day? I have a beautiful wife Uncle James and I could never just drop everything I have going with her!" James noticed his uncle smile over his statement and he began to wonder if the man standing in front of him simply gave up his life with his wife for the title of caregiver? "If I cannot be with Sarah, then there will never be another James born in the Jesu family!"

"James, are you finished defending your married status or the fact that a male heir has not been given to you and Sarah yet?" The eldest James chuckled softly. "When I was in training for caregiver, I cannot tell you how many times my Helen and I tried to have a baby. I too was anxious to have a son to name James but when I learned my beloved was barren, my brother got married and within a month, your mother found herself pregnant. I ask my brother to name you James, and led by the wisdom of the Lord, he agreed, so here you are, next in line to inherit the only known piece of fine carpenter's work made by the hand of our Lord!"

James looked down once again at the very special bench below him as the reality finally begin to sink it. The simple, but elegant love bench he was observing was actually built by his Savior. Just knowing that Jesus' hands had worked long hours making this perfect bench for the purpose of giving it to his brother James and it was called the miracle bench. Just how does a bench create miracles, James thought. There were so many unanswered questions, but this young man knew in his heart he was ready to learn all his uncle needed to teach him.

"James, forgive my mindreading son, for I have once again learned how you feel and the need to know everything there is to know about this magnificent work of art." Uncle James knew Sarah was waiting to know why he had called her husband over with such haste. The understanding uncle also knew James' beautiful wife was worried with anxiety because she could not have a son for the man she loved so deeply. "Son, the day grows late and sweet Sarah is by now pacing the floor with many questions of her own." Now was the time to show guidance concerning James' devoted wife. "James, Sarah is struggling with feelings of failure for getting pregnant. You made it clear to her from the beginning of your relationship that you had to have a son of your own blood and name him James."

"Uncle James, I have spoken many times to Sarah about this, to insure her we have plenty of time to conceive a baby. I don't know what more I can say to ease her worries." James knew from his uncle's facial expression that he was going to offer some advice, so the young minister would make it easy for him. "What do you suggest I do to help the woman I love?"

"Not conceiving a baby could be coming from several aspects James. Just staying anxious over the fact, she has to have a son and call him James. The mystery behind why every Jesu born named James must have an heir named James to carry on a family tradition." The gifted uncle reached over to touch his nephew's shoulder. "Maybe Sarah worries about being unable to have children and knows adoption is out of the question. Your girl is smart and has figured out that Helen and I could never have children so your father, my only brother and hope, did have a son and blessed me by naming you James. You only need to have the first James' blood flowing through your veins. Sarah is also aware you are an only child James, so the burden lies entirely on your success in having a male child."

James was caught up in his uncle's revelation about needing to have the first James' blood flowing through their veins. Speaking softly, as if he spoke the words out loud, he would be suddenly surrounded by men in little white jackets. "Uncle James, are you telling me that we are relatives to James, the son of Mary and Joseph, the brother of Jesus?"

"Yes James. Our ancestry goes back over two-thousand-years." The elder James took his nephew back to the tall hedge and when they stepped out they were back at the cottage. "There's no need to ask James. We simple came with a flash! I shall send you back to Sarah the same way. She is your mate James, so tell her all you know and the fact that one day soon, the two of you will move in with me. I'll not rush your promised day together and my hope is the happiness you share will bring forth a son." Uncle James gave a chuckle and turned his nephew toward the road. This time, you both may drive your cars here. We shall have all your things brought over the quicker way." The older man laughed when James looked around with uncertainty. "You are thinking there isn't enough room inside my cottage for your things! If I had to come up with enough space for all your furnishings, clothes and personal items, I'd never get it done! But James, with all the work being done with heaven's help, we both know, with God, all things are possible! Amen?"

"Amen Uncle James! I will inform Sarah about our moving in

with you. Our rent is due in two-weeks, the same about of time our landlord requires if we decide to move." James laughed, waved, then vanished.

CHAPTER 4

James had returned with his exciting news and after their loving greetings, he led his wife into the small den to tell her everything his uncle had shared with him. Sarah knew something extraordinary had happened on this sudden visit that had affected her husband tremendously. She noticed the difference in his face, that now somehow glowed with a heavenly aura.

"James dearest, don't keep me in suspense! What on earth happened when you were with Uncle James?"

"Sarah, I learned many things from my uncle this day! One of which is the reason why our family tradition calls for a male heir to be named James by every generation!" James could not control his joy and he wished he could just burst it out quickly to still his excited heart. "Dearest, do you realize my Jesu ancestors can be traced as far back as two-thousand-years?"

"Are you serious James? Dear Uncle James actually believes he knows who his ancestors were that long ago?" Although the good Christian woman knew her James, nor his beloved uncle had never uttered a single lie, this information sounded preposterous. "Maybe our dear Uncle James is starting to get senile and really meant two-hundred-years."

James could only laugh at his doubting sweet wife. "Beloved, if you think that is hard to believe, then my next revelation will be perceived as impossible for your bright-intelligent mind!" James laughed when Sarah smiled and gave him a playful slap on the wrist.

"Then, by all means James Jesu, let me see if you can top the belief that you know who your ancestors were two-thousand-years ago!" Sarah folded her arms and lend back on the sofa, never expecting the beautiful truth that she was soon to hear.

"Good, you look relaxed enough to handle what I am about to reveal to you, dearest Sarah." James took a deep breath. "First, the ancestor Uncle James told me about did lived on this earth over two-thousand-years ago and his name was James Jesu, the first James to start the family tradition." James noticed Sarah was listening closely and her beautiful smile she had earlier faded and a look of complete seriousness, filled her eyes. "I have the same blood running through my veins Sarah as the first James, who was the second son of Mary and Joseph." He paused as he watched his wife take a big breath before sitting straight up. "Sarah, Jesus is Mary and Joseph's first son and the beloved brother to the first James."

Sarah jumped up grabbing her trembling lips, the revelation striking her in the chest and knowing now the reason why James had insisted on them having a son so he could call him James. The devoted husband suddenly realized he had read his wife's troubled mind and walked over to hold her in his strong arms.

"Sarah, maybe I should not have told you so bluntly. I should have broken this wonderful news to you more gently." James felt his own tears flowing down his handsome face as he pulled her around to face him. "Sarah, this news was too incredible to hold within me! I just assumed you would feel what I had felt when Uncle James told me."

"My darling James, I am not upset by this incredible news you share with me and my heart is completely full of this heavenly blessing!" Sarah looked up into her husband's blue eyes, her heart filled with total love for him. "I just wasn't expecting to learn my husband is kin to my Savior and that you actually have blood from the virgin Mary, same as Jesus!"

"I too cannot get over that very fact nor the reason why there has been a James named in every generation since the first James." The young minister gave his wife a hug before walking over by the big window. "I still have a lot to learn from Uncle James before I can become the caretaker."

"The caretaker?" Sarah joined James at the window and noticed his attention was facing Zion. "Are you to become the caretaker of Zion? Where Uncle James lives?"

"I will be trained to be caretaker on Zion's property, but its not any place we saw when we visited Uncle James." James turned to gazed down at his faithful wife. "Uncle James showed me a secret garden today, one I never knew existed. It is called the Sacred Garden. A tranquil place hidden by the forest and is surrounded by unusual very tall cedars. The garden is in the shape of an arched church window, spanning ninety-feet long and sixty-feet wide. There is a beautiful manicured lawn over the entire space and the garden has only one thing placed in the heavenly arch. A small love-bench made from old wood by the hands of a gifted carpenter, over two-thousand-years ago."

"Jesus! You are saying, this Sacred Garden has a piece of furniture made by the Master's hand?" once again, tears could not be contained as they fell down Sarah's smooth cheeks. "James, you actually saw this bench that Jesus built?"

"Oh Yes Sarah and it looked as though it had just been made!" James felt her hands trembled in his and he wondered how she would take his next statement. "Sarah, maybe I should tell you what Uncle James wants us to do, tomorrow morning, instead of now. With all this other news I've told you, I haven't the heart to burden you with more."

"James Jesu, are we or are we not in this marriage together? Did I not agree to love you through better or worse?" Sarah took a firm hold of his shoulders. "What does Uncle James want us to do? He is a man of God, with unbelievable powers, due to this caretaker's job I would guess. So, James, whatever our uncle wants from us cannot be nothing but good tidings! I pray I am correct darling, but if you don't tell me, I will be up all night, wondering what it is he wants us to do!"

"We wouldn't want that darling." James laughed, feeling better about sharing the news about them moving. "Sarah, you have made it plain many times that you don't like this house." She started to object, but James held up his hand to quiet her. "I recall you think, the windows are too drafty, the old floors squeak when walked on, your closet is the size of a shoebox, yet the largest one in the house, the kitchen needs updating, the faucets drip, the shower sprays every way but down, the garage door always gets stuck half-way up, need I go on?"

Sarah laughed, knowing James had every complaint down perfectly. "Alright sweetheart, you got me, now let me refresh the reason you are not crazy about this 1960's ranch house we have rented since we tied the knot! The television reception is either blurry or green, the refrigerator never stops running and the icemaker has never worked, except for dripping on the old worn linoleum floor. All the doors in the house are swollen and have never closed, the basement floods with the smallest amount of rain, and if the yard had some real grass instead of weeds you wouldn't mind mowing." She laughed at his red face. "Shall I go own, James?"

"Let's face it, we both despise this house and I guess that is why we never called it home." James looked around and wondered why they had remained there so long. "What do you think of moving into Uncle James' Cottage at the end of the month?"

"So, that is what Uncle James wants us to do." Sarah laughed. "I love that old cottage James, but is Uncle James sure he has room for us and our things?"

"Sarah, you said earlier, Uncle James' faith made him have special powers and although he cannot make the cottage larger, his words, the Lord can." James enjoyed his wife's beautiful smile. "With God, all things are possible!"

"You know what I think husband, with everything you have told me about your meeting with that dear man, I absolutely believe in the miracle he spoke of!" She laughed as she glanced around the drafty room. "Although that cottage is far older than this ranch house, it has never fell to keep me warm in the winter and cool in the summer!" She gave her husband a wink. "Another gift from the almighty. Uncle James doesn't have an air conditioner at the cottage and he only heats with the one large fireplace in the large den. I can vision the Lord blowing cool breezes in the hot summer months and blowing warm breezes in the cold of winter!"

"I could not offer a better explanation for the warmth and coolness within the old stone cottage." James looked thoughtful for a moment. "I wonder just how old that cottage really is and come to think of it, I must remember to ask Uncle James when the bench appeared in America and how it arrived."

CHAPTER 5

Moving day arrived bright and sunny and the loving couple had joined Uncle James outside their 60's ranch house, glad the day had finally arrived. To keep Mr. Mason, the owner of the ranch house from witnessing their move without the aid of a moving truck, James had carried the keys over to his office earlier that morning and had promised to lock the doors when he left, before giving him a call that he was out. Uncle James looked around at the weed-covered lawn and chuckled.

"James, didn't you ever plant any grass seed on this yard son?"

"I gave it a try for the first year but the weeds just choked out the new grass and I gave up." James lifted his shoulders in defeat. "I was going to try again in the fall but Oscar Mason said he would plant some grass and ask me to just keep it mowed. He didn't know what he was doing either Uncle James, because when the so-called grass came up, it was clover."

"Well, you don't need to worry about the perfect lawn anymore James." The elder James gave a bright smile. "The grass is always blush and green at Zion and you will find it never requires mowing. A little bit of heaven on North-Carolina soil, I always say!" he waved his hand over the pitiful looking lawn. "You two can make one last trip around your old yard to tell it farewell while your things are transferred. There's no need for my darling niece to see all her things moving about this way and that, until they are sorted for the move to their new home."

"Dear Uncle James, we are so grateful that you want us to live with you in your warm beautiful home." Sarah gave her favorite uncle a hug. "You are the best!"

"Believe me when I say, I am the one who is grateful to have your pleasant company around." He returned her hug. "And remember, it is your home now, same as it is mine! Besides, I truly believe you will receive that miracle you've been wanting when you settle in our home."

James gave her a wink before heading toward the front door. "I'll welcomed you both at your new home after your drive there."

Uncle James disappeared inside the front door and closed it behind him.

James and Sarah gave each other a smile before strolling around the small yard one more time. James gave a soft laugh. "I should feel some kind of sorrow for moving from the only house we shared, but it just isn't any there."

"And the reason is, the only thing great about living here had absolutely nothing to do with this building or sad old yard, it was being together here for two happy years. So, we are not sad because we are taking the thing that makes us happy with us to Zion, each other!"

"My wonderful darling always has the right words to say." James stopped when they reached the front door. "It's hard to imagine all our things will be gone when we step inside this old house for the last time."

"But, from everything that has happened to you James since learning about your relationship with Jesus, I have no doubt the rooms will be bare, but the old floors will still squeak!" Sarah followed James in the empty house and laughed happily. "Another miracle! Maybe Uncle James is right darling. Maybe the Lord will give us our long-awaited son after we are in our new home!"

After driving down their new drive, the young couple had finally reached the cottage at Zion. Not expecting a huge change in the six-room cottage, James and Sarah could only stare in disbelief, even though earlier, Sarah's faith never doubted there would be room enough for them and their things. Now, standing there, gazing up at a stone cottage twice as wide and standing two-floors high, the couple were speechless. James finally broke the stillness.

"I never doubted the Lord would provide enough space for us darling, but I never dreamed He would make it three-times larger!"

"It was quaint and pretty before sweetheart, but now, it is a cottage out of a storybook! The size along is fit for a king!" Sarah smiled up at her husband. "But, since it was the King of Kings that built it for us, then I cannot imagine why we are so shocked!"

"My thoughts exactly, young lady!" Uncle James had opened the door to greet them and smiled out at James' red truck and Sarah's small Honda tucked away in the new garage. "I see you found the stable for your vehicles! Nothing escapes the Lord's attention!"

"There is no other like Him, uncle." James helped his wife set her personal luggage inside the door and looked around. "It's amazing how the new just blended in with the old cottage. It's still warm and enchanting, yet large enough to feel comfortable."

"We're glad you like it kids, since this is to be your new home from now on!" The elder James gave them a quick tour and they rejoiced at how their furnishings fit right in, as if they had always been there.

"Tell me Uncle James, did you arrange all this furniture yourself or did the angels assist you?" Sarah was half expecting to find their things waiting together for her and James to place around. Someone had made their welcome relaxing and extra special.

"Oh Sarah, my sweet niece, I cannot take any credit for the angel's quick work. Working and living at Zion is a heavenly pleasure, every second of every day!" Uncle James stopped speaking when a young lady stepped inside the room, a broad smile on her happy face. "Children, you haven't met the new addition to our beautiful Christian family. You both know my friendly helper Simon, who has a room on the south-side of the cottage. This very cheerful lady has been with me since you were here last year on Christmas day. Her name is Maggie Spillman and she has a gift for cooking. Her rooms are on the north-side of the cottage. As you saw, all your living quarters are on the eastside where the sun rises beautifully, viewed from your new porch and large-double windows across the back of the cottage. The entire upper rooms belong to you as well." The thoughtful man smiled over at the patient woman, and gave her a nod. "Maggie has prepared our lunch and has everything set up in the large dining room. We shall be right in Maggie."

The stout looking woman couldn't resist a chuckle as she greeted the elder James' family. "It is so good to finally meet you, young James and your beautiful young wife Sarah." She gave a friendly curtsy and before leaving for the dining room, she spoke to the senior James. "James, Simon and I will take our places and wait for your gracious blessing."

"Thank you dear." James watched her leave and took Sarah's arm. "James, my boy, come along and prepare yourself for some great food. I hope you're both hungry!"

"Starved Uncle James." The young minister followed behind his uncle and his wife. The lunch was a pleasant feast and this was another happy surprise for the young couple, since Sarah wasn't the best of cooks.

"Day two on your lessons James. Today you will learn both things you have questions about. The unusual tall cedar trees and how and when the miracle bench arrive in America." Uncle James had taken his nephew back to the Sacred Garden and had read the young man's mind for feeling sorry for Sarah, not being able to see the magnificent place with the bench the Lord had made with His own hands.

"Good uncle, these are two things I have wondered about as well as many others." James had stopped to look at the sacred bench and once again the powerful sense of praises swept through his entire being, as if a million butterflies just invaded his body. "Uncle James, Sarah really had her heart set on seeing the holy bench made by Jesus. I could feel how disappointed she was when you refused her entrance into this garden. What possible reason could you have to stop such a beautiful-loving-child of God from witnessing this awesome miracle setting in front of us?" James looked over at his uncle, tears for his wife in his devoted blue eyes. "I see no harm in it! Even Simon said he has been inside this Sacred Garden uncle, and he is no kin."

"James, after you have had your training, you will know why this special place has been set aside for the downtrodden, those who are in need of a miracle from the Lord!" Uncle James gently touched his nephew's face. "James, it is not up to me who Christ allows inside His Sacred Garden, nor is it up to you to choose. Our loving Savior alone calls his lost sheep to the bench, when they reach their last hope."

"Forgive me Uncle James, for overstepping what I do not know." James wiped his wet eyes. "It's just that I love Sarah so much and I want to help keep that smile on her lips as well as hope inside her big-giving heart. I know my dearest Sarah worries about not being pregnant yet and maybe it is my fought for sharing with her why we must have a son to name James."

"My dear boy, place your trust in the Lord and He will not let you and Sarah down." Uncle James had read troubled signs inside Sarah's mind and knew times would get far worse before they got better, but knowing with God, faith can move all kinds of mountains, Jesus would be there to save the day for them. "James, I will say this one time, then we must go on with the teaching. Your beloved Sarah will go through a hard trial but in the end her strong faith will help her survive."

"Uncle James, are you saying Sarah's life is in danger?" James suddenly felt anxious.

"James, the thing I see, will not happen right away, so you must not set your thoughts on what might happen son. Your Sarah will go through a trying time and it will bring her to the dark place where she thinks there is no way out. But James, trust me son, you cannot change destiny nor can you lighten her darkness son, this will take a much higher power." The caring uncle took his nephew by the shoulders. "Promises me, you will not try to alter your future, nor Sarah's. This is in the hands of God, not yours, son."

"Then I shall have to place all my trust in the One I chose to follow and pray continually that He watch over my beloved Sarah in her time of stress and trouble." James relaxed, feeling the Lord's presence and knowing his wife was in the hands of God, all would be well. He walked over and looked up at the tall cedars. "Uncle James, did these trees happen to show up with the bench?"

"Smart thinking young James and yes, that is exactly when they appeared." The elder James joined his nephew by the cedars. "These are the cedars known as Israel's glory. They were mentioned several places in the Holy Bible, a stately evergreen that palaces were built with. Even the Great Temple Solomon built used the majestic cedar. When the Holy lands could not stop the many wars against the Holy City, Jerusalem, the Almighty chose a new country to place His Miracle Bench in. A country where hope and freedom brought the tired and poor from every corner of the earth who longed for freedom. But most important, this new land proclaimed to be ONE NATION UNDER GOD, WITH LIBERTY AND JUDICE FOR ALL!" Uncle James stared over at the sacred bench. "Our nation wasn't a country of wealth when it first began. The war fought against England, the most powerful country in its day, made America poor in wealth, but rich in morals and faith. It was that faith in God that helped our struggling soldiers to defeat the greatest army known in the 1700's and early 1800's when they tried again. England had manpower and greater weapons, but America had God fighting for the nation the bible refers to as a land of freedom and with his mighty hand, he brought them down."

"Then after the wars with England, the bench and cedars appeared?" James had gotten drawn into the time America became the miracle bench's home.

"Actually, the sacred bench and surrounding cedars appeared after the first battle was won, when America proclaimed its independence in July of 1776. North Carolina was chosen because the present James Jesu, who was caretaker had had a vision of this state with both mountains and ocean, peaceful valleys and forest. It was one of the original thirteen colonies and was placed between two mountains of conceit, Virginia and South Carolina, who always pride themselves as being a step higher than their neighboring state." The elder James knew his nephew had a question so he paused. "Is there something you need to know?"

"Was there a purpose for placing the sacred items here after we won our independence instead of waiting for the second attack which I am certain God knew in advance would accrue?"

"As a matter of fact, James, there is a perfectly good reason why the Lord chose to place His miracle bench here after July 4th, 1776." The wise uncle glanced up into the heavens. "For the very reason you just stated. The Almighty God, who knows all things before they happen, knew the upset arrogant King of England would not give up the land he still claimed for England. God knew he would strike with vengeance and try to take down what he assumed was a lesser country. The mighty army of the king had attacked the capital in Washington and had set fire to the capital building after running the rag-tag army from the states away. They were about to set fire to the white house when the Lord intervene, showing His mighty power. Unheard of inside the heartland, away from the coast, God sent a hurricane that stopped the mighty army in fear as a new threat struck them, a strong tornado dropped from the sky and both powerful windstorms toppled cannons and blew weapons and horses away, soldiers tried to hide in fear. Just as the mighty Jehovah fought for the Israelites, God's mighty hand did battle for America, the nation under Him!"

"Wow! It is a shame to see this great nation moving away from the one and only God that help make it free." James knew Satan was working hard to win souls away from his creator, but the young man of faith knew Lucifer would lose in the end, just like the King of England when he tried to reclaim God's free land. "Then the caretaker from Isracl came with the sacred bench and cedars?"

"He did James. So that James was the first of our ancestors to live here at the cottage, which the Lord prepared for him and his family." Uncle James knew what his nephew's next question was so to save time, he just answered him. "To answer your question James, these things simply got here in a flash!"

CHAPTER 6

Sarah had made a trip to see her doctor and after pouring out her reasons for wanting to have a baby, without sharing the secret of her husband's ancestry, ask if there was anything she could take to enhance her chances at getting pregnant?

"Sarah, I had just assumed the reason you were incapable of getting pregnant before was your state of mind." Doctor Kelly Brandon had been the young lady's doctor ever since she was born and he had taken on her husband, Reverend James Jesu, a Jewish man who had once practiced Judaism, but found the Lord, and became a saved Christian. It was well known throughout the small town of Haven Brook, where he and Sarah had gotten married in the Glory Hills Baptist Church, that his father was Rabi Philip Jesu and still a leader in the Jewish Temple, while his uncle, Reverend James Jesu, was a very religious man with high Christian morals and a pillow of the community. The good doctor and family friend could see why Sarah had found such an upstanding man to fall in love with and why James Jesu had made the perfect choice for himself. "Sarah, I could tell ever since you wed James you have been anxious about giving him a son. The very fact that you were uptight every time you were intimate with your husband, made your chances of getting pregnant slim. Since you moved in with James' uncle, I could see a big change in your demeaner and you had finally learned to stop fretting the what if and started enjoying your romantic time with James." After checking her vitals, Doctor Brandon patted her hand. "I am certain the lack of getting pregnant is not from too little sex, since it obvious the love parks between you and James never goes out." Kelly Brandon pulled out his prescription pad and began scribbling down a medication.

"Doctor Brandon, so you think I just need some extra hormones or something?" Sarah had hope the doctor would recommend something to boost her reproduction system.

"I have written you a prescription for a new fertility drug and if taken regularly as directed, your chances for getting pregnant will be enhanced threefold." The family doctor gave the happy young woman the RX prescription and walked her to the door. "I expect to get a call from this soon-to-be little mother within the month."

"I shall call the moment I find out Doctor Brandon!" Sarah could not control hugging the older gentleman that had brought her into the world, just a wee baby. "I cannot thank you enough Doc!"

"Just enjoy making this perfect little son and remember to follow the direction carefully Sarah." The family doctor gave her a pat on the head, just like he had done ever since she was a cute toddler. "I would not want anything bad to happen to my precious little girl." He opened his office door and gave her a playful pat. "Now off with you and start making that baby so I can enjoy that beautiful smile of yours again!"

James had noticed the change in his wife when they made love. Now, instead of trying not to show her stressful reactions and stiff responses when they made love, Sarah was romantic and passionate, touching, feeling and embracing. She had become extremely relaxed and easy to arouse, that part he had never had trouble with where Sarah was concerned. His sexy wife never failed to turned on his manly feelings and making love to her was always exciting as it was enjoyable, the way God had intended for it to be between a man and his woman. So, when James met his uncle in the Sacred Garden for the third lesson, he could not contain his happiness.

"James, my boy, I do believe things are looking up for you and Sarah in trying to make a baby." The elder James could not resist his chuckle when his nephew blushed. "There's nothing to be ashamed of nephew. God has given a man and his wife great joys and pleasures when they are joined as one. Believe me, I know. Helen and I had many pleasant times trying to make a son, although it was unsuccessful. But that sad truth never stopped our love for one another and the Lord had a plan, so you were born and became the son I could not have." The man of great faith looped his arm around his nephew. "And dear boy, I could not love you more even if you were my own son."

"Thank you, Uncle James. That really means a lot to me." James had been observing the large-heavy book lying on the sacred bench and wondered when his uncle had brought it out. They had come out of the cottage together to make their way to the Sacred Garden and his uncle was not carrying it in his arms.

"I see you are wondering how the record book got out on the

miracle bench before we came inside the garden." The elder James led his nephew over to the bench and smiled down as the book began to open as if by magic.

"Now how on earth did that happen uncle? There is no wind blowing inside the garden and yet, the pages simply began opening and stopped at the very beginning of the massive book." James had not taken his eyes off the page, which appeared to be blank. "I can see no writing on this page, so do we just turn to the next page and start reading?"

"Lesson number three James, you cannot see the Hebrew script written on the page because it is invisible to the eye." Uncle James laughed when his nephew looked over at him forlorn. "As you must know by now James from trying to take this book to hold for your poor old uncle and found yourself sprawled out on the grass, things inside the Sacred Garden are not what they seem to be." Uncle James waved his hand over the large book. "We do not need to read this book, which has every story down for those healed at the miracle bench. Each recorded story simply comes to life and being caretakers of the sacred bench, we can witness everyone's story as though it had been filmed. And James, this includes when Jesus made the bench and showed it to Joseph, His earthy father."

"You did mention something about seeing Jesus' past come to life, but I wasn't expecting it to appear from this heavy book." James could never describe the strange, yet beautiful feeling he was experiencing, just trying to imagine what it would look like to see his Savior, the way he moved, talked, and looked."

"James, you do not have to imagine son. Soon you will know and the instant you see Jesus, there will be no doubt He is truly the Son of God." Uncle James smiled at the two chairs that had appeared behind them and after turning his nephew around to find his seat waiting, Uncle James could only chuckle over James' shocked face. "You will get use to things just appearing son, whenever we need something. God's angels are invisible most of the time and have the ability to produce whatever we need right out of thin air." The uncle took his seat and waited for James to sat down, after watching him first feel it, then slowly test it, to make sure it was solid before trusting it would hold him. "There, you see James, angels are heavenly wonders, sent to serve us not to trick us for a chuckle."

"Just be patient with me Uncle James. All this is new to me and surprisingly different from anything I have ever known." James relaxed in the super comfortable chair and turned to face the book when he heard the sound of birds and a hammer striking against tense wood. It was as though the page had lifted out of the book and grew into what could pass as a movie screen. Trees came into focus on the white canvas and James could actually see the birds he had been hearing flying from one tree limb to another. Then what appeared to be some sort of wooden shed became clear and the back of a tall man appeared, wearing a faded white robe and it was obvious he worn some sort of heavy apron.

When the man turned around, his heavenly blue-green eyes focused directly on the young man watching. James was speechless, thinking, I am actually looking into the eyes of Jesus. It's as though he can actually see me, but Uncle James said I would be seeing what happened in the past. James could not retain his smile, for he had never felt so much love pouring inside his heart as he was experiencing at that very moment. Then something amazing happened, Jesus returned the smile with one of His own. Without looking away from his Savior, James whispered to his uncle.

"Uncle James, this is so realistic! It's as though Jesus is looking directly at me! He smiled back when I gave Him a smile."

"Son, do not take your eyes off the Lord, for He can see you James and He knows your name." The nervous young man felt his uncle take his hand and he tried to relax.

"Should I speak to my Lord, uncle?"

"Yes James, you may speak to me. Anytime! Anywhere!" The Lord took James by surprise and he almost fell out of his chair. "Do not let your heart be troubled James, for I am your brother and friend, as well as your Savior. Listen to my servant, who is your uncle and teacher. He will guide you in all the things you must know and do. I will take you back to the day I finished making the miracle bench, brother James. You will witness the words between me and Father Joseph and later, on another day, you will faithfully watch me with my mother, Mary, when I ask her to give my brother James the bench after I have ascended into heaven to be forever with My Father, God."

James had felt the power of the Almighty sweep through his entire body, just by listening to his Lord and Savior speak directly to him. The incredible love the young man felt as Jesus looked into his eyes the entire time he spoke to him, was unlike anything he had ever felt before. James thought to himself, "this is what it must be like to live in heaven with this amazing holy man." The young minister had so much inside his heart he wanted to say to Jesus but all he could manage was "My heart is overflowing with love for you Lord and I feel so unworthy to be sitting in your presence."

"My brother James, I felt your love for me the moment I looked into your eyes when you were born and you felt your love for me as I laid down on that cross and stretched out my arms to feel the nails pierce through my hands and feet." Jesus gave James a warm smile and he took a step back. "As my servant, you will be a worthy caretaker James, so listen and learn. It is time for the journey from the bench to the cross. We shall speak at a later date, but until then, the pages have been opened and my past begins."

CHAPTER 7

YEAR: 25 A.D.

The carpenter's son ran his hand over his finished piece and gave it a smile for a successful, one-of the kind garden bench. Satisfied with his craftsmanship, he made his way quickly to his father's workstation and stepped in laughing. "Father Joseph, may I have a moment of your time?"

"You seem to be very happy over whatever you have been working with son." Joseph wiped the sawdust off his hands before looking up at his tall handsome boy. "Did you need my help with some problem?"

"No problem, sir, my work is complete." Jesus waited patiently before asking. "Father Joseph, if you can spare me a moment of your time, come and check out my new bench and tell me what you think of it."

"I would love to see the project that has kept you busy for almost two weeks, son." Joseph produced his own smile at his very special son. "So, you have been making a bench all this time. Is it anything like the one I built for your mother for her birthday?"

"The bench you made so lovingly for your Mary was indeed special and I shall never forget how happy mother was when you took her out to the garden to see it." Jesus and Joseph made their way into Jesus' workstation, where the seasoned carpenter had placed him after his training was completed. "Now father, before you see my design, I just wanted you to know I chose to keep it simple, yet give it a personal charm all its own."

Jesus stepped aside so Joseph, an expert in the skills of carpentry and known throughout Galilee for his fine work, could get his first glimpse at his son's unique bench, one Jesus had designed himself.

"What do you think? Will it pass the master of carpenter's approval?"

"Son, never have I seen a more solid piece of fine workmanship. You chose the strongest wood created by our great Jehovah, carved each piece to perfection and then your steady young hand took hours smoothing out the rough edges and ridges until it shines like the morning sun!"

"Yes, Father Joseph, I did all those things, to make this bench outlive many summers, withstand many cold winters, yet still it pleases the eye." Jesus walked over beside his fine work and gave it a pat. "Lasting and beauty are both fine traits sir, but it must past the hardest test of all. A bench that cannot be sat on is useless. Will it hold up with two people sitting on it? I designed it to hold two comfortably. By rolling the front of the bench and buffing it smooth instead of making the same straight front as other benches, those occupying the bench will find their legs drop smoothly with the rolled front."

"Son, there is only one way to test this theory of yours and then still trust it will hold up two people instead of one." Joseph looked down at the well-built bench and knew Jesus expected him to trust his handy work. After all, it was Joseph himself who had taught him everything he knew about being a good carpenter. Now his prize student was putting the teacher to the test. "It has always been my job to test out every stool or bench I made before letting my customer pick it up, so I would be delighted to try out your first bench." Joseph took a deep breath and slowly slid down onto the smooth bench. The hard-working builder closed his tired eyes and marveled at how comfortable and smooth his son's bench was. Now, feeling more confident in its stability, Joseph began to move slowly back and forth, testing for strength and waiting for any possible breaking sounds. After none came, the carpenter settled back with a big smile. "Jesus, you have past the single setter's test. For one person, it is spacious as well as comfortable. Why take the chance that it might break when two are seated, when it is special just as it is." The proud father let his hand run slowly over the smooth wood. "Jesus, never in my life have I sat in a setter this comfortable. Your smooth front will certainly take off son, should anyone afford such fine workmanship and luxury."

"Father Joseph, your words of praise mean a lot to me, but this bench will be one of a kind. There is not be another one made by my hands." Joseph could always feel the great love reflecting from the special son's blue-green eyes and he never doubted how much Jesus loved him. "You may use my design on any new benches you make sir, but this one is my only one and it must be tested for two, Father Joseph."

Joseph smiled and moved carefully to the far left to make room for his son. "I trust your judgement Jesus, to believe two grown men will be safe sitting on your special bench. Alright Jesus, if your new design will ever make it to the market for me to duplicate, you and I must test it now to make sure it will hold up." Joseph waited as he watched Jesus checking out the situation closely. The carpenter's eyes twinkled with mischief as he teased his brilliant son. "What is wrong son, are you up to the test or shall I call your brother James to try it out? You do have confidence in your own work Jesus, right?"

"Most certainly Father Joseph!" Jesus eyes glistened into a smile. "Have I not placed the heavenly Father's blessing on it? Did you not see how it remained in place when you moved over to one end and it never tilted over, but stayed firmly on the wooden floor?" With total confidence Jesus sat down, then to his companion's dismay, began jumping his body up and down on his end of the bench as it set steady in place. Joseph had grabbed on to the arm rest, another new feature, and thought for sure the bottom of their smooth seat would give away sending them both to the floor. Jesus glanced over and chuckled at his father's closed eyes and tight grip on the arm rest. "Relax Father Joseph, be at peace. I will not do you no harm, for it is not within me to do so." Jesus smiled at Joseph when he relaxed and saw the bench was still as sturdy as ever. "There is nothing bad within me, but the love that the Father sent me here with." Jesus gave a soft laugh, his hand gently patting Joseph on the back. "You need not worry about the strength of my bench Father Joseph, you taught me well. I have proved to be a good carpenter, so now I must hang up my tools and set my course to doing deeper things." The smile faded as Jesus grew serious, his previous mirth over his accomplishment for making a perfect sturdy bench now died away. With his heavenly eyes fixed straight ahead, Jesus's word came soft and clear. "My time here must come to a close. The Father hath called me to go forth and began my ministry to the nations. The son of man will no longer work with hands of a carpenter's son, but with hands of the great Jehovah!"

The lifelong carpenter sat up, a sense of deep remorse sweeping through his heart. "Jesus, must you start this journey so soon? You are yet a young man, barely in your thirties." Joseph suddenly felt the impact of what his precious son had just proclaimed. Had this mere carpenter assume that Jesus would remain with him and Mary and be like an ordinary man. "Forgive me Jesus, if my heart would wish a few more years with you, working beside you, hearing your words, seeing your loving smile. The thought of your leaving breaks my heart son, as I know it will your dear mother."

"It is for this reason I came into the world. I knew this day would not come easy, for either of us, Father Joseph." Jesus paused, as if he dreaded to share his next words with the man who had raise him and gave him so much love and training. "The near future will not be easy Father Joseph because I will not be the only one to leave this household." Jesus watched Joseph's questioning eyes, confused to who else would walk away from him and Mary.

"Jesus, my son, my heart is now troubled because I know not who it is you speak of. Who else in our family would find the need to leave when we are already heartbroken over your departure?" Joseph had not seen any signs of their other sons eager to leave the family nest. "Your brothers are learning the carpentry trade now with enthusiasm and your sisters are still happy dwelling among us. Please Jesus, tell me, of whom do you speak?"

"It is for your need to know, that I share this great lost with you, my beloved earthly father." Tears filled the heavenly blue-green eyes of Jesus as his hand gently touched the face of Joseph. "Soon, you will grow very ill and death will come quickly."

Joseph stood frozen for a moment, perhaps hoping this had been a dream, but the real tears flowing from his son's eyes knew this truth was real. "Jesus, time has flown and caught up with me. I too have reached fifty years of life, same age as my dear father when he closed his eyes in death." Joseph's attention went to their home, where he knew Mary was probably busy preparing the evening meal for her large family, with their daughter's assisting her. Now Joseph could not contain his tears, and father and son fell into each other's arms sobbing.

After several minutes, Joseph took a deep breath. "It is not for myself I cry son. It is the thought of leaving my beloved Mary behind to grieve both my passing and your leaving, to begin everything God sent you here to do. I will not be here to comfort her after you depart and without your loving arms to console her with your perfect peace, that can only come from you Jesus, my sweet Mary will mourn for me a very long time."

"Be at peace Father Joseph, I will not walk away while you are sick, nor after you close your eyes in temporary rest. I will see to mother and stay as long as I am needed."

"Jesus, you have always been such a good-loving-son." Joseph had wondered about his son's words about his death-rest being temporary, so he asked. "Jesus, you said temporary rest. Do you refer to the resurrection son, when all the dead shall rise at the coming of our Lord?" Joseph suddenly felt frightened over death being forever darkness and final. He had heard the Rabi in the temple speak about lying in sleep until the resurrection. Surely Jesus would know the answer.

Jesus had felt his earthly father's fear and he reached out to comfort him. "Father Joseph, be not afraid. This death only takes the sick body but your soul lives on still. Hear my words and be assured of perfect peace."

Joseph began to marvel over the sudden appearance of his son when he began to glow as heaven's light fell down over and around him. It brought back the visit from the angel Gabriel when he appeared to Joseph in the dream and told him to take Mary for his wife. That the baby growing inside of her was the son of God. Joseph thought, I did marry my Mary and raised Jesus as my own son. I could not love him more than I do. Joseph continued to think and he knew Jesus was truly special and was sent from heaven to save the world. To save the world? But, how, he thought?"

"How will I save the world Father Joseph?" Jesus had understood his thoughts and he knew what he was about to tell him would not be easy on the man that loved and raised Jesus. "All have sinned and fall short from the kingdom of heaven. So, the Father sent His son to take away the sins of the world. So, they that believeth in Him shall never die but have eternal life!"

"Jesus, how will you, being one man, take away so many sins son? Through prayers? Through hands uplifted?" Joseph touched his son's handsome face. "Jesus, I know you are the Son of God. Mary and I have had you with us so long sometimes I forget and feel you are mine and Mary's little boy. Please Jesus, tell me, what does God expect from you?"

"To be the perfect sacrificial lamb. The lamb without blemish. The one without sin." Jesus instantly saw the anguish on Joseph's face.

"Not like the sacrificial lambs killed on the priest altars? Surely the God of heaven would not send you down to die on an altar for all sinful humans?"

"Not on an altar, beloved. I will die hanging from a Roman cross for the sins of every man, woman, and child ever born, since Adam." Jesus' words came soft but powerful.

"My God, no! Surely your loving Father would never send you to suffer with agony on a Roman cross, my perfect, beautiful son!" Joseph cried, now the thoughts of his death, no matter the length of his illness, could ever be compared to his son's fate. Once again, his thoughts turned to Mary. "My beloved will have to go through all this sorrow without my strong shoulder for her to lend on. It will be bad enough, watching you leave this home, but Jesus, to watch her loving son suffer and die up on that cross, will be far more than she can bare." Joseph paused, suddenly remembering the day he and Mary carried the baby Jesus inside the temple and meeting an old man named Simeon. "Jesus, I was always there with Mary throughout everything that happened concerning you son. The man named Simeon told Mary that a sword would pierce her heart one day and seeing you crucified on that cross will make the old man's vision come to light."

"Father Joseph, I knew this revelation would be hard on you to hear, but I told you so you would know this death on the cross did not win! I will be buried and on the third day, I will arise bright and early in the morning and on that first day of the week, I will take you with me to heaven. Then after seeing the Father, I will return to earth for forty days to instruct my disciples, and see mother, then return to heaven until I go back to judge the world."

"Praise to God on High! All the dead shall rise on that resurrection morning! Because you live, we too shall live!" Joseph said softly, overcome with emotion. "Be sure to share this good news with your mother before she has to witness your death son." Joseph now understood the reason behind his son's death. "Jesus, you are saying, without the cross there would be no hope for mankind to be saved. What a burden you must bare upon your shoulders as you hang upon that cross. To take on the weight of every sin ever committed and the sins yet to be made."

Jesus closed his eyes and smiled, glad the truth was finally out. "Yes, Father Joseph, the choice has always been mine to except.

The Father and I are one, with the Holy Spirit. I left my heavenly kingdom knowing of my painful sacrifice to save my people from their sins. Our battle with Lucifer will not end until I return to this earth, to judge the nations. This will be some time away." Jesus patted the sturdy bench and gave a smile. "This bench I made is called the Miracle Bench and it will remain on this earth until my final return."

"Who do you plan to give it to son? This 'Miracle Bench will become the receiver's favorite gift. It is truly made by the master's hand."

"It does my heart good Father Joseph that you recognize my high status. And you are correct about the person who I will leave my bench too, because they will be the first caretaker of this bench that has been blessed with healing powers. It shall be used for many generations and many caregivers will be trained how it must be used. People will come to the bench because they are in need of a miracle."

"Then, your master's work is truly a gift to all mankind, my son." Joseph felt better about his fate, knowing Jesus would stay while he lay sick, then be with his Mary while she grieved his loss. The hard-working carpenter was not afraid of death anymore, knowing Jesus, the son he shared with the great Jehovah, would lift him up from the grave and take him to heaven as promised, where he would wait for his beloved Mary.

"Son, I wish I had enough time left to build Mary a bench like yours. I would call my bench, FOREVER MY LOVE SETTER, then sign it, your loving husband, Joseph."

"You shall have that special time then Father Joseph." Jesus smiled and kissed his cheek, placing inside him extra days and wishing he could grant him a longer life miracle. "My bench is also dedicated to my father and signed, under its belly!" Jesus laughed as he watched Joseph flipped the perfect bench over on its side to read the words his son had written.

Joseph smiled up at Jesus, too emotional to speak, thinking the Son of God had meant his heavenly Father would receive the dedication. The carved words the carpenter read softly would remain for all time. LOVINGLY MADE FOR MY FATHER JOSEPH! BY HIS SON, JESUS!

CHAPTER 8

Seeing the past come to life was both exciting and moving to the younger James, as he sat quietly eating his supper while his uncle and Sarah chatted about the change in the weather and the feeling of fall in the air. James' young wife had high hopes in getting pregnant now that she was on the fertility drugs and she had made herself a mental note that she would ask her husband why he had been so quiet during the evening meal. The devoted wife assumed James had a moving experience in the Sacred Garden and he was still overcome by whatever happened during his third day of training.

"Uncle James, I was taking a walk in the rose garden behind the cottage today and noticed, despite the chill in the air, the roses are faring quite well." Sarah reached for another one of Maggie's yeast rolls, and gave the happy cook an approving smile. "Maggie, I swear these hot rolls just scream for butter and I was hoping my new pounds were due to my getting pregnant."

"Sarah, maybe your appetite is another sign that you are eating for two now and that little baby boy growing inside you smelled that good bread I baked and wanted some for himself!" she chuckled out.

"Then, that would be a blessing, I'm sure." Sarah looked over at her husband who seemed to be miles away. "Do you think that is why I have such a growing appetite James darling?"

"What?" he glanced up and noticed everyone watching him closely. "I'm sorry Sarah, could you repeat you question sweetheart. My mind was completely consumed with my lesson for today."

"So, I gathered darling." Sarah reached over to pat his cheek. "We can share our day tonight with one another if you like."

James met his uncle's stare, and noticed his positive nod, then gave Sarah a relieved smile. "That sounds perfect darling. Then you will know why my head seems to be lost in a cloud."

After James shared his extraordinary day with his wife, she was amazed at what he had witness and understood why he seemed so far away in his thoughts. "Sarah darling, this caretaker's job is far greater than anything I felt possible. Jesus spoke to me Sarah! I saw him as clearly as I see you now. The massive book I told you about is like a living book to the past. I watched, through tears, as Jesus and Joseph conversed about the very bench setting in the Sacred Garden. I witnessed the closeness they felt for each other, saw the tears they shed due to the powerful words spoken by the Lord Jesus. The fact that Joseph was soon to die, the promise of Jesus, a devoted son, to remain at home until Joseph's death and until Mary no longer needed his comfort, concerning her great loss in losing the only man she had ever loved, except her own father of course. Then the moving dedication near the end of this past vision when Joseph assumed Jesus had dedicated his Miracle bench to God the Father only to learn after he turned it over where the carving was to read, LOVINGLY MADE FOR MY FATHER JOSEPH! BY HIS SON, JESUS!"

"James, my little stroll through the rose garden doesn't seem quite as magical now." Sarah touched her husband's face. "While I was marveling over the healthy roses, I was counting the days until my next period and was excited to know that it was due next week." Sarah sat up with excitement. "Do you know what that means if the due date comes and I don't have it?"

James gave his wife a bright smile. "It will mean, we just made ourselves a baby boy!" He grabbed her laughing at the prospect of her getting pregnant at last. "That little stroll just could be magical after all."

The next few lessons consisted of learning how to make a report in the Miracle book and James was surprised to learn you didn't need a pen for writing. Whenever a miracle accrued in the Sacred Garden, the caretaker would automatically find themselves watching inside the garden, book in hand.

"James, our job is to be there with the book held open toward the bench. The Lord will do everything else." Uncle James lifted up the big book and faced the bench. "Everything that happened to bring the person to the garden will be recorded in this book, for us to review anytime we like. Each individual's story will be named for that person. Such as the first miracle story we shall watch, titled: James, the first caretaker."

"Are you saying, James, the brother of Jesus, a son to Mary and Joseph, needed a miracle and found it at this bench?" the younger

James gazed down at the very bench he had watched in wonder as Jesus and Joseph were actually setting on it freely talking.

"James had always known Jesus as his older brother and his love and admiration for the gifted carpenter and speaker always lifted his spirit." Uncle James closed the massive book after showing his nephew how it must be held. "After Jesus left home, right after his father's untimely death, James had deep concern for his special brother and he had been hearing many rumors concerning him. These rumors disturbed James and he was in a constant battle with his enter-self, as he tried to figure out just who Jesus really was." Uncle James surprised the young minister when he began sitting down and there wasn't a chair in sight under him. James' reflexes caused him to reach out quickly, only to come short of catching his smiling uncle when a chair was suddenly waiting for him.

"Darn! What just happened? I just knew I had to rescue you before you took a spill on the ground!"

"It is what the Lord called, having faith the size of a mustard seed, young man." The happy uncle patted the empty space beside him. "Care to demonstrate your faith in the unseen? If your faith is strong enough to believe you can take a seat where there is no chair, you just might find a soft surprise waiting."

"Alright uncle! I truly believe my faith is as strong as your own, therefore, I will take a seat next to you and have faith that I will end up on a comfortable chair instead of the soft grass." James took a deep breath and commenced to sit down. Before he hit the grass, he felt the soft cushion under him and gave a chuckle. "The invisible angels have once again supplied our needs."

"You are correct young James and while you slowly lowered yourself in faith, with your eyes closed, I suppose in a prayer-like-state, the Miracle Book has once again turned the pages for us to view the next chapter, Jesus' last words for Mary before he began his ministry." The page moved up, same as before, and this time the young preacher could hear humming. It was the sound of a woman, softly humming a mournful song. James sat up when the raven-hair girl came into view and he knew the moment he saw her sweet beautiful-sad-face staring into space as she went about her household duty of hanging out the family's linens, it had to be Mary.

Jesus had stood back listened to his mother's beautiful sad

melody and the tears in his heavenly eyes matched her own. Mary was aware her son would be leaving and the heartache she had felt for losing her dearest Joseph, now seemed to return, three-fold. What would she do without her rock to keep her calm and filled with the sweet peace she had always blest others with whenever they departed from her sight? How would she carry on as now the only parent to all her and Joseph big family? Jesus stepped up and took his mother in his strong arms.

"Mother, when I go I will not leave you helpless and hopeless. I will install inside you the strength you will need, not only to be the head of your big household with confidence, but I shall grant you even greater strength to face my final days as a human man."

"Jesus, you speak of the reason the Father sent you down to earth in the first place, don't you, my adorable son?" Mary's tears came easy, for the thoughts of losing her special boy cut into her very soul. "This is what Joseph, your dear earthly father, was referring to when he told me before passing, 'our special gift from God will tell you something that will break your heart, as it did mine, but this thing he must endure and you must witness without my support, shall be the greatest gift given to all the human race'."

"Father Joseph is a wise man and he speaks what is true to the only woman he had ever desired to be his wife." Jesus led Mary to the last gift her husband had given her before closing his eyes in death, and they sat down on the smooth, double bench. "You know I must start my mission to seek out the twelve men I chose long before I came down to earth, to be my twelve disciples. I chose to have twelve followers, same number as the tribes of Israel. So, once taught, once they have received the Holy Spirit when I depart from them, they can go forth to teach the gospel of the New Testament, filled with words by the Holy Spirit, so all generations, both Jew and Gentile, can learn of me and be saved through me." Jesus reached for Mary's hand. "This mission will last for three-years and at the end of the third year, during the Passover Feast in Jerusalem, I will enter into the great city, riding on a colt. Thousands of my followers will be shouting my praises as they throw down their cloaks on the road in front of my journey. They will be waving palm branches and shouting heavenly praises and singing hosannas. The priest will grow even more jealous and angry and seek a time to arrest me." Jesus took a deep breath, knowing the next statement would tear his mother's heart into, but she needed to know everything. "They will find the perfect time to take me prisoner." He watched his mother stand up and take a step back, shaking her head.

"Please Jesus, my beloved boy, can your loving Father in heaven not altar these things you are seeing that will happen to you?"

"Mother, believe me when I say, it is He, my Father who will set these things into motion so that the end results can be accomplished." Jesus stood up and gathered both Mary's hands in his. "Hear me out mother. Once you know why this is the only means to the end, you will understand why I must go through with my Father's plan. And before I tell you, know this, this decision did not come easy for my Father nor I. We discussed it at great length before we knew this could be the only way to save all our earthly children from their sins."

"Please forgive my words regarding your perfect Father and my great Jehovah. Jesus. I have always known the great love given by our holy Creator and I know it must have been the hardest thing he ever had to do when He sent you down to earth, to be born as a baby to a humble young girl. To know what your fate would be and to be the One to make it happen, could not have come easy. I know heaven is a place where sadness does not exist, but to watch his only Son suffer so much agony and not be able to help him, would break any father's heart into."

"Then you know in your heart what I will go through. After my arrest, I will get beaten, flogged, crowned with twisted thorns, then nailed on a cross." Jesus opened his arms when Mary fell into them weeping. "You weep now, Mother, as you will weep beneath my cross on the day I am crucified to take away all the sins of the world." He pulled her at arms-length and smiled down. "Dearest mother, after lying in my borrowed tomb for a while, I will rise on the third day! The Lord God cannot remain dead and the same body I die in, I will arise in. Mother, I am the resurrection and life, whosoever believes in me, though they die, yet shall they live. The human body dies because it was made with clay, but the soul of man was created in heaven and it never dies! The morning I arise, I will lift Father Joseph from his sleep and he will be taken to heaven to wait your arrival when I come back years from now to take you home."

41

Mary had a beautiful smile replace her sad and sorrowful face. "Then this sword that will pierce my heart, spoken by old Simeon, will come when I watch my perfect little boy suffer and die. As I watch weeping, I must silently sing inside my heart, my son who died so all could be saved, will arise, my Savior and Redeemer!"

"Bless you mother! For you, like my beloved earthly father, know who I am and now, why I came down to earth." Jesus kissed his mother before looking down at the bench. "Father Joseph made his bench just like mine, except of course for its name and who the receiver was."

"That's right! Joseph did tell me he copied your new design because you had given him permission." Mary smiled down at her precious gift. "I love Joseph with all my heart and I know how much he loved me, as well as all our children." Her small hand reached up to caress her handsome son's face. "But, Joseph always had a special kind of love for his oldest son, same as your mother has for you. He was such a good father and he tried to spoil you when you were small by building you toys from scraps of wood he had left over. I could tell he loved to watch you giggle when he placed a carved donkey or sheep in your little palm. When you were just a baby, Joseph was a very watchful and attentive father to you. He knew of your importance and being the man of our family, he felt responsible for keeping us safe and protected."

"I remember mother." Jesus noticed her surprise look, causing him to chuckle. "Dear lady, even though I was but a baby and then a toddler, I can recall everything about my past childhood with you and Father Joseph. The moment I was born, I can still see your beautiful face looking down smiling, with so much love I knew you had to be my mother. Then Father Joseph peered over your shoulder and laughed with joy. All the wooden toys meant a lot to me, because I knew my earthly father had made them with his own loving hands and I knew my laugh would return my love to him."

"Amazing!" Mary shook her head as she thought, I wonder if he remembers just because I reminded him about what happened when he was small?"

"You think I remember these things because you have told me." Once again Jesus laughed when she looked up surprised because he had read her thoughts. "I remember the small group of shepherds that came to the stable and speaking to the small shepherd boy. I recalled weeks later when three wealthy Magi appeared on camels bringing gifts and worshiping me as the newborn king! I recall going to the temple and hearing Our servant Simeon, who had been praying to us to let him live long enough to see for himself the long-awaited Messiah, and recognized me before giving his blessing, before telling you about the sword that will pierce your heart. There was an older woman inside the temple who also started giving praises and telling the worshipers about me." Jesus gave his mother a smile, knowing his parents had never spoken about any of those things until now. "I could go on mother, but, I need to tell you the other reason why I came out to speak to you."

"Of course, son. Tell me what is on your mind." Mary was glad he had stop reminding her he knew everything because he was the Son of God, so, of course he would know.

"You know about the bench I made and showed Father Joseph, to get his approval on its workmanship." He smiled when Mary nodded her head. "What your husband did not tell you was I made this very special bench for one purpose. To draw those people to it who are in need of a miracle. I named my bench, the Miracle Bench, because whoever is led to it by the light, will be blessed with the miracle they are searching for. You will find its name and who it is dedicated to carved beneath the bench in my script and signed by me, much like your devoted husband did for you with his bench."

"Who will be given such a powerful gift son?" Mary glanced down at the bench Joseph had made and wondered where Jesus's was. "Do you keep this special bench hidden somewhere?"

"My bench sets waiting inside my workstation and I will remove it out of sight until the day I return to heaven after being with my disciples for forty days and telling you goodbye." His eyes held serious words, that he would give his mother. "After I am gone from the earth, I will send down the Holy Spirit to remain with you and all who believe in me. Whenever a miracle is in need for the bench, I will appear to the person in need of healing, whether in the body or soul. This bench has been blessed and it shall remain on the earth until my final return. The person I have chosen to be the first caretaker of the Miracle Bench had to be some person I could trust with such a big responsibility. The Holy Spirit will fall down on him with a flame once he has excepted who I am and why I came to earth."

"Tell me Jesus, who will be gifted with this special honor? Is it someone I know?" Mary knew the person who received this master's work made by the hands of Jesus, must have been having doubts as to what Jesus really was."

"Mother, once again your thoughts are correct. My brother James loves me deeply. Of this, I have no doubt, but once I began my ministries and miracles, James will hear rumors from our town's people, causing him to get confused as to who I really am, when all he knew me as was an older brother. He will struggle with this for a long time, even after I have been crucified, but James will find himself being led by the Holy Spirit to the Miracle Bench, and his story will be the first in the record book. I shall appear to James and all his doubts will melt into beliefs. He will even be chosen to write the twentieth book of the New Testament, where his Epistle will be a plea for vital Christianity."

"Then what you ask of me shall be done Jesus." Mary hugged her beloved son tightly. "I will give your brother James the Miracle Bench, knowing the Holy Spirit will watch over both James and your special gift to humanity and teach him when the time is right for everything he needs to know."

The present younger James watched the screen disappear and the book close. The first story would come next for the young minister, but for the moment, the lesson was over and both men named James, walked quietly back to the stone cottage.

CHAPTER 9

Once again, James was taken to the Sacred Garden and this time he would get to witness his first miracle story. The angels had provided two chairs in front of the sacred bench and the book lay shut, waiting for the elder James to instruct his nephew.

"James, since you are new to the caretaker's job, you will share your first year's experiences with me, your trainer. You will find when a miracle will accrue and we find ourselves waiting inside the garden, book in hand, opened to record everything it sees, we shall be invisible to the person who is receiving the healing from the Lord. Do you have a question about our roll?"

"I have one questions Uncle James. Whose job is it to hold the big book open while the miracle is taking place?" James once again gazed down at the super big heavy book, knowing ever whose job it was, they would have to hold it open a long time and he had not tried to hold it ever since the weight of it pulled him to the ground.

Uncle James glanced down and chuckled, recalling the shock from his nephew when he tried to take the heavy book to hold for him. "Not to worry son. When the trainer and his student are present for the recording, each of us hold a half, standing side-by-side with the record book open between us."

"That sounds positive and a much safer and steadier way to hold it up." The younger James laughed and settled back in the soft chair. "Will we be sitting or standing?"

"Standing, of course." The elder James smiled when the book opened automatically. "A servant of the most-high God always stands in the presence of Jesus, the Christ."

The young minister lifted his hand to hide his embarrassed face. "Can we see the first book now, Uncle James?"

The experienced caregiver chuckled and settled back as the page lifted into a screen and the first story title game up in bold letters.

Book 1: JAMES, THE FIRST CARETAKER
After hearing his fellow town citizens make fun of the

carpenter's son, James had remained inside Joseph's old workstation, working non-stop, trying to take his mind off the cruel gossip spreading throughout Nazareth. He continued to attend all the services held inside the temple, never having missed a single day of worship since he was old enough to attend with his beloved Father Joseph. James considered himself a man of deep faith and had asked his elder brother many questions regarding the words spoken by the Rabi when the sacred scrolls were read. James knew he could always draw wisdom from Jesus and the true fact that his brother seemed to know the scriptures better than the religious teachers. James had always been amazed at how Jesus could quote any verse in the Holy Word by heart and he never fell to delight in the stories told by his big brother, which all led to a special meaning.

The day Jesus showed up in Nazareth had given James mixed feelings. He had missed this special brother and to see him again was a blessing. But the event that happened in the synagogue on the sabbath day, was one that would haunt the brother of Jesus for a very long time. The time had come for the Rabi to read the day's scripture or ask someone in attendance to open the sacred scroll and read. When Jesus was asked to stand up and read the scripture from the book of Isaiah, James recalled slumping down in his seat, hoping no one would make fun of the brother he admired and loved so deeply.

Standing in front of all the familiar faces he had grown up to know, Jesus opened the book and found the place he chose to read.

"The Spirit of the Lord is upon me, because he hath anointed me to preach the gospel to the poor; he hath sent me to heal the broken-hearted, to preach deliverance to the captives, and recovering of sight to the blind, to set at liberty them that are bruised, to preach the acceptable year of the Lord." Jesus closed the book and gave it again to the leader before taking his seat. He noticed all the ones in attendance had their attention on him, so he began to speak to them.

"This day is this scripture fulfilled in your ears."

The large group of men had listened to his gracious words and marveled at what he had proclaimed. One man looked around at the silent men and spoke up. "Is not this Jesus, the son of Joseph, long gone from us and Mary who has lived among us since she was a child?"

Jesus had known their heart and the fact they would not except him for who he really was, but he had chosen to make himself known to them anyway. "You will surely quote this proverb to me, 'Physician heal thyself': whatsoever we have heard done in Capernaum, do also here in thy country."

"That is exactly my argument Jesus!" A stout man near the door shouted. "Show us one of your so-call miracles if you are able!"

James sunk down in his seat, closing his eyes in fear as he listened to his eldest brother and the town citizens going back and forth. When things turned quiet, he opened his eyes to see Jesus looking around at the familiar faces.

"Verily I say unto you, no prophet is accepted in his own country." James could hear mummering throughout the synagogue causing his brother to stand. "But I tell you of a truth, many widows were in Israel in the days of Elijah, when the heavens were shut up three years and six months, when great famine was throughout the land; But unto none of them was Elijah sent. Instead he was sent unto Sa-rep'-ta, a city of Sidon, unto a woman that was a widow. Likewise, many lepers were in Israel in the time of Elisha, the prophet; and none of them were cleaned. Only Naaman the Syrian."

These statements cut at the heart of every man that heard his words and they were filled with wrath. As James witnessed the angry mob turn on his perfect brother and had rose up to thrust him out of the city, the anxious younger brother feared for Jesus' life. Following close behind the crowd, that kept him and his other brothers pushed back, he watched in horror as they led Jesus unto the edge of the hill, whereon the city of Nazareth was built, planning to cast him down, headlong. When James and his brothers, along with some of his brother's disciples, finally managed to push their way up to the front of the angry crowd, they noticed all the confusion as heads whipped around and back-and-forth, trying to find the man they had drag to the city drop off. Jesus had passed through the midst of them and went his way without a single man seeing him.

James closed his eyes with thankful praises after hearing from the anxious group that Jesus had simply vanished from their sight. He felt the town citizens watching him and his brothers, needing an explanation as to what had happened to their strange brother. James could sense the fear building on his younger brothers and knew, being the eldest left behind, it was up to him now to defend his family.

"Why do you look at us, brothers of God? Are we too gifted with the same powers as our beloved brother? Is there anyone of us that can perform miracles like our saintly brother?" Tears filled James blue eyes. "I have yet to witness a miracle done by Jesus, but knowing my perfect brother, I doubt it not! Once I witnessed what others had been blest to see for themselves but I was only a recipient of the wine my brother had made from water." James waited until the laughter had died down. "Friends, if you still let me call you such, because of your disbelief and doubt, you shall never have the beautiful blessing for witnessing any miracle done by Jesus. I fear the lost for healing loved ones will be gone but an even greater loss for not believing will hinder your salvation. I still search for the answers as to what exactly my brother is, for only knowing him as my big brother all my life. What I do know is Jesus is no ordinary man. His wisdom goes way beyond even the greatest religious teachers or leaders I have heard. He can quote the scriptures by heart, as you must have noticed this day. Even now you seek to find natural reasons how my brother escaped your sudden condemnation for him and took it upon yourself to harm God's special gift to all mankind." James suddenly felt a new kind of strength, one he had never felt. "Brethren, I may not know exactly what my sinless brother is and why he can hear the call of God, then go to do His will. I might never witness one of his miracles for myself, but I know they are real. What man among you can turn water into wine? Make a cripple walk or a blind man see? Is there one among you who can feed 10,000 men, plus women and children with only a few fish and loafs of bread, a young boy's lunch? Is there any of you who can bring the dead to life, or drive demons out of a person? Have you ever walked on water? Nay, not a one of us! But this man called Jesus can and did, all those things and so much more! Do I believe my brother has done these miraculous things? Yes, my brothers, I believe in him with all my heart and I know Jesus is so much more to me than just a brother and friend. I shall never stop searching for God to fill me with the answer to the questions that have settled into my heart and mind. "Lord, who is this man I adore? What is this man's purpose for being born? "Why is he so different from the rest of our family, my brother whom I love so deeply? And why does my heart and soul rejoice at the very sight of Jesus and I feel the great need to fall down on my knees at his feet and worship him?"

James grew silent and was expecting mocking and laughter coming from the large group of men, but instead, there were dropped heads, many feeling shameful for their previous actions toward Jesus, others considering the strong words spoken by the usually quiet brother James, and feeling that they had acted with too much haste after hearing the words Jesus had directed toward them. Now calmed down, the men could see the young man they had known as the carpenter's son, had only spoken the truth about their bad behavior toward him. Each man could not explain what had happened to Jesus when the hands that gripped him felt the obvious strong tugging from the tall young man until they reached the cliff, where he simply vanished and all they felt was the air and emptiness left in their grip.

As time swept by, the horrible news came that his perfect brother had been arrested by the chief priest in Jerusalem, and taken to Pontius Pilate for judgement. James had been horrified over the outcome and crucifixion. Knowing his loving mother had been there to suffer through this tragedy without him by her side, tore at his very soul. After speaking to his brothers about taking care of the family business and watching after his sisters that had not gone with Mary and John, one of the twelve, James packed his few belongings, left a letter for his mother and his wife, then departed up into the hills, to fast and pray. The broken man would remain away until he was older.

When James reached forty-years-old, he finally came down and was led by the Holy spirit to an unknown garden that contained only one object, a beautiful bench. James had been looking down as he made his way back home and when he finally glanced up, he found himself in a beautiful garden, surrounded by the cedars from Salem, a place of peace.

James studied the garden for a moment, trying to recognize the place, perhaps as being altered since he left. After studying the tall cedars, James realized his mother's garden could never have grown such tall cedars in such a short time. James had left when he was twenty-eight, so the trees had only twelve-years to grow after getting planted. And if they had been planted the same year he left homc to find the answers he was seeking, they would be smaller. James recalled his last thought and mumbled out loud.

"Find the answers I was seeking?" he gave a sarcastic laugh. "The only fact I learned was what was safe enough to eat up there on that hillside and where to find the water I needed." James moved closer to the bench. "I wasted all those years searching for the truth!" His face lifted to the heavens as he shouted. "And all I found was starvation, loneliness, and absolutely nothing about my dead brother!"

James fell on the ground, unable to stop the tears that fell from his tired-sad eyes. Between sobs he continued to speak to God. "Why? Why did Jesus have to die? He was the most perfect, the most innocent, the most loving and generous man I knew! Why did they kill my beloved brother? Why God? Please tell me now or take my miserable, wretched life and stop this torture!"

"James." Came the soft familiar voice, that cause the unhappy man to jerk his head up and look around at the empty garden. Had he only imagined hearing the voice of his beloved brother speak his name or was he simply going crazy. "James, follow the light." Once again, the calm familiar voice he knew so well.

"Jesus?" James arose slowly to his feet and saw the light his brother had told him to follow. Was this the first sign from heaven, James thought. Did God hear his plea asking for death. Was this a light from heaven to take him up to where Jesus surely was.

"James, my brother, death has not come for you. Just do as I say and follow the Spirit where it leads you. There, I shall meet you."

"Then I go with haste, dear Spirit. Lead on to the place where my brother is waiting." James was surprised to find himself standing in front of the bench, just a few feet away. "This is where I meet Jesus?" James glanced around at the empty garden and smiled. "I'll just stand here and wait until something happens." As soon as his words came out, James felt a strong source of power push him gently down on the bench. Startled, the young man looked out into the empty space for whoever or whatever pushed him down. Before he could respond, he let out a gasp when the form of a man suddenly appeared in front of him. Recognizing his brother, the instant he became visible, James tried to jump up to give him a hug, but found it impossible to move from the bench.

"James, you cannot move from the Miracle Bench once seated,

my beloved brother. I have felt your great sorrow, thinking me dead forever, and I have heard your many questions about who and what I am." Jesus glowed with the light from heaven as he spoke lovingly to his brother. I have known of your struggling over the fact that growing up with me beside you every day as your big brother, has made believing the truth of who I have always been, hard on you. Now, the moment has come for you to know all things about the man who was born of Mary, your mother also, making us human brothers. Believe me James, the love I gave you throughout your life was real. As you got older you could see I was different from the other children of Mary and Joseph. You marveled at my great wisdom and how could anyone know the holy book by heart, word-for-word. Then I left to begin my ministry and you heard how I did great wonders that no man had ever done before." Jesus' eyes glistened. "James, you know what the prophets said about the Messiah, how he would be born of a virgin. The truth is Father Joseph, who I admire and love deeply, was not my flesh and blood father." Jesus could see reality was starting to sink inside his brother's heart and soul. "The blessed virgin, named Mary, did conceive a son, given to her by the Holy Spirit, through my real Father and they told her as well as Joseph, by the angel Gabriel, you shall call his name Jesus, and He will save His people from their sins."

"Jesus, you are the Messiah! The Christ!" James had felt like falling on his knees in front of Jesus' feet and worshiping him, and now he knew the reason. "Please tell me Lord, what happened after you were crucified on that horrible cross?"

"James, that was the reason I came into the world. I went to the cross by my own free will to carry with me every sin ever committed since Adam and Eve, up until the last person born when I return. The Father sent me down as the lamb without blemish, without sin, to die for everyone who will believe in me and ask for forgiveness. To walk in my light and to tell my redemption and sacrifice to all the nations."

"Jesus, I will gladly carry my cross for you and share the good news wherever I go." James finally felt alive again and knew now what he wanted to do with his life. "Jesus, I sense you have a very important job for me to take on. If so, I am more than willing to give my all to you, my Savior and King!"

A broad smile fell on the Lord's handsome face. "You asked about what happened after the crucifixion, so you must know. After dying on the cross, I was laid in the tomb of a man named Joseph, and I arose from the grave on the third day, early in the morning on the first day of the week." Jesus held out his hands and showed the wholes where the nails had pierced his perfect hands. "They killed this body James and, in my resurrection, I remain in the same body, the same body I have always had in heaven with the Father and Holy Spirit, who will remain with all of you until I return to take you home to heaven where Father Joseph now waits, happy in his carpenter job."

"Then, what we enjoy doing on earth, can be done in heaven?" James would wait for his instructions from Jesus.

"Most things brother, just not the task I give you." Jesus gave him a reassuring smile. "This bench you are sitting in is very special James. If you hadn't ran away, then you would know through mother that I made the special bench and placed a very powerful blessing on it. She would have informed you that I wanted you to have the bench and wait for my instructions for using it. You are to be its first caretaker and keep records on every person who is led to the Miracle Bench. You will need no script to write with, for the book has also been blessed and will automatically record a living record for you to review whenever you choose. People in need of healing will be led to the sacred bench by the light, same as you were, and I will appear to heal whatever they may need. There will be many different reasons for needing a miracle and many will be unbelievers. This bench has been given eternal life so it will remain in perfect condition until my final return."

"By your saying my job as caretaker will last until you come again to take me home to heaven, so who shall I leave the bench to?" James had felt this job was both blessed and rewarding.

"You have a son name James. He will be trained by you to become the second caretaker of the Miracle Bench." Jesus knew James was ready to take on this important roll. "The book will amaze ever caretaker when it comes to life and you can actually see the person's life become real again. You will be trained by the angels and they will remain with every caretaker. A stone cottage will be built for you and your family, and all the other caretakers after you. These men must remain in our family line and every generation must name a son James to be trained for the job." Jesus took a seat next to his brother so they could hug. "My brother, you will never be alone, for I am always with you. There is one more thing you will leave with all people. I want you to write one of the books for the New Testament, concerning me. There is no need for you to ponder over what words you should write James, for your Lord and Savior will fill your heart and mind with every word to write. They shall be read and studied for all generations throughout every nation on this earth we created. Peace and love my brother." With one soft kiss on the cheek, Jesus was gone.

CHAPTER 10

Sarah was up and dressed when James woke up. After spotting her waiting by the big window, gazing out at the first rays of sunlight, the handsome young man sat up stretching.

"Sarah sweetheart, what gets you out of bed so early this morning?"

Giving her faithful husband a big smile, Sarah jumped up with excitement and dashed over by the bed. "Finally, you are awake, sleepyhead! I've been bursting inside with anxious happiness with some hopeful good news!"

"You're pregnant?" James, now wide awake with the great morning news, dived from the covers and grabbed his wife, laughing. "How far long are you? Have you started showing yet?" the young preacher pulled back to look at her flat stomach. "Too soon for mommy-fat!"

"James Jesu, will you please calm down and try not to wake ever soul still asleep in our home." Sarah loved to see her husband so happy, but she must make him understand this could be just another false alarm, and her monthly is just late this month. "Did I not say, some 'hopeful' good news?" The pretty-young woman gave her mate a playful slap when he narrowed his eyes. "I won't know for sure darling until I see doc this morning, so he can verify my diagnosis!"

"Doctor Brandon sounded sure of the fertility pills when he same as said: on your next visit, you would be a little mother." James walked quickly to the closet and pulled out a casual suit. "When is your appointment darling? I will go with you to hear the great news myself. Then we can have breakfast at that little café we love, to celebrate!"

"Listen to you, already acting as though you're going to suggest going by the Smoke Shop to order a box of cigars, with IT'S A SON, printed boldly on the wrapper!" Sarah looped her arms around her husband's neck. "Now, just hear me out James, didn't I hear you and Uncle James discussing what your training lesson would be today and that you would begin right after your usual seven-o'clock breakfast." The cute girl chuckled at his serious face as she sat down and started putting on her shoes. "Didn't you tell me last night before we went to sleep, how excited you were about today's lesson? Something about meeting another high-ranking person from the bible?"

"Alright, you're right darling, as always." James hung the suit back in the closet and took out the box his uncle had given him the night before, and sat it on the bed. "Uncle James said my jeans and sweaters were fine at the beginning of my training, but now that I know what is expected of me, my attire must be appropriate for the caretaker's job."

"So, your uniform is inside this big box?" Sarah finished fasting her shoes and made her way over beside her husband. "Go ahead James, open it, so I can see how my handsome husband must dress to be a caretaker."

"Sarah, if the caretaker wears what Uncle James does, I cannot see much difference between my jeans and his kaki pants. Although my sweaters are various colors and his is always white, I just don't know what the big deal is about." James stared down at the closed box, his fingers resting on the lid. "no-one will ever see us anyway standing in the garden. We will be invisible to them." James gave a sarcastic laugh. "We could be standing there naked for that matter. Who would know?"

"Jesus Christ will know James!" The couple jumped when they turned to see Uncle James standing in the doorway, pointing at his watch. "The vast group of angels would know as well. Do I need to go on, young nephew?"

"No uncle, I catch your meaning as I gather we are running a little behind time this morning." James took his wife's hand. "I was merely joking about prancing around in the nude sir. To be honest, I would be embarrassed in front of you alone." James opened the box and found it empty. "It appears I wasn't the only one joking about wearing nothing." He glanced at his wife who had noticed the empty box as well. "Did I wait to long to dive into my kakis and white sweater, Uncle James?"

The uncle finally gave a chuckle after checking himself over, wearing his usual kakis and white sweater. "Son, these clothes I wear is what this household sees before we step inside the sacred garden. You could even wear those pajamas out the door and down the path, but the moment you step inside that wondrous garden, your caretaker vestments will appear. The ones that covered your body the moment you opened the sacred box."

James and Sarah looked over his young body and only saw pajamas. "So, if these invisible vestments are on me now, and will appear when I step inside the Sacred Garden, why haven't I ever seen your vestment change from those kakis and sweater?"

"It was not your time to witness the robes and vestments James, other sacred items left by James, the first caretaker." The elder James smiled over at Sarah, reading her anxious wandering if she was indeed pregnant with a son at long last. "As for you, young lady, do not place all your hopes in one try. You must keep the faith Sarah. God will not let you and James down. He knows your needs far better than you or James does." The gentle man's eyes sparkled with faith. "There is a time for every purpose under heaven, child. Just hold on to that truth Sarah. If you just put your trust in the Lord, you will find yourself singing those very words from the holy scriptures, made into a song to lighten the darkest moments in your life." Uncle James turned to his nephew. "See your wife gets away safely then meet me in the dining room. Her appointment is Doctor Brandon's first one." He disappeared out the open door.

"Uncle James is right Sarah. You must never give up hope with God in control of our lives." James escorted his nervous wife down the stairs and out to her car. "I suppose no breakfast for you means Kelly is having blood work done on you, just to be sure the outcome." Before James helped her inside her Honda, he gathered her into his arms. "Sarah, my deepest love, if by some chance, you aren't with child, please promise me that you will not lose faith. I am certain, same as Uncle James, God has a reason for waiting until the time is right, should this be another false hope. I never should have made you think you had to give me a son, never considering the fact that maybe we couldn't have a baby right away. What I'm trying to say darling is, whatever the outcome is, pregnant or not, my deep love for you will always remain the same. You are the beautiful thing that makes me whole, my love and I shall always need you Sarah, in my life forever."

"Thank you, James. I have never doubted your love for me and I love you just as deeply." She looked up, tears in her beautiful eyes. "It is because I love you beyond ending that I want so badly to give you the son you have spoken about wanting from the moment we declared our love for each other." She reached up to give him a kiss and gave him a sweet smile. "You mustn't worry about me sweetheart. I'll not deny I hope the test come back positive but I won't fall apart if there's no baby, yet. I too believe the Almighty has a time for everything James. You just enjoy your lesson and I will let you know if there is anything to celebrate when I see you." Sarah got behind the wheel and drove away, leaving James whispering a silent prayer up to God.

Sarah had been examined by her doctor and she waited anxiously in his office to hear the outcome. Up until that moment, the good Christian girl had held on to her hope for being pregnant until she saw Doctor Brandon's solemn face when he stepped inside his office holding her chart.

"You have bad news Doctor Brandon? There is no baby, is there?"

"Sarah, this is very unexpected and I would give anything if it was just an error with the slides." He reached for his lifelong patient's trembling hand and the good-hearted man could not miss the tears welling in her eyes. "I ran the test through the lab three-times Sarah and the results were still the same."

"Please doc, tell me! You are scaring me." Sarah sat up, eyes wide with uncertain fear. "Tell me it's the same problem as before? That I am trying to hard! That the fertility pills need to be switched to another kind. There has got to be a way, in this modern world, that I can get pregnant!"

"That's just it Sarah, you can't get pregnant sweetheart. You can never get pregnant." The doctor saw panic fall over her face as her fingers clutched her handbag so tightly her knuckles grew white. "Sarah, there are other ways for you and James to have children."

"Yes! You can take my eggs and fertilize them with James's sperm and have the embryo placed inside a surrogate to carry our baby for us!" The brief hope she felt faded with the doctor's negative head shake. "Please tell me, what other way can James and I have a baby Doctor Brandon?"

"I was referring to adoption Sarah. There are plenty of couples unable to have children and adopted children can feel like they're your own if you get them as an infant." Kelly Brandon noticed Sarah's head shaking swiftly back and forth as she said upset.

"No! Never would an adopted son work out for James! He needs his own flesh and blood son doc!" Sarah pulled her hands free and jumped up. "If I cannot give my beloved the son he wants, then I'm useless to his needs!"

"Sarah darling, that is preposterous! James loves you and he will never blame you for not giving him a son!" The upset doctor hit the desk. "Is James so selfish that he makes you feel useless for not giving him this son?"

"Just tell me doctor, what is wrong with me? Why can't I have babies?" the usually calm and sweet girl flew into a rage, knowing the real reason her beloved needed his own son and angry that this man she had always admired had put the man she loved down. "Isn't there some type of operation I could have to help my problem?"

"Nothing can help your problem, Sarah. It is completely out of any physician's hands" Kelly knew he had to tell her the hard truth. "Sarah, there are no signs of any eggs inside your ovaries. You are completely dried up child. That is the reason you stopped having your monthly period. Your cycle has shut down. I am so sorry Sarah. God knows if there was anything I could do to help you reverse this I would."

"Then, I am just like Sarah in the bible and Elisabeth." Sarah stood up in a daze, head spinning over the tragic news. "They both received a miracle when they were older. I just cannot hold out for my chances to receive such a blessed miracle."

"Sarah, I told you there was not anything I can do for you, but being a Christian, there is always hope where God is concern." Doctor Brandon gathered her trembling hands. "Jesus is the great physician Sarah and if James needs this son due to a religious reason, and by your reaction when I put your loving husband down, I'd guess he does need a son. Perhaps another heir to name James, since that's his uncle's name. Pray for that miracle child. The God who loves you will hear your prayer and grant you whatever you ask of Him."

Sarah wrapped her arms around the only doctor she had ever known. "Thank you, Kelly. I will pray for that miracle and who knows I just might catch myself singing." She started to leave after the nurse peeked in to tell the doctor his patient was waiting. "Kelly, I would appreciate it if you don't tell James what you told me. At least, not until I can find a way to break the news to him myself."

"I promise." He watched her moving slowly toward the door. "Sarah, remember what I told you about those strong drugs. Please see they are properly destroyed. We wouldn't want them to end up in the wrong hands."

"Don't worry Doctor Brandon, I'll get rid of them, I promise." She had a faraway look as she added. "I'll make sure every single pill disappears. Goodbye old friend." The doctor had a bad feeling as he watched the little girl he had saw grow up walk away.

"I made you a promise Sarah, not to tell your husband." The doctor spoke to himself. "But, you must forgive your old friend child, that is one promise I cannot keep."

CHAPTER 11

"James, I can see you are worried about Sarah. Son, there is nothing you can do except show her how much you love and support her. The rest is in God's hands. He has a plan for the two of you and this plan has something to do with giving Sarah the baby she so desperately wants. Just be patient, keep praying and never give up your faith in what the Almighty can do." Uncle James had walked beside his quiet nephew all the way to the secret entrance of the garden and had stopped to address what had been bothering James. "Son, once we step inside the Sacred Garden, we shall become the caretakers of the Miracle Bench. It is important that you have a clear mind once inside and all your thought must be on your lesson. Always be aware that we are never alone inside the garden James, and I am not referring to the many angels that serve us there."

"I'm ready Uncle James. I know to become a caretaker, one must leave all worries at the Lord's feet and carry out the duties that lie before us." James felt at peace after his uncle's faith-fill words of hope and assurance in laying your burdens before the Lord and replace them with the mantle of faith. "My heart knows God will watch over Sarah, to keep her safe."

"Happy day!" the elder James waved a hand toward the thick hedge. "After you young James. Today's lesson awaits and once again, we shall find ourselves back in Jerusalem, over 2,000-years-ago."

After uncle and nephew stepped through the hidden entrance, their robes and vestments were visible, and after checking himself out, James felt more reverent about the caretaker's job. Seated on their usual chairs, both men watched the great book open to the next story and instantly the page floated out into a big screen.

STORY# 2 HEALING THE SOUL OF PONTIUS PILATE
Ever since the crucifixion of the man called Jesus, the governor of Judea found himself having great difficulty with sleeping. Much of his anxiety came from the same nightmare that plagued his restless dreams, whenever he grew too tired to stay awake. His mood swings

would change on a mite. One minute his usual demanding mind-set, then turn quickly to almost childish frighten behavior, where tears flowed down the normally stern face, ready to announce a harsh sentence to a criminal or murderer. Normally active and romantic at night to his beautiful wife, the haunted man who had ordered the death of this man he had wanted so desperately to set free could not bring himself to enjoy the pleasures of life he once enjoyed.

Seeing the change in her husband, Pilate's faithful wife knew it was time to offer him the help he so desperately needed, and she felt she was the one to offer it. Susanna had heard Pilate's ravings during the dark hours of the night and there was always one man's name that came out. Susanna had heard many things spoken about this Jesus and what she heard had touched her heart so much, she desired more. So, unbeknown to her husband or anyone else living and working within the governor's palace, the brave wife of Pilate disguised herself as a Jewish woman and sought out the man from Galilee. After hearing him preach and witnessing her very own miracle, she was compelled to follow him whenever he was close by. Then to see him standing before her husband's judgement seat, she knew she must try to warn her husband not to have anything to do with the man she had grown to love and believe to be truly, the Son of God. Who else could proclaim the powerful words he spoke or quote scripture with no words to go by. What man had ever been able to bring a dead man back to life and one who had laid in his tomb for days. Lazarus had lived just a few miles away from the Holy City and once before Jesus had visited the family in the small town of Bethany. Susanna had followed a small group of their friends to their big home and had eaten at the same table as Jesus. There, Pilate's wife had heard the Lord speak for the first time. Being excepted by Martha and Mary, the sisters sent her word when their brother Lazarus grew ill and their message stated they had sent word to Jesus, so he could heal his friend. Lazarus grew worse and he died before the man from Galilee arrived. Susanna knew she would stay with the other mourners for as long as the sisters needed her. Her husband was busy preparing his soldiers for any unrest during the approaching Passover, so she would not be missed for some time. The devoted new follower of the Lord would risk punishment from her Roman husband before she would miss any opportunity to hear and see Jesus.

Hc finally arrived and Martha met him, weeping uncontrollable, and asking him why he came after it was too late for her brother. Susanna recalled the sadness that filled Jesus' beautiful eyes as the sister asked him: "If you would have been here, my brother would not have died!" Then she heard the Master say: "Your brother will arise again." It was clear to Susanna how much Martha and Mary loved Jesus, but their hearts had been broken, Martha responded back: "Yes Lord, my brother will arise again, on the day of resurrection! The resurrection of us all!" Thinking back to the Lord's next words brought tears to Susanna's eyes as she heard him again plainly say: "I AM THE RESURRECTION AND THE LIFE, HE THAT BELEAVES IN ME, THOUGH HE WERE DEAD, YET, SHALL HE LIVE!". Susanna remembered the new flood of tears as she watched this loving man weep, then ask: "Do you believe this Martha?" Knowing, by faith, who this man was, Martha answer: "I believe if you would have been here my brother would not have died. But, even now, if it be thy will Lord, I believe I shall see my brother again, by your word!"

Susanna walked to her big window and could see Golgotha, the hill where Jesus had died on the cross. On that horrible day, she had only been able to take one glance at the tragic scene, before falling to the floor weeping. Susanna had heard Jesus' proclamation, I AM THE RESURRECTION AND THE LIFE! And as she lay on the floor weeping she could hear his voice proclaim this statement over and over in her head. At that very moment, Susanna remembered his words: After I am crucified, I will arise again on the third day. Susanna did not have to be there to believe that Jesus would come out of the tomb, she knew, by faith, Jesus Christ, the Son of God, would live again. And when the soldiers reported what happened at first light on the first day of the week, Susanna could only stand hidden behind the door to her husband's grand-hall and listen with joy.

Now, she had watched her husband suffer long enough and the Roman physicians would be of no help. She knew his problem did not consist of any illness. What her husband needed was a revelation for the reason his constant thoughts were about this man called Jesus. Susanna found Pilate alone inside his chamber, staring out into the moonlet sky over the hill where he had watched the innocent man die.

"Pontius, I have seen your anxiety growing with each passing day and it breaks my heart to watch you suffer."

"My beautiful Susanna, then do me a favor and rid me of this anguish that eats at my very soul!" the strong man glanced back at her and noticed the gentle calm that fell around her. "Oh, my sweet wife, to be able to feel the peace you seem to possess. Give me your secret so I too can be at peace, instead of this thing that eats away at me, day in and day out! I pray for sleep to come to me, but as soon as it does, the nightmares return and I can still behold the man hanging on that cross that I ordered him on!" Pilate felt his wife's soft hand on his back and the tough man fought back the tears that he had tried to hide from everyone, including her. His position did not leave room for a weak man and Pontius had always considered himself, a perfect governor, whose methods always frighten the average citizen into behaving and following his strict Roman rule.

"Pontius, you saw something different in this Jesus and as he spoke such profound words to you, where you not captivated by his astounding eyes, that seem to absorb your whole being?" Susanna paused as she watched her husband drop his head before nodded an affirmative. "Speak the things that are on your mind beloved, so that I may help you."

"You, help me?" Not use to a woman asking for control of his problem, much less, trust a female to possess such knowledge, the high-ranking governor managed a soft chuckle. "What would a female know about such matters, wife? You speak as though you may know something about this Jew I condemned to die by crucifixion."

"If you will find it in your heart to believe my words to you, then yes, Pontius, I can ease your mind concerning your nightmares about Jesus." Knowing the truth about her risen Lord, Susanna had no fear to speak about the one she knew had died not just for her, but for her husband and everyone else who would believe in Him that he was the Son of God. "The truth is, Pontius, I am the only one inside this palace that CAN help you."

"Such brave and bold words my wife speaks!" Pontius turned to face her and noticed her strong resolve and strength did not coward away from his stare. "My beloved is serious and she declares she knows more than my great-high-paid Roman physicians!"

"On this matter sir, I do! These Romans know nothing about who Jesus really is!" Susanna stood her ground, unafraid.

"And you do?" The smile now dropped from her husband's mocking face and was replaced by a serious one. For a few tense moments, the governor of Judea stared down at his loyal wife and could only see love inside her eyes. "Why would you risk your life for my well-being Susanna? You know going behind my back to learn of another faith, other than our Roman beliefs, can prove deadly."

"I am aware of the risk I am making Pontius, but I would do it again if it meant saving the man I love from damnation!" Susanna stood bravely, knowing the Lord was her shield and strength. "Husband, even though I came out with what I have done, only to save you from any more torment, I can face death knowing that even though I die, I will be resurrected by my Savior!"

"Resurrected? By what Savior, Susanna?" he took hold of her shoulders. "Who is it you speak about?"

"Jesus! Jesus Christ is my Savior and the Son of God!" Susanna's eyes lit up with the love of Jesus. "Don't you see Pontius, you may have ordered Jesus to the cross, but remember what he told you. Say it, my love. What did Jesus tell you? Do you remember Pontius?"

"Do I remember? That is all that consumes my thinking Susanna! Our conversation repeats itself over and over again inside my head!" Once again Pilot moved to the window facing Golgotha, the words spilling from his lips. "I had met with the high priest, Caiaphas and his group. I immediately noticed the man wearing a simple white robe, his head dropped. I thought how tired he looked, as if no sleep had closed his eyes since this angry mob arrested him. Caiaphas was demanding that I judge him and stated he was a criminal. I told the Jews to take and judge him for themselves, according to their law but they declared it is not lawful for them to put a man to death. He claims to be King!" Pilate closed his eyes and he could see the face that haunted him, the loving face of Jesus. "Then I ask Jesus, are you the king of the Jews?" he answered me.

"Do you say this thing yourself, or did others tell it to you about me?"

I was wanting the whole matter to be over so I gave him my answer. "Am I a Jew? Your own nation and chief priest have delivered you to me. What have you done?" then he answered

"My kingdom is not of this world. If my kingdom were of this world, then my servants would fight, that I should not be taken by the Jews. But, now is my kingdom not from here."

I was totally confused to his meaning, so I ask him, are you a king then? Once again, he answered

"You say that I am a king. To this end was I born, and for this cause, I came into the world, that I should bear witness to the truth. Every one that understands the truth hears my voice."

Then I ask him, what is truth?" Pontius turned to look at his wife. "I know there was some meaning in his words, but so help me wife, the Gods refuse to help me! I speak to them but they remain quiet."

"You shall never here the gods you worship Pontius. They do not exist because they are false gods!" Susanna could see a hint of anger growing in her husband's eyes so she came to the real God's defense. "The reason you did not understand the words of Jesus Pontius is because you are deaf to what is true. Even now you doubt the truth I shared with you about the statues you worship! The one and only God reigns in heaven husband and unless you change your heart and turn away from these false gods you worship, you will spend your eternity in the never-ending lake of fire with Satan!"

"My wife grows bolder! Can this new faith you have make you dumb or incredibly unafraid?" he remained calm, the need to know what Jesus meant by the words he had spoken to him. "If you can translate the words spoken by Jesus, I shall hear you out. If not, I will not hesitate to call my guard!"

"I have naught to hide and I knew the moment you spoke the Lords words what he meant." Susanna stood bravely. "The kingdom Jesus was referring to that was not of this world is heaven, where he reigned even before creation of this earth, with His Father and the Holy Spirit! They are one God, three in one. The servants he spoke of who would fight for him are the angels of heaven! The truth is there were 10,000 of his servants around him while he hung on that cross! Should our Lord have chosen to come down and not die so we could live, the angels would have easily destroyed the earth. When you ask if he were a king, he proclaimed to this end was I born. He was saying, the Son of God came down to earth as a baby to be the Savior for all the people by dying on the cross for all our sins! This was his cause, and he preached this truth for three-short-years knowing his destiny."

"That statement by Caiaphas bothered me the most!" Pilate fell into his seat. "When I ask the priest why they wanted this Jesus crucified, he said because, he made himself the Son of God!" the usually calm man buried his head in his hands to weep. "I tried to convince the angry mob that the man did nothing wrong! They would not hear it! The harder I tried the louder they cried, Crucify him! Crucify him!" Desperate and unsure of just who this Jesus really had been and the cold fact that it was his own order as Governor of Judea, to give the man's final sentence to be crucified, Pilot order his wife to leave him so he could be alone to think.

Obeying the word of her husband, Susanna gave his worried face one last caress before starting to the big chamber door. Turning briefly, she spoke one last time, in hopes it might kindle some type of spark within the staunch Roman's heart. "Pontius, I speak as the woman who loves you dearly. Just speak to this man now, in your chamber, quiet and alone. Jesus will hear you, for He has seen your torment and He loves you even more than I do. Whether or not you believe it possible, even should you doubt he can hear you, I promise, if you try, Jesus will respond." Susanna watched him close his eyes to give a mocking laugh before turning to stare at her.

"Wife, how can a man who was crucified and died on our cross, be capable of hearing my pathetic cry, much less answer, by any means? What is this Jesus now anyway, a spirit, to haunt my nights even greater than they already are?"

"Pontius, do you recall how mesmerized the soldiers were who had witnessed the tomb of Jesus, in which you had sent them to guard, was opened by an invisible force, as the ground shook as though there had been an earthquake? How they proclaimed they were blinded by the incredible bright light that shined from the open tomb?" Susanna almost glowed with the marvelous news. "Beloved, Jesus, the Son of God, is not dead! He arose on the third day, just as he had told his followers! Ever since our Lord and Savior went back up to heaven after being with us for forty days after his resurrection, He left the third part of the Almighty God with us, the Holy Spirit. The true God is Triune, Father, Son and Holy Spirit."

"If this Jesus is gone back to where his kingdom is, and heaven is definitely not of this world, who is telling you all these preposterous things about him?" Pontius tried to remain focus as a loyal Roman, but his heart and mind were screaming for the truth. The governor paused in his thinking as he recalled the past words spoken from himself and Jesus. Not realizing he was speaking softly a loud, he said "I came into the world that I should bear witness to the truth. Everyone that understands the truth, hears my voice." Pilate turned to his wife. "Susanna, after Jesus spoke his words, my heart was moved to know more, so I ask, what is truth? This Holy Spirit he left behind, is he the one that fills your head with this knowledge of his staying for forty days before ascending back to his kingdom?"

"Jesus had many followers as he went around teaching and giving miracles to those in need, but the Lord had chosen twelve men to be his closes followers. Those twelve men were called disciples. This group was with Jesus throughout His three-year mission and it was one of His twelve that betrayed the Lord to the chief priest, Caiaphas, for forty-pieces of silver." Susanna noticed her husband trying to fight the fresh tears that welled up in his serious eyes. "Pontius, I know you are confused to this true belief, but the person I heard preaching these things about Jesus knew everything first-hand. He was one of the first picked to walk with Jesus. A mere fisherman by trade, and the Lord declared to the man name Simon, his brother Andrew, and brothers James and John, I will make you fishers of men. All four men left their nets and families to follow the Messiah. Jesus changed Simon's name then to Peter and called him MY ROCK! In a way, it is the Holy Spirit I hear when Peter speaks the truth of Jesus, unafraid, because the spirit of God came down on the disciples like a flame, then filled them with His very presence."

"Then, I shall do as you say and call out to this man I watched die! I shall see if he responds to my words." Pontius Pilate stared coldly at his wife. "Know this woman, if there is no response from this dead man within two-minutes, I will send my guard to have you arrested for treason against the Roman gods! Do you understand, Susanna?"

"I am not afraid Pontius for I too have been blessed by the presence of the fire above my head and now, the Holy Spirit reigns inside this temple!" Susanna swept her hands down over her body. "Pray with a sincere heart Pontius and the Lord will hear your cry.

If you ask anything of the Almighty God with a hard heart, I can grant you, He shall not hear your cry. I leave you now to make your choice. If you choose a heartless-doubting remark, be ready to spend the remainder of your life tortured over your decision to have Jesus killed, regardless to his words to ease your pain. If you choose to humble yourself before God, who is far greater than the mighty Tiberius Caesar, and speak all that is in your heart, for His ears alone, then you will get your answer." Susanna turned and walked from the room.

Everything grew quiet as Pontius Pilate made his way over by the large window overlooking the last place he had witnessed Jesus' bruised and bloody body hanging up high on the Roman cross against the dark-stormy sky. As his thorn-crowd head hung down to the right, Pontius remembered his dark hair blowing out gently in the howling wind. He recalled the sudden trembling of the palace when the earthquake struck and the distant sound of the massive Jewish temple curtain tearing down the middle. This sort of thing had never happened before at a crucifixion, he thought, but all the other times the men being crucified had been justified in the death order. All but this one man. He had known Jesus was innocent of any crime, and he tried several times to set him free. The Jewish leaders were determined to have him killed and Pilate could find no fault in Jesus at all. The priest had worked the large crowd of people to yell with them Crucify Him, over and over, so loud, they almost drowned out the smaller group yelling Save Him! The strict governor had felt some hope for releasing Jesus after he had him whipped, hoping that would satisfy the 'religious men' but they wanted more and wouldn't be satisfied until he got the death sentence. Then they brought up the scare tactic, to use Pilate's emperor, Tiberius Caesar. Threatening that if he did not kill Jesus, who had claimed to be the king, would make him a traitor to his king, Caesar.

"That's when I ask for a bowl of water to wash off my part of this setup murder, planned by Caiaphas and his group. I called out that I wash by hands of the blood of this just man, and the angry crowd just shouted back, then let his blood be on us and our children!" Pilate felt tears stinging his eyes. "What more could I have done Jesus? I told you I had the power to crucify you or the power to release you!" He paused, as the words of Jesus filled his mind.

"You could not have any power against me, except it were given you from above. Therefore, he that delivered me to you has the greater sin."

"Jesus, why would anyone from your kingdom decide to send you to be crucified and place such a burden on my shoulders? You were telling me the leaders of your people did the greater sin. Did you mean, that even if this thing was not my doing after all, I still had a lesser sin, but sinned against you no less?" Pilate fell on his knees, his head dropped to the floor. "I am so confused as to what to believe Jesus! I have been taught ever since I was a toddler, to worship all our Roman gods, who we can see in the stars. Now my wife tells me they are fake gods and there is only one God and this Caiaphas mentioned you admitting you were the Son of God!" the tears fell in small circles on the floor as he jerked up his head, speaking between sobs. "Please Jesus, help me to know this truth you spoke about. I cannot explain why, but I know you can hear my cry. I want to know and believe like my Susanna!" A breeze blew over the tormented man, causing him to look up at the open window. A stream of light came into the room and lit Pontius' face. He stood up slowly on trembling legs and looked out to find a horse saddled and waiting for him in the light.

Without hesitation, Pontius Pilate went quickly to the courtyard, to find it empty of guards. Not stopping to wonder what happened to the night guard, the governor of Judea jumped on the unfamiliar stallion and within minutes it had stopped around a big hedge. The light moved through the green hedge, so Pontius followed it into a big garden surrounded by tall cedars. The light had come to a stop at a beautiful smooth bench. Unsure of the meaning of what had just happened and were he was, the brilliant man assumed since the light was at the bench, then that's where he should be.

After taken a seat on the comfortable bench the light in front of him floated up into the form of a man. The usual-tough man took a big breath when he saw just who had led him to this garden. Unable to speak from the shock of seeing the very man he had ordered to be crucified several months earlier, he could only stare into the same blue-green eyes that had watched him give the order.

"Pontius, you seek to know this truth I spoke of and to remove the guilt that has been torturing your very soul for sending me to the cross."

"Yes Jesus, I am ready to know this truth that has filled the heart of your many followers. As for my guilt, I carry it with me night and day. The nightmares of that Friday afternoon, replays itself over and over in my dreams! I knew you were innocent and I did nothing to stop your death!"

"This thing that happened to me was planned in heaven by my Father and me, so we could save our people from their sins. You were part of the great plan Pontius. I had to come to earth and be born of a virgin, grow to go forth to preach the word to the poor and needy, to bring sight to the blind, open the ears of the deaf, make the cripple walk, drive out the demons of Our enemy, Satan, from the innocent and bring the dead to life. My main purpose for coming to earth was to save the world from the sin Satan had started through our first man and woman we created, after creating this earth. The stars you chose to worship were created by the Holy Three in One as well. The Father God, the Holy Spirit God and myself, the Son of God, also God!" Love radiated from the Lord. "Now you know, there was nothing you could have done to stop the crucifixion. I was the only person, born of woman, without sin, so I had to take on every sin ever committed and those sins not yet made, onto that cross and die for them so those who believed this truth, that I am the Son of God, then they confess their own sins, my death and blood on that cross has given them life eternal." Jesus looked down before saying. "Pontius Pilate, what is it you desire?"

"Lord Jesus, I am a sinner, probably more than most, and I am asking you to take away all these sins from me because I truly believe you are who you say you are, the Son of God! Forgive me Jesus so I can have this life eternal with you when I die."

Jesus reached out and touched the head of Pilot then gave him the blessing of forgiveness and everlasting life!

CHAPTER 12

The instant James returned to the cottage from his lesson in the Sacred Garden, he rushed inside the door to find Sarah, anxious to hear what the doctor had said. Maggie spotted the young man looking around the large down stair rooms so she informed him that his wife had returned sometime after noon and went straight up to their private rooms saying she needed a shower, then a nap before coming down for supper.

"Thank you, Maggie. I guess my girl couldn't sleep much last night, feeling too excited over the hopes that this time Doctor Brandon would have good news for us. She was up before the sun this morning to share her excitement about having a check-up to see if she was expecting a baby." James glanced up the stairs. "I'll go check on Sarah now. Thanks again for the information!" The young minister made his way quickly up the wide steps and found his wife lying on their bed, hand over her closed eyes. Not wanting to startle her, James walked over quietly and sat down on the bed next to his wife. He gently touched her face and spoke softly.

"Sarah, are you alright sweetheart?" seeing her eyes flicker open, James gently took her hand down to hold and returned her smile when she smiled up. "I came straight inside the cottage after our lesson and Maggie told me you got home after noon, then came up to our rooms to have a shower and I can see, a much-needed nap." Concern began to fall on James' face after noticing Sarah did not have the same joy she had entertained him with that very morning. "What happened between your cheerful morning with me and dragging back, obviously unhappy, almost seven-hours later? Bad news at the doctor's office?"

"It wasn't what I wanted to hear darling but after some breakfast at the diner on Fifth Street and some light shopping in Haven Brook, I came to terms with doc's diagnosis." Sarah gave James' hand a pat before getting up to stretch. "Fact are facts and no matter how much you want to change his outcome the facts always win out!" Sarah walked to the window and glanced out. "The cold fact is I am not yet pregnant darling and mother nature was just playing a mean trick on us. I felt those irritating gramps the moment I left the Doc Brandon and now we must wait at least five days before we can try again." Her eyes still focused out the window instead of her trusting husband, Sarah felt bad about her lie, but she recalled the nurses warning about her dryness causing great pain without the aid of her new prescription, a cream to make her feel natural when making love. Sarah's anxiety caused her to feel sick and the thoughts of food made it worse. She knew if Jack knew her symptoms, Jack would swear she was indeed pregnant and the doc made a wrong diagnose, so Sarah would make up another reason for not going down with the group for dinner. The truth was, Sarah just didn't want to hear all the others voice their opinions to help her and James get pregnant. Sarah had bigger problems weighing on her tortured mind. James wanted and needed a son. His very own son and Sarah knew she was incapable of giving him a baby. She would study her options when left alone to think.

"Sarah, your mind seems to be far away. Please sweetheart, you know you can tell me anything and I will listen, never to judge the woman I love." James walked over and pulled his wife into his arms. "Sarah, you are the most important person on this earth to me and if there is some kind of problem concerning us having a baby, please Sarah, do not shut me out. We can, through the grace of God, work it out, together. You need not go through this alone sweetheart. Together, we can make the right decision. Remember the old saying Sarah? When God closes the door, He opens the window! I know my loved one far better than she thinks and I can see you are fighting a battle by yourself." James lifted her chin. "Darling, is what you told me the exact words Doctor Brandon told you?"

"Yes silly!" Sarah gave a soft chuckle and playfully slapped his arm. "James Jesu, now why on earth would I start lying to you over something as important as our having a son?" Sarah walked over to her drawer and pulled out her flannel pajamas. "Now, you just go downstairs and enjoy your supper with the family. I am still full of my extra big breakfast from the Haven Brook Diner, not to mention exhausted from all the window shopping."

James goosed her waist, causing her to giggle, then he glanced around the tidy room for any sign of packages. "So where are all those shopping bags from all that window shopping beautiful? There are usually eight or ten setting around when you hit the stores."

"I just so happened to put away the few things I purchased and the bags are folded and placed in the bag tin." She pulled back the bedclothes and propped up her pillows before retrieving a book from the full shelf. "Give everyone my apologies and tell them I'll build up a nice-big appetite for tomorrow evening."

"I'll eat with the family alone then, and come right up afterward to tell you about my interesting lesson." They exchanged smiles before James left the room, still feeling unsure of his perfect wife's story.

Unable to get her mind on the book in her hand, Sarah closed it and slid from the covers to try out her new cream. The dryness made the application painful at first, but once the applicator was inside, she inserted the cream. Sarah hid the tube under other items in her bathroom drawer and noticed the bottle of fertility drugs. She lifted them up to read the warning directions, speaking them softly to herself.

"Take only one capsule with a full glass of water every night, for fifteen days, then stop. Never take more than one! They could prove fatal!" Sarah felt her fingers tremble. "Always take with a full glass of water! NEVER TAKE THIS DRUG WITH ALCOHOL! IT WILL BE FATAL!" Sarah slipped the bottle back in the drawer instead of throwing them out like her doctor had ask. "Sorry doc, these pills may be my only way out so James can remarry someone who can give him the baby boy he must have." Glancing behind her, to make sure she was still alone, Sarah took out her small key that locked the bottom drawer where she kept her jewelry. Opening it, she glanced down at her latest purchase, a fifth of vodka. Just in case she chose that route it would go quickly.

James had finished his meal and was getting ready to climb the wide staircase when the doorbell rang. He called out to the family, still enjoying coffee and table talk. "I'll see who is at the door. Just enjoy each other's company." He made his way through the hallway and opened the door to find a serious Doctor Kelly Brandon waiting, holding a brown bag obviously filled with something in the bottom. "Doc? What brings you out here tonight?"

"James, can we speak in private. I am concerned about Sarah."

Suddenly James was worried about his wife as he glanced back up the stairs. "Please Kelly, come in and tell me what is wrong with my wife."

"How was Sarah acting when she got home?" Kelly Brandon glanced up the same staircase, hoping he could speak to James without his sweet patient's knowledge.

"I was in the secret garden when Sarah came home doc. Our houseguest and cook told me my wife arrived back after twelve and went straight up to our rooms."

"Twelve? Did Sarah tell you what she was doing all that time after leaving my office at seven-forty-five?" James noticed how the doctor held on to the brown bag.

"Sarah said she was hungry and went for breakfast at Haven Brook Diner on Fifth Street, then after did some window shopping. I inquired about the missing shopping bags and she told me she had put away the few things she bought as well as the bags." James looked into the doctor's concerned eyes. "I had no reason to doubt my wife doc. Sarah has never lied to me before."

"And Sarah has never been given such bad news before either James. Did Sarah tell you what her diagnosis was James?" the doctor moved around nervously.

"She told me she wasn't pregnant and she had come to terms with the facts that we would have to keep trying." James noticed the concern deepen on the doctor's face. "She also told me mother nature had just played a trick on us, so now we had to wait before trying again." James took a tight hold of the doctor's shoulders. "For the love of God, tell me what you are holding back from me! What is wrong with my Sarah?"

"James, Sarah is barren, dried up completely! There are no signs of eggs in her female organs." Tears came to the doctor's eyes as he watched this good man tearing up. "James, Sarah cannot give you this son you want and obviously need. I have never seen the sweet girl so torn up as she was when I broke the news to her." This time it was Doctor Brandon grabbing James's shoulders. "James, I am worried about Sarah's mental state right now. I am afraid she may try something desperate!"

"You are not referring to suicide, surely?" James moved toward the door to glance up and could hear music playing on their radio. "Kelly, how did you come to that conclusion, just because my girl was upset over this tragic news? We have spoken at length about this possibility and the fact that nothing is impossible for the Lord!"

"Sometimes when people feel there is no real solution for a

problem this final, they turned to dark thoughts. Sarah feels useless to your needs James, so to help get what you need, knowing she cannot have a baby, she thinks, if she were out of the way, then" the doctor paused so James could finish the statement.

"I could get married again? Married to someone just to give me this son?" James fault the urge to dash up the steps to confront the women he could not replace in order to have this son. "Kelly, what makes you think Sarah is capable of taking her own life? She is a good Christian woman and she knows suicide is breaking God's law!"

"Yes, when Sarah is thinking straight, she would never choose suicide as a way to fix the problem she feels responsible for." Doctor Brandon gripped the upset husband's shoulders. "Listen James, I have known that girl all her life and I can read her actions. Perhaps I should not have told her without you there. Then maybe she would not have felt so worthless about being able to give you, the one thing you had ask for. A son to call James." Now the doctor was gazing up the stairs, recalling what made him start worrying about Sarah's state of mind. "James, I had thought at first Sarah had received the news graciously and had planned to tell you everything, until she started to leave my office."

"Kelly, what was different this time that made you suspect Sarah was in trouble?"

"The way she said goodbye. Normally she would smile and say, see yah, doc! Not this morning James.

There was a faraway look in her eyes as she glanced around, never really giving me eye contact, and said. Goodbye, old friend!" the doctor stared down at the bag in his hand. "Most people would never take note to her words, but James, when Sarah said those words to me, I knew at that instant, this beautiful young lady was headed for trouble."

"What's in the bag doc?" James had noticed the doctor not taking his eyes off the brown bag. "Is it some kind of medicine for Sarah?"

"No, my boy. This bag contains dirt. I want you to go straight up to your wife and ask her to hand over her fertility pills! She should have exactly five left. I counted the days she was on them until she stopped, thinking herself pregnant. It was ten-days. I gave her fifteen pills in her prescription." Doctor Brandon opened the bag. "Put the five pills inside this dirt and stir it over them, then take the bag and lose it someplace in the trash." The doctor looked up seriously.

"You believe Sarah is planning to take some of these pills, doc?"

"I know Sarah is planning to take all five pills James and if you have any alcohol inside this house, lock it away now!" he passed the bag of dirt to the young minister. "One pill alone is fatal with alcohol, five means instant death! Do you understand?"

"Thank you, Doc, for the warning. I'll see to the house wine, then retrieve those deadly pills so they will not be a temptation for my beloved Sarah." James walked the doctor to the door, anxious to get upstairs to his wife. "I'll speak to Sarah and make her understand how much her life means to me and the honest fact that I would never want to live without her next to me." The young man watched the doctor leave, saw to the wine cabinet getting locked, then dashed up the steps. Unknowing Sarah had just overheard her husband's conversation with their family doctor, he would not know the medicine had hurriedly been switched with some old pain medicine she had meant to throw out.

"Sarah, Doctor Brandon just informed me that we needed to throw away those fertility drugs since they cannot help you get pregnant." James walked with Sarah to their bathroom to collect what he assumed was the dangerous pills and had her toss them inside the bag of dirt. "I guess you forgot the doctor telling you to throw them out."

"No, I did not forget James, I just hadn't had the time to go out to the shed for some potting soil to put them in." She gave her husband a beautiful smile and he couldn't understand why the doctor had been so absolute over Sarah's behavior. "What else did doc tell you darling? He had agreed that I would be the one to tell you what he found."

"Then, why didn't you Sarah? Why tell me we could still try to have a baby when the doctor made it plain that you could never have children darling." James watched her walk away, and toss the empty pill bottle in the trashcan. "When were you going to tell me the truth sweetheart. I would never hold something like that against you. Sarah, you must know by now, if things look hopeless, God can make anything we ask of Him come true. You must never give up that hope Sarah, no matter how bad you're feeling right now. My love for you is the same and it will never change. If by some freak reason you cannot give me a son, and all else fails, I will never stop loving or needing you in my life. I married you because of my deep love I feel when we are together. Believe me darling, if I had to choose between you or having a son of my own, I would always choose you Sarah!"

"I believe you James, because I know how much you love me. Don't you see darling, I love you the exact same way and this is why the desire to give you a son and name him James would be the greatest proof of my undying love for you." Sarah went into his open arms feeling the tears she had been holding inside welling up in her eyes. "My darling James, I would do anything to make you completely happy."

James closed his eyes, afraid of her meaning for anything. "Sarah, believe me when I say, you are what makes me completely happy! All I need is for you to be by my side forever."

"I promise to pray for strength to get through this loss of never being able to bare you a son, my dearest James." The hurt was too deep to ignore, but Sarah knew her loving husband truly loved and needed her. Could she still go through with her plans, knowing she could never have the son she had hoped for and another James to be ready to take on the caretaker's job one day. There would be much prayer before her final decision, knowing once it was done, there would be no coming back.

Joan Byrd

CHAPTER 13

James had felt better about spending his morning in the Sacred Garden after his long talk with Sarah and the fact that he had left her to spend the day with Maggie, canning the leftover summer vegetables to set aside for the winter months. Even though the young man had tried hard to hide any signs of worry from his uncle, the man of faith saw right through his nephew.

"James, I am sorry Sarah got such a drear report from her doctor but never lose faith son in what the Lord can do when all seems hopeless." Once again, both caretakers stopped just outside the garden. "This may be hard for you to hear James, but Sarah must fight this battle alone with her Lord. She puts up a good front in front of you and the family, but inside, the beautiful girl is fighting dark emotions and her inward thoughts are only on helping you achieve your dream. Sarah feels like she is standing in your way son, so before the Lord can open her eyes to see her bright future with you, she must reach the dark bottom."

"Uncle James, are you saying Sarah will try to take her life so I can remarry to have the son I need?" Jack suddenly felt the urge to run back into the cottage and stay by his wife's side every second until she heard God's voice of hope. "Tell me uncle, how can I concentrate on this lesson when my thoughts will be on my wife?"

"James, there is a special transformation that accrues inside the Sacred Garden once you are fitted into your robe and vestments. No one who has been caretaker before us can explain why we become more like the angels, but nevertheless, it happens." Uncle James knew his nephew would feel the Holy Spirit's peace once inside and his heart and mind would know Sarah was in good hands, so he need not worry about her. "I can see these things clearer than you son because of my faithful commitment to this job for so many-years. Seventy to be exact, since I was twenty when I started learning how to be a caretaker. Sarah will not try anything this day James. She is in the process of trying to come up with another safer plan so she can remain with the one she adores. I am afraid after a long-drawn-out mind search, Sarah will come up empty and resort back to her first decision."

"Then, it won't be by taking those deadly pills, Uncle James. I watched her dump all five out into the paper bag, filled with dirt, I was holding."

"James, my boy, you must learn there are some women who are very talented at acting and your Sarah is one of the best at that. Remember when she gave you the big 30th birthday surprise party and had all the invited guest to dress up like a favorite actor. How she spent the entire night playing the perfect Marilyn Monroe." Uncle James smiled over the remembrance of Sarah decked in a shapely long dress wearing a blonde wig. "This is a determined young lady James and she might have considered the doctor telling you what he found and switched her pills, then acted innocent."

"If she did switch those pills, I guess I'll never find out, since I burned the brown bag, pills and all, in your fire pit." James had not considered his sweet wife tricking him into thinking he had the deadly pills safely out of her reach. "I cannot make her feel that I don't trust her Uncle James. If I accuse her falsely she might snap back into her depression, thinking I don't love her as much as I claim. Even if you're right and she did switch the pills, confronting her about it could trigger her anxiety even higher." The young man looked at the thick hedge, hiding the secret entrance. "But, you're right uncle. Sarah is a smart girl and she would never do something this devastating without a lot of prayer. Prayer to the only One that can help her find her way out of the dark."

Inside the Sacred Garden both caretakers sat relaxed in their usual chairs, feeling at peace from the heavenly transformation. The big record book opened and the white page floated upward to reveal the next story.

STORY: SAVING BARRABBUS

New candles had been replaced inside the wall lantern that dimly lit the cold-damp dungeon, that set directly under the wide courtyard of Pontius Pilate, governor of Judea. The prison cells that held four prisoners each, rose from floor to ceiling with a double thick stone wall, ten foot tall. The massive timbers stretched the full length of the large room's ceiling and the strength from the extra thick stone that held the courtyard up, was an easy feat for the genus Roman stone masons. Long-narrow open windows made their way across the top of each side wall. The floors were also paved with rough stones, making the prisoners cots move back and forth, while they tried to sleep on the worn-out coverings. The cells had heavy-thick bars, just wide enough for a hand or foot to pass through. Near the far end of the long prison hall was some of Pilates meanest captives, four out of one hundred determine rebels, who's mission was to take down Roman depression on their people, Israel.

Usually quiet during the Jewish holy week of Passover, the prisoners and Jailors suddenly noticed an uproar up in the courtyard. Trying to take a nap and fighting to make his cot stable, BARRABBUS grew angry over the sudden interruption and slung his feet around.

"Hey! Jailer, what is all the commotion going on up in that courtyard?" he narrowed his eyes at the jailer nearest him, sitting propped up against the wall in front of his cell. "Are you hard of hearing, you, Roman dog? How is a person supposed to sleep in this stinking rat hold with all that yelling going on overhead?"

Aggravated over the intrusion that disturbed his own nap, the beefy guard stared over at the shaggy-hair man, now up and standing at the bars. "Watch who you call a dog when it was you who got caught for acting like a wild animal!" The stern face looked up toward the ceiling where the noise was coming from. "By the great yelling overhead, my guess would be some poor unfortunate thief got caught robbing those celebrating Jews and they have arrested him, now want our governor to judge his punishment." The hefty man walked over and smiled down at the unsmiling face of BARRABBUS. "They are now demanding for justice, because it is now the Jews that have been robbed, not the Romans! Like you and your band of brothers committed! There was not a single Jew yelling for your arrest BARRABBUS! Why was that? Can you give me a good reason?"

"I can and believe me, you, Roman dog, I would do it again if I am broke free from Pilate's rotten dung heap!" BARRABBUS made a tight fist and held it up. "The Jewish people respected us for trying to rid our land of you Romans! Why should we need your King Caesar, when we will be getting a real king! A Messiah!" the brave man moved as close to this guard as he could. "We fight now so we will be ready for His coming! Then our king will drive out our trespassers and set us and Jerusalem free from Roman depression!"

"This messiah you speak of will be no threat to Rome and neither will you BARRABBUS. Should your foolish men on the outside try to break you and your men here free, they will find themselves behinds these prison walls with you, if they are still alive after their failed attempt!" The guard walked back to his seat, eyes still on the enemy.

"You misjudge my men, you oversize rat! They would not be foolish enough to come inside Pilate's grand grounds to free me and the boys. They just sat back and wait for the perfect opportunity to strike."

"Our brave leader is right!" Markus had been listening, along with his other comrades and he had noticed how quiet the crowd had gotten up overhead. "Listen how silent the people have become." Suddenly a thought came to the young follower. "BARRABBUS, you don't suppose the people were calling for your release, do you? It is Passover and Pilate sets one prisoner free every Passover, remember?"

The brave leader laughed at the thought before slapping his friend's back. "Set me free? Old friend, the only way Pontius Pilate will set me free is by nailing me to one of his crosses he delights in using!"

"BARRABBUS is right boy! Your old leader won't go out carrying his meager belongings, he will leave this prison dragging his own cross!" the jailer chuckled. "People will be jeering for him though, those Roman citizens he robbed and left dying in the streets."

"Pity! I did not take more before my arrest!" BARRABBUS grew quiet when he heard the roar of the crowd again overhead. "I am confused over this trial above us. Why would Pilate agree to having a prisoner brought in for him to judge during Passover? He has never permitted anyone inside his courtyard during our holy week."

"Mum! Now that you mention it bad one, you do have a point!" Once again, the guard stood up to stare at the ceiling, as though he hoped to see just who was so special his governor allowed him in during Passover. "The powerful Pontius never takes anyone to trial during your Passover. He concentrates on keeping peace in the streets and making sure no riots began to stir up the influx of travelers in Jerusalem."

"I guess we shall know soon, Tarsus!" the other guard pointed to a Roman soldier headed down the wide stone steps, with two escorts. "What do we owe the pleasure of your company, Captain?"

"I have come for BARRABBUS!" Strong and tall, the captain of the guard turned his attention on the shock faces inside the prison cell. "Pilate has called him up to the courtyard! Release the prisoner so I can take him at once!"

"By all means, take him out of my hair!" The bald man fumbled with the large group of keys before finding the right one to unlock the heavy bolt. BARRABBUS walked out and rubbed his hand over the slick bald head while laughing, and while the soldier tied his hands secure he continued to laugh.

"It appears you lost your hair a long time ago old man!" the brave leader smiled back at his friends. "Don't let this Roman dog take away all your fun boys! I am off to only God knows what?"

"Just get a move up those steps BARRABBUS and cut out the cute remarks!" The captain of the guard took the convicted criminal up on the courtyard and he tried to shade his eyes from the bright sun he had not seen in over five-years.

Within the large crowd, there were sudden cheers from somewhere in the middle of the large group of people that had gathered. BARRABBUS's old comrades had been present at ever release to see if their leader or one of the other three men captured, would be set free during Passover. The group of ninety-six men were elated to see their leader again after so many years.

Pilate looked out over the large crowd. "People of Judea, it is our custom to release one prisoner during your Passover. You see standing before you two prisoners! To my left stands a man who had been imprisoned for over five-years for murder and stealing! His name is BARRABBUS. To my right, is Jesus, your king!" Pilate listened to the uproar coming from the large crowd. "Who would you have me release unto you? BARRABBUS, a harden criminal? Or will you therefore have me to release this King of the Jews?"

"Then the crowd yelled out, drowning out the voices calling for the release of Jesus, and with demanding voices said. "Not this man, but BARRABBUS! Release BARRABBUS!" the ninety-six rebels pushed their way up to the front yelling even louder for their leader to be released.

Pontius Pilate looked out at the angry mob, suddenly growing with anxiety over the situation. He had assumed these people would see this man Jesus was innocent and compared to the murderer they just called to be released made him have a sick feeling. The governor held up his arms for silence, as his soldiers made themselves known to help quieten the crowd so their governor could speak.

"Then, what shall I do with this man?" he waved his hand toward Jesus while BARRABBUS watched and listened with his own confusion. Then the captured rebel heard the crowd's loud cry.

"AWAY WITH THE MAN! KILL HIM! CRUCIFY THIS MAN!"

BARRABBUS watched with mixed emotions, knowing the crowd had just called for his own release, yet even this tough fighter could not see anything bad about this innocent looking man. What could he possibly have done to brought on such hate from so many people? To go against the emperor armies and government of the Romans, was one thing, but for Jewish people to be against one of their own seldom happened. He stopped his daydreaming when he heard the governor call for silence.

"To satisfy your anger, I will order for this man's flogging!" Pontius Pilate snapped his finger for the captain of the guard. "Release the prisoner and see to this Jesus's punishment!"

BARRABBUS felt the soldier grab his arms to cut away the ropes before sending him away in the crowd. He stumbled down the steep steps and made his way through the throng of angry people. Half-way to his comrades, the bold man stopped and turned to see what was happening to the man that had looked into his eyes after he was declared free. BARABBAS heard laughing and shouts of terrible things to this Jesus, who had been led down into the grassy vista in front of the courtyard. The soldiers had tied the man with the incredible eyes to a post, while two-muscular men waited with flogging whips, capable of ripping a man's skin off. While a third man called out numbers loudly, each man took his turn at slinging the sharp-covered whip back to bring it quickly down on the strong tan back of Jesus. With each painful blow, the soft-spoken man jerked in agony, but never yelled out. As the counting grew up to the high thirties, even those Jews watching had to turn their heads from all the blood that flowed from the painful blows. BARABBAS, who was used to seeing a lot of blood shed at his many battles could

Joan Byrd

not resist his own anxious expression as his hand covered his mouth.

"Why, for God sakes? Why contemn this innocent looking man with the most alluring heavenly eyes I have ever witnessed!" BARABBAS felt hands grab him.

"BARABBAS, our great commander, God has answered our prayers!" A young man resembling his cellmate Markus stood smiling just inches under his tall frame, while ten more rebels walked up. "What are you doing down here captain? Come! We have got a place just on the edge of the old city where the rest of the men await the news!"

BARABBAS glanced back to the open vista and noticed the soldiers had already removed this man Jesus and took him back up to Pilate. "What news is my men waiting for? Surely you did not know I would be set free today!"

"This was not our purpose for being here, captain." An older soldier stepped up to give his leader a thankful hug. "We were just killing some time until the festival was past, but this was not our mission for being in Jerusalem."

"I cannot see any of you men being here for religious reasons, like the Passover?" the leader of the determined fighters smiled at their faces of dismay. "Not to worry comrades, my five-years in that rat hole did not convert me to priesthood!"

"Speaking of priest, did you catch the boldness from the high-priest, demanding Pontius Pilate to kill Jesus because his laws do not permit such things!" Jude laughed. "You should have heard the pompous Caiaphas leading the crowd in angry shouts to crucify the poor man."

"Why would Caiaphas order the death of this man?" BARABBAS once again looked toward the courtyard and found it empty. "Surely someone with such innocent eyes, reflecting so much love, could not have broken any laws of God."

"We shall know your answer very soon captain." Once again, the older follower acknowledged his leader's concern. "We left two men to report on Pilate's decision over this man's fate. It appears the Governor of our provenance feels the same as you sir."

"I did notice that, just the short time I was there to witness theses strange happenings for myself. For some reason, I feel responsible for the man's fate."

"It is funny you should mention feeling responsible

84

BARABBAS. The real reason we came to Jerusalem was to carry out our well hatched plan to save your life." Jude acted sure of their laid-out plan to save their leader from sure death.

"Looks fellows, I appreciate your bravery to overtake the heavily guarded palace of Pontius Pilate to free me and your fellow comrades, but any such plan you made would have been deadly and foolish." The big brawny man slapped young Jude on the back. "It appears my release saved all you from either getting killed in the attempt or captured yourself to join me in Pilate's nasty, dung filled prison."

"My good friend, do you really believe that I would have let your men carry out such a one-sided battle, ninety-six men against Pilate's four hundred?" Masa looked up seriously. "I was second in command, so your men followed my orders same as they had your own. Young Jude speaks about your fate after the Passover. Our inside spy has kept us well informed of your status in prison and he learned that Pilate had chosen you for crucifixion, along with two of your men."

"It was a great plan BARABBAS, you would be please with!" Joel bragged. "A few of our women would cause a distraction while you and our brothers carried the crosses down Cobble Stone Path, the narrowest street in all of Jerusalem. The city dwellings there are tight together and the unrulily followers must hurry around the path and wait to resume their insults. It is there the soldiers, usually ten or twelve, are alone with the prisoners. This is where our women will be causing a loud commotion just ahead, so the soldiers will halt the walk as a few go to move the women from the street. All of your men would have been waiting to give a surprise attack and after freeing you and the comrades, with your weapons back in your hands, we can take care of business and be done quickly. No one will suspect anything until they see the streets remain empty!" Proud and cocky, the young man laughed. "It would have been a pleasure to put down all those Roman dogs, captain!"

"Then, if that was Pilate's plans for me, I guess having to set me free must have been very painful for the important man!" BARABBAS joined in the laughing and stopped abruptly when the men left behind at the courtyard came running up, excited over what had happened. "Speak Thomas! Did Pilate release Jesus?"

"He would have preferred to, but Caiaphas was determined to

have him crucified!" Thomas spoke between breathes. "The governor asked Caiaphas for a reason, since he had taken Jesus inside to speak to him alone, then came out telling the priest he had found no wrong in him. You will never believe what that high and mighty priest charged the man from Nazareth with."

"Tell us, for God's sake!" BARABBAS felt sick over the harsh punishment. "Caiaphas is known for being a stickler for small things, like washing of your hands. What could a man like that do to make Caiaphas demand death?"

"Caiaphas said loudly, for everyone to hear his charge against Jesus: HE MADE HIMSELF THE SON OF GOD! Those were the priest's words captain, and after hearing from others who have witnessed this Jesus in action, I can almost believe it is true."

BARABBAS stood staring toward the courtyard where he last looked into those heavenly eyes, words could not form in his mind the feeling he was having, nor could he understand what they meant. He knew he could not just walk away and take up where he left off. All he could hear inside his head was two words, follow him. Jude broke his concentration.

"What kind of luck is this captain? That man has taken your place on that cross. It will be this Jesus dying instead of you!" The young man laughed, happy his leader was free. "Sir, we can return to our dwelling on the edge of town and bring this good news to our waiting comrades!"

"I am not quite ready to leave the market Jude. I think I shall stay behind for a while longer while you and the boys returned to your comrades and relate the news that has you so excited." Appearing back in charge, BARABBAS motioned for the men to leave except his second in command. "Masa will remain with me! Go now!" he watched them leave and started walking toward Golgotha.

"We leave for the deadly hill, do we not?" Masa stepped briskly to keep up with his leader's long strides. "Must you see the poor man die such an agonizing death captain?"

"Do not you understand what I am feeling right now friend? This Jesus is dying in my place and I will not rest until I know the reason!" without stopping, the mighty fighter suddenly felt small and unworthy.

Back down in the prison, the captain of the guard once again returned. The jail guard rose from his chair quickly, knocking it over, surprised by a second visit so close together.

"Begging your pardon Sarton, I was not expecting your presence so soon. Have you another prisoner for me or perhaps, brought the harden devil back to be a torn in my side?"

"Neither! I have come to get my two chosen prisoners for crucifixion, to hang on either side of the man Jesus! You may rest knowing BARABBAS will not be coming back! The people have set him free for the Passover custom and chose crucifixion for this Jesus!"

"Your guard will see fit not to let that murderer back near me to take revenge for his long stay here, correct?" the hefty man pulled at his tight tunic when the man over him only stared down. "Who will be suffering this day sir? Which prisoner do you desire I release to you?"

Sarton walked down the long row of jailcells, looking over the nervous men. He stopped at the middle cell and pointed to the stern face watching him closely. "You! Jose, a murderer of women and children! This day you face execution!" the proper soldier moved on slowly down the row of inmates, while the jailer released Jose to the soldiers with his captain. Sarton stopped again, this time at the last cell, where BARABBAS' men stood close together, wondering which one would soon be dead. "Markus, you are very young to have followed this murderer we had to free. Perhaps, it should have been you instead of your big leader. Then this choice would have been far easier for me." The stern soldier turned to the Jailer. "Release the boy for execution. Maybe while he suffers on our Roman cross he will regret following this BARABBAS!" he watched his men pulled the young man from the cell and tie up his hands. The harden soldier watched as the three men said their sad farewells, then he laughed. "Not to worry men, it will not be long before you join your young friend in the grave!" Sarton gave Markus a shove up the wide steps and disappeared with their young friend.

BARABBAS had watched as Jesus pulled his heavy cross down the streets of Jerusalem and as he watched he could vision it being himself dragging the weight, knowing what lie ahead. Always filled with uncanny strength and steady sureness, the big man found himself having to fight back un-natural tears that filled up his eyes.

Watching with concern was his life-long friend, Masa.

"Old friend, why torture yourself like this? There is nothing you can do to help this man."

"Masa, I know this may sound strange coming from me but, if there was any way I could take his place right now, I would!" BARABBAS had to sniff back the fresh tears. "If I could but take away some of the pain he is bearing! How could this happen to such a good man? I have the desire to go to Caiaphas and demand him to stop this insane madness before it is too late!"

"It would be of no use my friend. Caiaphas is headstrong and believes himself to be the most religious man alive! Why, the things that are reported about Jesus are only good things! Never has the man did anything against the Almighty God. If anything, the way he speaks, the words he has spoken, could not come from man, but from the One in heaven."

"Masa, what sort of things do you know about this Jesus? I must know!" BARABBAS came to a stop as the soldiers reached the hill of Golgotha and he instantly noticed young Markus hanging to the right of where they would place Jesus. "Dear God in heaven! Those devils have crucified the boy!" with a shaky finger, the anxious man grabbed his friend to steady himself. "Why Markus? Did they choose this innocent young man because they could not have me? First, it was this pure man Jesus, now Markus, the son I never had!" the big man could not control his tears now. Just watching the young man, he had taken in and grown to love as his own. "So, help me God, someone will have to pay for this!"

"BARABBAS, listen, Jesus is speaking." Masa had looped his arm around his big friend's shoulders as they grew quiet to hear what he was saying.

As the cross settled down heavily, jarring Jesus' body and racking it with horrible pain, his voice came clear "Father, forgive them, for they no not what they do."

Below the cross two soldiers divided the clothes Jesus had been wearing. There were people standing around belittling Jesus and the rulers also stood watching, made fun of him, with words like, "He saved others, let him save himself, if he be the Christ, the chosen of God." The soldiers also mocked him, coming to offer vinegar instead of water and saying "If you are the King of the Jews, save yourself!"

BARABBAS looked up to read the sign being nailed at the top of Jesus' cross and being educated in several languages he noticed it was written in Greek, Latin and Hebrew. He spoke the words softly to himself. "THIS IS THE KING OF THE JEWS." Hearing one of the criminals hanging with him, he looked up to see the man on his left railing at Jesus.

"If you are the Christ, save yourself and us!"

Then BARABBAS heard his young friend's voice rebuking the other criminal harsh words. "Do you not fear God, seeing you are in the same condemnation? And we indeed are rightly judged, for we receive the due reward of our deeds! But, this man hath done nothing wrong!" Markus looked over at Jesus and found his peaceful eyes were on him. "Lord, remember me when you come into your kingdom."

Then Jesus said unto him. "Verily I say unto you, today shalt you be with me in paradise."

BARABBAS felt his tears flowing down like his young friends and took a step forward when Markus looked down and spotted the man he had always admired crying for him as well as his Lord next to him. No words were spoken between them but the love that reflected from their eyes spoke what was in their heart for each other. Then they both broke away when the sky grew dark around the sixth hour and darkness was over all the earth until the ninth hour.

The wind blew strongly and the sun was darkened and somewhere in the distance, the temple veil was ripped in half while the earth trembled. Then Jesus' voice called out in the howling wind "It is finished. Father, into thy hands I commend my spirit." And having spoken these words, he gave up his ghost and was dead.

BARABBAS felt a great loss, never to have known this righteous man who had shown great wonders and spoken words given from heaven. Now this Jesus was dead and the strong leader who had fought for his people's freedom, felt responsible somehow. It should have been himself dying up on that cross, not a man of God. He paused, recalling the reason Caiaphas wanted him dead and how frightened everyone, who moments earlier called up mocking words to Jesus, became when the day turned as night when the anger of the Almighty stormed down over the land. BARABBAS could hear voices offering comments as his attention was on the blood-covered man who's head now lay drooped to the right, his once glorious hair blowing out and around the crown made of twisted thorns. Next to him, Markus was barely hanging on to life, so seeing the centurion was checking out the status of Jesus, amazed by his quick death, had called for a spear in which to pierce his side to make sure, BARABBAS slipped up under his young friend's cross and reached up to caress his nail-pierced feet.

The brave young man looked down, taking painful breathes he managed a smile for the man that took him in and treated him like a son. BARABBAS strained to hear Markus' weak voice. "I never told you this before BARABBAS, but I love you." He coughed up blood, and managed to say "You will remember me?"

"My son Markus, I could never forget the young man that has filled up this empty heart of mine." Tears came easily now for the once tough man that laughed at men when they grew sentimental. His heart was breaking, not just for this young boy that brought him back to life after the loss of his dear wife while giving birth to his dead son and for this man, who died in his place and had claimed to be the Son of God.

"My good friend is confused over this holy man beside me." Now Markus spoke as though he were normal and felt no pain. "BARABBAS, search for the truth! You shall find it! A man called Peter can help guide you, but you must believe, Jesus is truly our Lord! The long-awaited Messiah!"

"Markus, how could you possibly know this, seeing you were in the same cell with me for the years this Jesus did all those wonders told me after I was released?"

"Because my friend, these truths were written on his glowing face when he looked into my eyes and told me today I will be in paradise with him!" Markus painfully turned his head to see the limp head of Jesus. "Even now, his body only sleeps and soon, Jesus will rise from his sleep, to be our resurrected King!" Markus let out a loud-painful cry when the centurion broke both his legs with a heavy pole, after pushing BARABBAS out of his way.

Never witnessing any crucifixions before, BARABBAS grabbed the soldier's arm and shouted in anger. "Why in the name of God, did you have to torture this young man even more? What kind of animal are you? Have you no feelings in that Roman body of yours?"

Made by the Master's Hand

Masa, afraid his old friend could be arrested again, ran up to grabbed him back. Unable to looked at their young comrade dying, the older soldier spoke politely to the serious centurion holding the heavy pole. "Please sir, my friend is having a hard time watching his son suffer and die on this painful cross. I pray that you overlook his actions toward you and I shall see that he remains out of your way."

The soldier stared down at the familiar face, then back up at the young man, who's breathing now was coming less and less. "Very well, see that he behaves! I was merely carrying out my orders to make sure all prisoners are dead before the Jewish Sabbath! The hours are unwinding quickly to the seventh day of the week and all corpse and crosses must be down by then!"

"What is to become of these bodies once they are taken down?" BARABBAS asked with respect, for his friend's sake.

"This King, now dead, will be laid to rest in a borrowed tomb, at the request of one Joseph of Arimathea, a counselor of faith." The soldier looked down uncaring. "As for the other two men, they will be thrown on the remains of past criminal's bodies." He pushed them back. "Now, stand back and let us carry on with our duties!"

Backing up out of the demanding man's way, BARABBAS looked up as Markus was taking his last breath. "My son, I will take you home and plant your feet next to my Salena and baby boy."

Even in his pain and near death, the young man smiled down at the father he never had. "My old body shall rest beside my family father but" Markus looked up and saw glory, the weak smile now bright as the ray of light that fell on his handsome young face. "But my soul shall be alive in paradise with my Lord forever!" he closed his eyes in death and opened his eyes with new life.

"BARABBAS, my friend, we shall wait and take young Markus back with us for a proper burial." Masa looked around for the man in charge. "I will go and arrange his removal, while you wait here."

Never taking his eyes off both Markus and Jesus, BARABBAS did not notice the centurion headed his way. "Hey! You there, give us a hand with this man's body!" the brave leader was surprised to see he was speaking about the King of the Jews. "Now, before I have a change of heart and have you arrested for disorderly conduct to an officer!"

"What is it you want me to do? I can see four strong soldiers waiting to assist with his removal! This man cannot weigh all that much, even though he stands higher than most men."

"You sir are now under my authority to do as I command! Now, stand at the front and be ready to take hold of the body, then see that it is delivered to his mother, kneeling just beyond the cross!" BARABBAS turned to find the woman he had spoken of and found Mary, being supported by a strong Jewish man and another woman on her other side. The small group of mourners were weeping bitterly as they watched the one they all loved be taken down. BARABBAS turned back quickly when he heard the head soldier snapped out threatening. "Pay attention to your job Jew! There is time for joining this man's family before you collect your own dead!"

"I am ready! Hand down the King to me, gently and with the respect he deserves unlike the brutal acts given him while he lived!" finding his bravery, the muscular leader showed his disrespect for the evil empire of Caesar by casting his eyes up on the body of Jesus instead of the angry ones staring down with hate. BARABBAS could feel his hate-fill eyes staring down at him and he gave a sarcastic laugh as he glanced up smiling. "You are safe to show your hate for me around your comrades, but the greatest army built by your Caesar will never defeat" he caught Jesus in his waiting arms before ending with "This one man, who sleeps in my arms!"

The scowl on the centurion's face changed into a smirk, as he laughed. "This ex-prisoner BARABBAS, has been locked up too long! His mind is completely wasted. He has dreamed dreams of make believe so long he now lives out his fantasies in real life!" Still laughing, the soldier waved BARABBAS away then continued taking down the cross that bore Jesus.

Mary watched as the man she had seen released earlier carrying her son to her. She found a smooth rock for a seat and sat down, then held out her arms. "Please kind sir, place my son into my arms like I held him when he was my baby boy." Drawing closer, the man who had been released instead of this loving man he carried, only felt love flowing from this beautiful woman whose tears would not be stopped until she could see him again. With tender slowness, BARABBAS gently lowered the sacred body onto her waiting arms. Instantly, Mary began cradling Jesus as she swayed back and forth, weeping uncontrollably and through her sobs a sweet lullaby came from her lips. "Little lamb, filled with love, sent down from glory, high above. My precious son, my precious child, sweet Jesus Christ, so meek and mild. I always loved my little son, you gave your all till you were done. Till you awake, now you must rest, and sleep sweet Jesus, sleep in sweet peace."

Months later, BARABBAS sat staring at the three headstones in his family garden, a broken man. Time behind bars and his anxiety over feeling guilty from the death of Jesus, plus the loss of his young friend Markus, had made age mature faster for him and now with his long thick hair mostly grey, his men felt they had lost their leader to depression as they stood back watching his daily tradition for visiting the graveyard.

"The captain spends more time with the dead than he does with the living." Young Jude had finally gotten over the brutal death of his brother Markus and now he felt as though he was losing BARABBAS as well. He noticed the others trailing back toward the house they all shared with their brave leader. He ran to catch up and stopped next to BARABBAS' oldest friend. "Masa, cannot you speak to him and see what we can do to bring him out of this dark place he has wondered into?"

"I know what BARABBAS needs young one, to find out just who this man Jesus was." Masa glanced back to his old friend pushing himself up with a strong walking stick. "If we could find this man called Peter, Markus saw in the face of Jesus, I believe he could tell him all he needs to know. I have sent out scouts to hunt for him and hopefully bring him back here to help our sick friend." Masa saw BARABBAS wondering to the garden. "This mental anxiety has affected the captain's physical health as well. I am afraid if he goes on like this much longer, he will not make it."

"At least he seems to be moving further out on the property." Another man spoke up watching their leader walk toward the wooded area. "Surely, these walks are good for him and his walking stick is sturdy enough to hold up his frail body."

They stopped speaking when a man ran from the house, so they met him half away. "Masa, Simeon has found this man, Peter. He was a follower of this Jesus and now preaches about his resurrection from the dead!"

"Then, this is great news Simeon has found! This is exactly what our captain needs to hear but it must come from this man

Peter!" Masa looked around when Simeon came out, dirty from traveling. "Where is this Peter? Did you not bring him with you Simeon?"

"I did ask him Masa, but the man is busy speaking in the courtyard of the temple! And, you will not believe this, when he speaks, no matter a person's language, they can understand his words. He claims it is the Holy Spirit that speaks through him!" the man smiled. "It makes a man feel there is hope at last and not just for the Jew, but for the Gentile as well!"

"Jude, go find BARABBAS!" Masa grabbed the young man laughing. "Help is just a few miles away in Jerusalem, the same place Caiaphas arrested and had Jesus killed! Now, the Lord Himself is speaking through His disciples right on Caiaphas' front porch declaring He is alive!"

As Masa packed a few of their things for travel to Jerusalem, Jude came dashing back inside the house, frantic written on his worried face.

"Please, do not tell me we are too late and that you found BARABBAS dead?" Masa felt his own anxiety building until he noticed Jude shaking his head negative. "Then what is it? He refuses to go?"

"I would not exactly say he refuses to go sir since he already has gone! I cannot find BARABBAS anywhere on this property or beyond walking distance." He tried to catch his breath. "It is getting dark outside and if he wandered off in his condition, who knows where he will end up."

"We need to saddle up the horses and spread out until it grows too dark to see." Masa felt his past happiness was short lived. "If we have no luck, we will try again tomorrow, first light."

Going the opposite direction from his men, BARABBAS had been captivated by a beam of light that shown through the forest, so he had gotten up to follow it and see where it led. The long walk took him down a narrow path, well-lit by both the full moon and the guiding light ahead of him. His journey came to an end when he found himself standing at a high green hedge. Pausing only briefly, BARABBAS once again noticed the beam of light just inside the hedge, so he stepped through to find a beautiful green vista surrounded by tall cedars. There was nothing in this secret place except for a beautiful bench where the light had stopped at. The smart man knew something had led him to this place and whatever it was, it waited for him at the bench. BARABBAS moved over slowly, cautiously looking around for a possible attack. None came, so he felt more at eased and took a seat on the bench.

The moment BARABBAS sat down the light began to swirl around to form a man and the moment he became visible to the brave leader, he recognized the man on the cross. He had seen this man die and even carried him to his grieving mother. Did not his mother and Markus speak of Jesus only sleeping and that he would awake. Jesus smiled into BARABBAS's confused eyes, the same heavenly eyes that had looked at him in the courtyard of Pilate.

"BARABBAS, my friend, be not afraid, for I am real, not a ghost! I have seen your suffering and have come to heal you, that you might believe that I am the Christ, the Son of God! I witnessed your tears for me as well as young Markus, who now dwells in paradise just as I said. I have watched you and known of your hard heart and the ease for killing your enemy. Yet, you were never there to hear my words of guidance, such as, you are to love your enemies and pray for them. To do unto others as you would have others do unto you. This hate and killing placed you in prison, but my son, you are still inside a prison. A prison of guilt and despair over believing I took your place on that cross because you deserve it, not I."

"Ye Lord, it was I that was to be crucified after the Passover Feast then I felt my joy for being chosen for freedom slip away when I realized who was taking my place." BARABBAS broke down. "Why should the Son of God have to suffer on that Roman cross instead of a harden criminal who was set to be crucified anyway for actual crimes committed?"

"BARABBAS, I did take your place on that cross, as I did every man, woman, and child born on this earth, by taking all your sins as well as every sin committed or will be on that cross with me, the only one born without sin. I willingly died to save the world from their sins so they could live again in glory with me."

"Lord, what must I do to be saved, a man with far too many sins to count?" BARABBAS felt at last there was some hope for him.

"Though your sins be as scarlet, they shall be as white as snow if you ask for forgiveness for those sins and believe in me, that I am the Son of God who truly is my Father as is the Holy Spirit, who planted the Father's seed in Mary, the virgin."

"I have sinned Lord and I pray that you take away all my sins because, I do believe that you are the Christ! The Messiah! The Son of the living God!" BARABBAS lifted his head, tears rolling down his weak face.

"BARABBAS, stand!" the Lord waited for the weak man to rise. He stretched out his hand and offered the healing blessing. "Your sins are forgiven and will be remembered no more! May the strength you once knew flow through your body so that by faith, you are healed!" eyes locked in love, Jesus ended with "Go now, my friend, and show kindness to the less fortunate, pray for your enemy, who is lost from the truth you now hold, lift up the fallen and look toward happiness. Teach those under you about me and seek out one of my own to learn of the things you missed out on. One day, my words will be written same as the Old Testament words, so generations from now, all my people, Jew or gentile, can know of me. My peace I leave with you and when I go, you shall find yourself beside your own front door. Go straight in and ease the worried minds of your friends who have been in search of you." Jesus gave one more smile and lifted his arms. "Just show all you meet the love I showed you and life will be filled with joy! I leave you with my mother's words, sweet peace. She sang them beautifully, while I lay cradled in her arms."

CHAPTER 14

"Sweetheart, how was your day with Maggie?" James had noticed Sarah's smile as she made her way over wearily to greet him at the door. "My girl looks tired. Just how much canning did you get done while I enjoyed my lesson?"

"When Maggie greeted me in the big kitchen she asked if I was ready for a fun day of canning. Naturally, always ready to try something new, I chimed in with a cheerful, YOU BET!" Sarah gave a soft laugh. "Then I noticed a twinkle in her bright eyes as she motioned me to the walk-in pantry and pointed out two shelfs containing dozens of empty quart canning jars. There was no stopping the dear lady then as she pulled out a stool and climbed up to hand down jars for me to take to the kitchen counter."

James laughed before asking. "Just how many quarts did you can this morning?"

"How long have you got?" Sarah giggled and goosed her husband's waist. "We 'put up' twenty quarts of green beans, twenty quarts of stewed tomatoes, twenty quarts peas, ten quarts of corn and thirty quarts of beets, Maggie's favorite. So, now with our one-hundred quarts of vegetables, and Simon's harvest of potatoes, sweet potatoes, onion and dried pinto beans in the root cellar, plus Uncle James' hams and shoulders in the smoke house, we are prepared for the winter months!"

"There is one thing for certain, we won't be going hungry this winter." James pulled Sarah into his arms, understanding why his beautiful wife was worn out. "All that day of canning certainly wore me out from just listening."

"And I promise you won't be unhappy from all the fine meals I will be stirring up from little Sarah and my hard laboring over the hot stove all the live-long day while you two gents went about your caretaking business!" Maggie walked out from the kitchen drying off her hands and dragging just a wee bit herself.

"Tell me Maggie, who taught you how to can all those, different kind of vegetables?" James gave his wife a wink when the cheerful woman cackled out. "Was it your mama or perhaps one of your

97

great-cooking grandmothers?"

"I guess you don't know about my past yet Mr. James but until that miracle book enlightens you, I can assure you it wasn't any kin that taught me canning. The truth is, I haven't ever seen my birth mama since I was five and God only knows where my daddy is. I got shoved from foster home to foster home until I got tired of getting whippings and molested by some of those so-called Christian men whose wives just looked the other way." Maggie gave another chuckle. "I guess them home bodies got tired of their old men climbing on them all most every night. Why, I could hear them old spring mattresses squealing up and down!"

"Maggie, must you go on and on gossiping about those sinners from your past?" Simon Granger stepped in the room shaking his head. "Why, if Mr. James hears you speaking about that stuff around his kinfolk here, he just might send you packing!"

"I was asking Maggie who had taught her how to can so many vegetables and I guess bringing up her mother sparked bad memories." James tried to calm down the situation since he felt somewhat responsible for bringing up her past. "You never did tell us who taught you about canning or cooking, for that matter. You're very good at both."

"That is a gracious compliment Mr. James. I learned all my fine skills while I was in the Raleigh Correctional Institution for women. I went in for murder when I was sixteen years old and escaped, with the light of the Lord, when I was twenty-seven, one year ago."

"And Maggie has learned to be honest since her prison days, haven't you dear?" Uncle James had been listening, knowing his nephew would soon learn how this cheerful lady had gone from a moody, angry young woman to a giving loving woman.

"Yes sir, Mr. James! When goodness and mercy, comes into your heart and you are blessed to have loving people take you in and show you how much they care about your life, you begin seeing yourself in a positive way and actually start loving yourself for the first time. No more that angry person but someone who can feel happiness and glad to be alive!"

STORY: MAGGIE SPILLMAN'S LAST HOPE

"Maggie Spillman: #3377123." The jail clerk issued the young sixteen-year-old her prison number and ordered her to get in line with the other prisoners. "Ladies, the prison van is outside to take you to the Raleigh Correctional Institution. Enjoy your long stay!" nodding to the escort officers, two men and two women marched the inmates out to the van.

RALEIGH INSTITUTE FOR WOMEN

"You ladies will be learning skills to help in the prison. We will have no complaining for doing labor! Just be grateful that you are not in the men's institute! Their labor is much harder than yours will be, if you behave and do your jobs! Anyone who gets out of line, will be put on latrine duty for your entire stay, and for some of you, that is for life, no chance of parole." The warden's eyes fell on Maggie "Right Spillman? Only sixteen will give you a heck of a long time scrubbing out toilets, so you best co-operate with the matron over your group." Hazel Rollins lifted an eyebrow when an African American raised her hand. "Questions Ella Mae? What gives an inmate a right to ask the top brass in this place a question?"

"Ma'am, I was just wandering if I would have to work beside that young murderer? I hear she done went and stabbed a black man and that is why she is in here." She glanced over at the stone face of Maggie Spillman, who was taking in her words. "I have seen the way she looks at me. You know, with hate in her eyes! I'm just scared that she might try and stab me cause I'm black and that is the gospel truth ma'am!"

"The gospel truth?" Maggie spit out each word. "It ain't the color of your skin missy that I despise, it's all that religious garb spilling from your mouth!"

"Since the both of you don't get alone, I feel it best to place you next to each other and" the warden got in their face "WORK IT OUT!" Hazel Rollins went back to the front of the group. "I will start Spillman, Brown, Wallace, Turner, and Clayborn in canning. Your instructor will be Wanda Jones and ladies, you will find the cannery surrounded with prison guards just in case one of you get out of line. Since 3377123 is fond of knives, she will be using a dipper instead to fill up the canning jars. Those girls Pealing and cutting up the vegetables will be in the other kitchen."

IN THE CANNERY

"Inmates, my name is Wanda Jones. I will be teaching you how to can your own food, should you get out of prison. Those staying incarcerated for a long stay will be helping keep the prison supplied with can vegetables for the winter months. When you see other prisoners enjoy the good vegetables you helped put up, you might take some pride in yourself for accomplishing a good job." The instructor pulled out her short list. "Spillman and Brown will be filling the quart jars, then place in the canners to seal the lids before removing. Wallace and Turner will be in the prep kitchen pealing and cutting up the assorted vegetables for canning. Clayborn's job is to steam the vegetables lightly and carry the pots in to the fillers." The stout woman clapped her hands. "Ladies, get to your post!"

Maggie and Ella Mae stayed out of each-others way for the first two-weeks, but as time went by they began to wonder about each other. Maggie broke the silence.

"Hey girl, what are you in here for? You seem to already know why I'm in this rat hole!"

"I got tired of being hungry, so I stole a loaf of bread from the local grocery store." Feeling she may have been wrong about this inmate, Ella Mae glanced over and shrug her shoulders.

"You mean, that grocery store turned you in to the cops? Just for stealing a loaf of bread?" Feeling angry for her partners mistreatment just for being hungry, Maggie grabbed a lid and gave a tight tug. "How long you in for?"

"Stealing is stealing in the law's eyes and I got the max for first offence." Her cute face found reason to smile. "At least I'll have canned vegetables for ten-years and I won't go hungry."

Maggie stopped and stared up at the guards, watching them closely. "Ten years! Just for taking one lousy loaf of bread!" Maggie picked back up the large dipper and filled the next quart. "I hope you got an expensive name-brand loaf!"

"Wouldn't have mattered anyway. They caught me for I got out of the store. Then they took the bread, tossed it in the garbage can and called the police."

"Those no count devils! If there had been any descents inside their selfish bodies they would have let you keep the bread and offered you a job!" Maggie felt bad for her friend, but she would be out in ten-years but not Maggie.

"Maggie, why did you kill that man? Did he hurt you in some way?" Ella Mae felt she had a friend inside these prison walls and it made her feel safer.

"I was placed inside his foster home when I was ten and his old

100

lady worked at night while he stayed with four of us, all foster children, two boys and two girls, no kin." Maggie thought back. "he'd start drinking whisky from the minute Mrs. Stalls left, then he would send us all to bed. I shared a room with Elsa, a scared five-year old while the boys, Billy and Randle slept upstairs in the attic." Anger draped over the young girl's eyes. "I lay in bed shaking in fear, knowing that big ox would slip inside the bedroom, naked and with a monstrous hardon."

"Oh, my God! Did he rape you Maggie?"

"Not at first. He would just slip up to my side of the bed and lower the covers, then reach inside my panties to feel around, and later, slip a finger inside me." Ella Mae notice tears coming in Maggie's eyes. "The next night, he got bolder and rape me! The big ox raped a ten-year old child every night his old lady worked, then went back to his room to read his bible!"

"Girls, it is alright to talk to one another, just don't stop your working!" Wanda Jones had caught the new friends talking, but never heard what their conversation was about. Had she had taken the time to listen, she might have been gentler with the young sixteen-year-old.

Time past, and the two best friends became fast with their canning job. Knowing now all the girls she was in charge of, were dependable and not as dangerous as the head warden had led on, Miss Smith decided to rotate the job positions, so their work would not get to boring. Now feeling it safe to placed Maggie at the cutting table, she gave her and Ella Mae the prep kitchen duties, kept Jane turner in there to replace Gayle Clayborn with steaming the vegetables and taking the large pot to the canning room.

"Now Maggie, you and Ella Mae can start out the peeling and cutting at a slower pace until you catch on. Those paring knives and peelers are pretty sharp, so you must be careful until you get used to using a cutting board."

"Yeh Spillman, cutting on wood is not as easy as cutting a man's body!" Faye Wallace gave a sour face. "I'm just glad I will be working in the other room, far from your knife, blade killer!"

"Faye, that will be enough of that kind of talk!" Wanda Jones took the girl's arm. "You girls will show good manners in my presence and treat each other with dignity! Is that clear young lady?"

"Yes ma'am, I will treat Spillman with respect as long as I am in your company." Wallace stared at Maggie. "What I do or say on my own free time, will be another matter!" the rude woman laughed when the matron walked her to the cannery.

After they had been left alone, Ella Mae stared toward the cannery. "I can spot trouble, friend, and something told me the moment I saw Wallace that she spelled trouble!"

"The word that comes to my mind is dangerous." Maggie had carried the washed carrots over to set between the big boards. "There are all kinds of people in this world Ella Mae, and Faye Wallace is the bully kind! She will slip around and make serious trouble then put the blame on the person she is after. In this case, me!"

"Well, just let the overbearing bully just try a stunt like that and I'll be on her like bees on honey!" The petite Ella Mae narrowed her eyes causing Maggie to laugh. The cute black girl turned to looked at her friend. "Pray tell, what is so funny? You do not think your best friend is going to sit back and watch that big bully, blame you for something she's done, do you?"

"I was just trying to picture my tiny little friend taking on the Hulk!" Maggie noticed Miss Jones coming back to check on the progress and she noticed Ella Mae hadn't peeled one carrot. Maggie gave her friend a nudge as she slipped several peeled carrots on her board. Ella gave her a thankful smile and started cutting the way Wanda Jones had showed them. They passed the matron's approval.

Two years had passed, and summer had brought in a lot of sweltering heat, which made a few of the older female inmates irritable and Faye Wallace happened to be one of the worse. Jealous over Maggie and Ella Mae's youth, now only eighteen each, gave her even more to bitch about while she sat staring out from the prison yard bleachers.

"Look at the little jerks, always laughing and hitting or throwing some stupid ball! I's like to smash a hard ball right in Spillman's pretty little face!"

"Now, why would you want to go and do that for Wallace?" Frankie Franks took a drag from her cigarette and gave a deep cough before laughing. "If you just wait until her and rag doll go for a swim in the exercise room, just prance over and push her head under for about five minutes! You might have wrinkled hands for a while but throwing that ball could break them pretty-long fingernails."

"Cute Franks, real cute! Drowning the little creep would be too final and I need her around to harass until I get my green light to get out of this joint!" This evil woman had failed at her first attempt to get the 'little bade killer' in big trouble and found herself in detention for a solid month with very little to eat and absolutely nothing to do but climb the cells walls or try to sleep the time away on the warn out single cot. "My new plan will surely put the irritating brat away for practically all summer!" Seeing her young enemy look her way, the scheming woman just reached into her prison shirt pocket and pulled out a cigarette and lit it.

"How are you going to set up the kid this time Wallace, short of murdering someone yourself to point the guilt to the blade killer?" A rough looking middle-aged woman set filing her long fingernails while chomping on chewing gum.

"Carter, even if our genus here managed to make her own hit job and in prison to boot, how on earth would she blame the crime on that poor innocent looking man killer?" Frankie spoke with a deep tone, between coughs as she lit up another cigarette. "And then there's the obstacle of getting hold of a knife in a place that is well guarded." She carefully pointed out the twenty men with riffles in the watch tower and around the prison yard wall.

"Ladies, if you can be called that, my none-fail plan will be carried out day after tomorrow with the knife I borrowed from my job in the prep kitchen." Knowing her friends interrupted while she was speaking, the irate woman held up her hand for silence. "Let me finish or it might be you who'll get set-up." Faye gave a sarcastic laugh when she noticed them hold their mouths to keep from speaking. "That's better. I overheard the janitor tell Mr. Miller, over maintenance, that a Mr. Jackson would be coming by on Friday at 5:00p.m. to work on the air-conditioner unit. As you are aware, five o'clock is when the workforce switch shifts and during all that commotion when we are usually in lockdown, I will be having toilet duty. Lucky me, my turn! I'll start my job at the south side and work my way down to the last bathroom at the north end, right next to the maintenance room. After Mr. Starch, the morning janitor and Mr. Miller, his boss, show Vince Jackson down to the furnace room, they will leave to change shifts with the night workers. I'll slipped in behind my victim and stab him in several places that will make him pass out, but I won't hit anything that might kill him. To make them think it was the blade killer, I'll plant the items I took from off her yesterday while she was in the shower."

"May I speak now?" Frankie waited for a nod. "How will they suspect the young jailbird when she will be in lockup?"

"You really don't expect me to be that stupid, do you 'friend'? Little miss perfect will be assisting the prison maids with sprucing up the warden's office while she is giving new orders out for the prison guard." Faye Wallace gave a satanic smile as she watched the friends waiting for the prisoner's mail to be handed out and the carrier waving them off again. "The poor things, always waiting uselessly for a letter from the outside, but never receives a single one, between them. Losers, that's all they are."

"But not our fearless leader." The short haired lesbian had taken her usual spot behind her mate and was slowly rubbing her shoulders while listening to the conversation between their small party. "My beauty here gets at least three letters a week, sometimes more. Lace made a lot of friends in the streets!"

"You bet I did, sugar, and you better believe old Lace baby will pick up where she left off when I get out of this trapped heap!" Wallace took out another cigarette as Racy Fletcher reached around to light it for her. "Thanks Fletcher, I owe you one!" she turned to give her partner a wink before hearing her named called out from the mail carrier. Giving a big wave over her lover's head, the homosexual pointed down at Faye. The prison mail delivery carrier, handed up four letters before continuing with her rounds.

Giving another deep cough, Carter glanced down at the sender's name and address. "You received four letters from these same men almost four months ago, and every week there are other groups of repeating men sending you letters. If I kept up a count of different names, I'd guess near 100 men are sending you letters."

"Wallace was a high-paid prostitute before she got busted Carter, so that counts for the addresses being similar." Frankie had been told about their leader's previous occupation before getting arrested, but she could not understand why all her clients wrote her letters now that she was in Prison and couldn't work. "Wallace, the thing I cannot understand is why these gentlemen are writing you when you are unable to sale them what they're after. Surely they're not making appointments for when you get out of this joint."

"Do you really think the prison would allow me to make any

kind of future appointments, especially to set up an hour session for delivering sex instead of a haircut or a root canal?" Giving a hardy laugh, the hateful woman tore into the first letter and read it quickly, then folded it back into its envelope. "My dear Frankie, I have no doubt all these loyal customers will once again give me business when I am released but to answer your question about why they are writing when I am unable to 'sale' them what they are after. You recall my telling you I had overheard about Vince Jackson, the repair man coming tomorrow around five. Well, the truth is, I have found a very good friend, who has a fairly high position here at the prison, and it turns out he has a problem with gambling and owes a lot of money to this underground gambling casino. The owner of the casino is a Mr. Sal Abernethy and my old business partner. Under his pen name Sal Pal, he made arrangements with my prison spy for me to continue my drug business in the streets of Charlotte and my customers write me when they want a new order. Under innocent names of course. Things like baby Janes or sweet dreams. I pay my snitch very well and he keeps us supplied in all these cigarettes you ladies enjoy and I keep him out of trouble with Sal."

"As for setting up Spillman for the attach on Jackson, Lace's new guard friend will be stationed on the north end and is prepared to give the Warden his report about seeing the Spillman girl slipped out of her office and head toward the furnace room." Racy Fletcher had already been filled in with her lover's perfect plan.

CHAPTER 15

IN CELL 9

"Maggie, I just can't understand why mama hasn't written me. Not one letter." Ella Mae sat slumped on her bed. "I never got the chance to go back home after taking that bread. I left her in bed feeling weak, because she hadn't had nothing to eat in two days, same as me. I promised her I would find some food and come right home." Tears dropped from her sad brown eyes. "You don't suppose mama thought I had abandoned her like my daddy did when he left and never came home?"

"Ella Mae, surely your mama knows how much you love her and how you had always been there for her." Maggie walked over to sat next to her friend and placed an arm around her. "Didn't the authorities get in contact with your mama after they arrested you? You were underage then and they should have called her and paid her a visit."

"They did ask me for our phone number but we didn't have any service since the telephone company cut us off for not paying our bill on time." Ella sadly shook her head. "We didn't have much money after mama got laid off working in the cleaners. What little bit she put away went for rent and oil bills to keep warm. Poor old soul, I guess they went by to tell her and she felt as hopeless as I did, having no money to even get a cab or bus fare to come to the court house at my hearing. God only knows what has happened to her. She may even be living out on the streets by now, a homeless person, sick, lonely and hungry." The tears became sobs as she buried her head in her lap.

"Why do people have to be so mean to one another? All of these worries would not exist if that jerk who manages that grocery store would have just gave you that loaf of bread instead of throwing it away." Maggie stood up and walked to the cell bars and looked out at all the other inmates. "How many other women are in here for stupid little crimes when there are hundreds of horny men outside these walls raping and molesting innocent children! People read their Bibles daily but do they really see the words written in red. Why can't everyone just follow that one rule to 'do unto others as you would have others do unto you'!"

Faye Wallace carried through her assault to set Maggie up for attempted murder. The paid-off guard reported the crime and told the warden what he had seen before Vince Jackson was stabbed by a paring knife. The dirty guard laid the handkerchief containing the objects left behind by the attacker.

"I had these things tested in the lab Hazel and they have Spillman's fingerprints all on them." Harvey Waters stood at attention in front of the head warden. "Like I told you, I saw #3377123 slip from your office and race down toward the basement."

"If you saw this young inmate leave my room in so big a hurry Mr. Waters, why didn't you follow her? That is your job, correct?" Hazel Rollins had saw the change in Maggie Spillman and trusted her to help clean her office.

"At the time, I only assumed the maids had saw a problem with some mechanical device and had sent the girl to fetch the janitor. Up until this attack, Miss Spillman has kept her nose clean. Watching the warden lift up the different found objects with her white gloved hand, he began to grow nervous, knowing this woman was brilliant at her job. "Is there a problem about the found items ma'am?"

"It just seems rather odd that the young lady would have these particular personal items on her person knowing she would be scrubbing the floors in my office."

"Don't most ladies like to make sure they have their comb, hand mirror, and wash rag, most likely to keep her hands wiped off while working." The guard swallowed, wishing she would dismiss him. "The weapon was from Wanda Jones' prep kitchen, where Miss Spillman had last worked during the fall months."

"The report states no fingerprints could be found on the paring knife, so the attacker had planned the attack but why? Why would Maggie Spillman try to kill Vince Jackson, a repair man from Jack's heating service?" The warden looked up at the nervous man. "It appears all the evidence is pointing to Maggie. I will have her brought to my office tonight and see what she has to say. You may be excused for now. There may be more questions later."

THE WARDEN'S OFFICE: 7:00P.M.

Hazel Rollins read the report to the serious young lady who

stood listening to the false words. The warden closed the file and slid the handkerchief containing her things across the desk for Maggie to identify. "Do you recognize these things Maggie?"

"Yes ma'am, they are mine and were stolen from the shower room while I was taking mine. I have my suspicions of who took them, but being unable to prove it, I kept it to myself." Maggie had grown to admire and respect this woman, who had shown her some kindness and trust. "Ma'am, how is that man, Mr. Jackson? Please, tell me he made it."

"Why would someone, accused of stabbing Mr. Jackson care about his condition?" Hazel Rollins had known other inmates who disliked one of the other inmates do things to blame them for, but up until this brutal attach on a service worker, no one had used attempted murder for getting even.

"They wouldn't care ma'am but I care, because I am innocent. I know I was set up for this hit job and my guess is the same person that stole my personal things from my carry bag." Maggie had grown used to getting set up for things due to growing up in foster homes, but this incident could get her deeper into trouble. "Miss Rollins, I cannot prove who stole those things from me, but the same woman also worked in the prep kitchen with Miss Jones. Please ma'am, you must believe me. The maids can tell you I was with them the entire time we cleaned your office. Did anyone asked Mildred and Mae if I left early?"

"Mr. Waters states in his report the maids remember seeing you down on the floor scrubbing before they went into the file room to dust off the shelfs, where they remained for thirty minutes before coming back out to see you holding the mop bucket." The warden glanced up over her glasses to see Maggie nodding her head. "The guard stated he saw you slip out the office door and run down the hall toward the basement where the service man was working alone. Water's stated thirty-minutes would have giving an expert slayer plenty of time to attack their victim and return to the office."

"And did that liar tell you he saw me return just in time for Mildred and Mae to catch me holding the mop bucket, filled with the dirty water from the entire office floor I finished after their big feet got out of my way?" Maggie noticed the warden try to hide her smile. "If you ask me ma'am, that fat guard is in on this set up, because there is no way that bastard saw me come out of your office, much less run down the hall to stab a man I could not possibly know was there! Why, in the name of God would I wish this hardworking stranger to die? Or bring my comb and mirror with me to work on floors with only a couple of shaggy-hair maids watching me instead of a handsome prince charming?"

"My thoughts exactly!" Hazel felt now even more positive of this girl's innocence but she knew the only way to prove it was to speak to the victim himself and get his part of the story. "Maggie, I believe you dear but until I can prove who the attacker really was, I must make it appear you have been put in suspension. To keep your friend from being upset, I'll have her brought to my quarters as well."

"Are you saying, I will be staying in your personal quarters Miss Rollins?" Maggie had never been treated with so much trust before, she felt totally surprised.

"That is exactly what I mean child." The warden walked around the desk to take Maggie's trembling hands. "Maggie, if I seemed hard on you at first, I just hadn't had the time to read your file. After reading what that man did to you and that young five-year-old who slept with you, I could understand why you were driven to self-defense. I feel the punishment was way more than you deserved so I will do whatever I can to help you. For now, we must make the one that set you up think she got away with it and I'm pretty sure who did it too, but we must be absolutely sure. The woman we think is guilty has many bad friends who will do anything to help her. In the end, we shall find the right person, then we can arrest Harvey Waters for aiding and abetting a crime."

Four days later, the victim was able to speak to the authorities and Hazel Rollins was present at his bedside to ask the questions. "Mr. Jackson, tell us everything you remember that happened the evening you were attacked at the prison's furnace room."

"I had just arrived and Mr. Miller showed me where the inside unit and the outside unit was for the air conditioner. After he left, I got busy checking out the furnaces cooling system when I felt a sharp pain in my back and heard a female's low voice say, the blade killer strikes again." The man shuttered, recalling her breath at his neck as she cut a gash in his leg, then arm. "She wouldn't stop stabbing me! I called out for help, but she threatened me that is I didn't shut up she would slit my throat. I thought I was dying!"

"Mr. Jackson, we know this is not easy, but we must find the right person to charge for attempted murder." Hazel knew she needed some other kind of clue that would help free Maggie from the crime. "Were there any kind of personal things you recall about your attacker? A hand perhaps, coming around to stab your front. Hair touching your back? A particular smell or scent? Shampoo? Perfume? Anything Mr. Jackson."

"As a matter of fact, I did notice a very strong smell of tobacco smoke and come to think of it, her breath had a distasteful smell of cigarettes." He looked up hopeful. "Will that help you narrow down your suspect ma'am?"

"Mr. Jackson, if you didn't have such a bad cut lip, I would kiss you right now!" The warden finally let out a sigh. "Now we can charge the right woman for your bad incident. Thank you very much and be sure, your hospital bills will be taken care of." Hazel Rollins finally had exactly what she was after to bring in Faye Wallace for setting up another inmate by the attempted murder of Vince Jackson.

CHAPTER 16

EIGHT YEARS LATER

Faye Wallace had been sent to Raleigh's maximum-security prison for women after being charge with the arranged crime to set Maggie Spillman up for attempted murder. The beefy guard that helped her with the set-up was given a lighter sentence of ten-years for telling everything he knew concerning Wallace. Beside the ten-year stay in prison, Harvey Waters now had a record and could never work in law again.

Ella Mae Brown's ten-year incarceration was almost over and the best friends were having a hard time parting after being together for all those years. Maggie solemnly watched her tearful friend pack her small bag. She slipped from the bedside and walked over to her small cabinet to get something she had always treasured, a small child's golden book of fairytales.

"Here is something you may pack, to remember me by. It might seem childish, but it is the only thing I have from my childhood." Ella Mae gazed down at the worn book in her friend's outstretched hand. She did not see an old well-used worn-out book, instead what Ella Mae saw was her very best friend's most treasured memory of her mama, probably seated by the small sweet Maggie, reading with a mother's patience until the sleepy little girl fell to sleep.

"Oh Maggie, what a big heart you have! But, I could never take the only thing you have left that reminds you of your mama, when you felt safe at home where you were always loved."

"Ella Mae, mama died when I was five, then my daddy remarried to a sour old woman who hated children, so daddy put me in the foster home society. This was the only thing I was allowed to take with me when I left home and I chose it because it did hold special memories with my mama. But, things are not safe inside this terrible place and my next cell mate might be a pickpocket or a thief or just some jealous person who wants it for herself, then threatens me if I try to get it back." Maggie placed the book in her friend's hand. "Please friend, I truly want you to have my treasure and perhaps one day you can read it to your little girl and tell her about

111

the friend you had to leave behind."

Ella Mae placed the old book carefully inside her small luggage, then turned to hug the only best friend she had ever had. "Maggie, I don't want to leave with you still inside here. You don't suppose Miss Rollins would let me stay?"

Maggie couldn't resist her laugh as she squeezed her dearest friend. "Ella Mae, I want you to walk out of this joint with your head held high, knowing you have served your time and now you are a free woman. Stealing a loaf of bread because you and your mama were starving was never that big of a crime and most fine-upright people could have gotten by with community service for taking bread! If anyone's guilty here, it was that store manager that called the cops on you. Most likely because you were a young black girl so he never considered the reason behind your taking the bread. Why, if that jerk would have been a good Christian man, he would have heard the Lord say to him, I WAS HUNGRY AND YOU GAVE ME SOMETHING TO EAT! Instead, Mr. high and mighty store manager threw the bread away in the trash and had the poor hungry child of God, tossed in jail!"

Finally, something to laugh about, Ella Mae chuckled. "Then, that is exactly what I will do Maggie! I will give my very best friend one tearful hug, pick up all my worldly treasures, and march out of this prison, a free woman, to go where I choose and do what I want!" she giggled. "Except of course stealing a loaf of bread again! After I find mama, I am going to look for a good job, that excepts released prisoners with a very light record. Then I am going to start climbing the latter to improve myself by first getting my high school diploma. I'll choose a college suited for me and make something out of my life! In the course of my climb-up, maybe I'll meet the man of my dreams and get married so I can have that baby, a girl I'll name Maggie after my best friend and read her fairytales every night from my most treasured gift."

Maggie had stood listening to her friend's perfect future dreams and the smile on her pretty young face revealed all the love she had inside for Ella Mae. Yes, she would miss her friend being with her every day, but the once troubled child had a reason to smile. Maggie knew her friend would be happy and she knew now when she looked for the mail carrier, she too would receive her own special letter from the best friend she had ever had.

Made by the Master's Hand

Despite all her long letters from Ella Mae carrying out everything she had dreamed about, including getting married and having her little girl to name Maggie, Maggie found things had gotten worse since Miss Hazel Rollins, the warden, had been transferred to an even larger prison. The new warden had come as surprise to the ladies on cellblock seven. Up until Miss Rollins' stent there, all the wardens had been women. Now, the state was switching things up by placing men over the women's prisons and women over the men's. Richard J. Hackler turned out to be a shifty, hard-as-nails, womanizer, in a place with plenty of willing women. The new warden liked a variety of women and with his high position, and knowing he could tempt them with things they wanted, Hackler could get them to do almost anything for him.

Hackler had the habit of making his rounds, mostly for checking out the next woman he desired. He would step up at the cell to speak to the inmate that drew his attention, many of the women on cell block seven would deliberately flirt with the warden as he past their cell, giving him little jesters or striking a provocative pose. Seldom had the handsome hunk been rejected by an inmate or they would find themselves on permanent toilet duty and scrubbing the nasty bathrooms out. But there was only one young lady he desired above the others, but she refused all his advances and up until the present time, he did not have this one punished. The word quickly spread throughout the prison and it wasn't long before all the inmates despised Maggie Spillman and wanted her out of the way. Overhearing their plans to kill his choice girl, Richard Hackler had her removed and brought to his private quarters for safe keeping. Having her this close and unable to leave, the sex-starved man planned his attack.

Wine had been brought up to the warden's fancy dining room to be served with a gourmet meal, for two. The experienced lover knew how to charm a lady into his bedroom and great wine over candlelight never failed to seduce any young blooded female. His way of speaking and being the perfect gentleman for attending to the lady he entertained would give the lady confidence that he would behave.

"Miss Spillman, I hope you understand my reason for bringing you up to my private quarters." They had been served by his personal butler and now it was just the two of them, dining on steak, potatoes and a small salad. Richard reached over to top off her wine, then his own. "I find the cell block is far too dangerous for you my dear. I have heard all the threats on your life and some way I feel I may be to blame for all these women's jealousy toward you."

"Mr. Hackler, please, do not take this wrong, because I am truly grateful for your concern over my life sir, but I am very capable of taking care of myself." Maggie laid down her fork to blot the steak sauce from the lips. "I have taken care of myself since I was five years old and it really seems odd to have a man protecting me when it was because of a man that I am inside this place for life. Can you understand how I feel?"

"My dear Miss Spillman, I really hate to think some stupid bastard took advantage of you when you were still a child, but you mustn't put every man in the same category with that devil." Richard reached over to touch her hand laying on the table and looked into her eyes. For a moment, Maggie felt like he might really care something about her, but she still didn't quite trust her new warden, so Maggie slipped her hand out to pick up her wine.

"This is very good wine Mr. Hackler. I don't recall ever having this before." She quickly went back to eating to avoid his alluring eyes watching her. "How long are you going to keep me up here sir? I've got a life sentence and I'm sure you would like your privacy back so you can carry on with entertaining the ladies."

"Word does get around Maggie." The warden pushed his plate away and picked up his wineglass. "Would you believe me if I said you were the only women I wanted?" Maggie almost got choked on her wine from his bold statement. "It's true Maggie, I believe I am falling in love with you."

"In love? With me?" Maggie had never been told that before and it sounded strange coming from this handsome warden. "You know what I think sir? I think you only think you're in love with me because you cannot have me! If I gave in to you or maybe even thought I was in love with you too, just as soon as you won your conquest over me, then I would be tossed back into the lion's den!"

The handsome warden sat back laughing. "Maggie Spillman, you are about the most charming young lady I have ever met!" Richard sat back up and took her hands. "If I had the pleasure of making love to you, I can assure you, I would be under your spell for the rest of my life."

"That sounds like a lovely fairytale Mr. Hackler, but I can never see our warden getting married to one of the prisoners and I can assure you, I will never be just a lover."

"For starters young lady, start calling me Richard and cut out the formalities. If we are to be lovers, then newlyweds, we must start by addressing each other by our first names. Do you agree darling?" He got up and walked around the table to collect Maggie in his arms. "Before, I said I thought I was falling in love with you, Maggie, I have never felt like this for a woman ever before and I know it's love." Richard lowered his head and kissed the willing young lady who had fallen in love over candlelight.

TWO WEEKS LATER

Maggie awoke and looked over to find the bed empty, so she sat up to check the bedside clock, 2:00a.m. Worried about Richard, she slipped from the covers and into her robe, then slippers. The bathroom was dark so she just assumed Richard had gone to the kitchen for some water or milk. Cracking the bedroom door open, Maggie noticed a light on in the guest bedroom so she tip-toed to the door and peeked in to see Richard on the telephone speaking to what sounded like a woman. She remained quiet to listen and hoped it was a relative, a sister or mother perhaps calling from out west on a different time zone.

"Cindy darling, you know I cannot have you and the kids come to stay with me here at the prison. How many times have told you this?" Richard paused to give the caller time to speak. "Sweetheart, you know I love you and the kids! I didn't make the rules for this prison darling. This is a prison for harden criminals who happen to be women and if they see you and my kids living as though everything is normal, they could get dangerous and try to harm you." Once again, the woman spoke. "Cindy, you are getting paranoid! I told you why I haven't called you for three weeks! We had some trouble here at the prison so I had to get it under control, that's all. All the other inmates had it out for one young lady and I had to separate the angry mob from her. It took a lot of personal protection to help keep her safe but things are quietening down. I've had a long talk with all the ladies and they were happy with what I promised them."

Maggie stormed in the room, angry for being lied to and used

115

and felt his last statement meant she would be push aside just like she had stated. "Just what did you promise those willing broads?"

Wide eyes and shocked, Richard motioned Maggie out before trying to calm down his wife. "It's not what you think Cindy! Please, just listen to me, that girl is only the one I am protecting! My quarters are large and the young lady sleeps in the guest room! I must have woken her up and hearing I made a deal to give her enemies things like free cigarettes for a month has her worried I will just place her back in harm's way. You know I would send for you if I could darling. I will take some time off and come home so I can show you just how much you mean to me."

Maggie had gone back to the bedroom to gather her things and return to the other room until morning. Then she would return to her cell and take her chances with all the inmates until she could plan her escape and get out and away from Richard Hackler.

Finishing his call, the irate man searched his unit until he found the third bedroom door locked. Angry for getting him in hot water with his wife of twenty-years, Richard pounded on the door until Maggie slung it open.

"I have nothing to say to you Mr. Hackler, so you can just get your cheating ass back to your bedroom and leave me alone!"

"Maggie, I couldn't tell Cindy how I really felt about you. She might try something stupid, like she has in the past! My wife is not well." Richard calmed down after seeing his young lover's body through her robe. "It's you I really want Maggie. You I love."

"Then divorce your wife and marry me Richard!" she watched him drop his head. "That's what I thought! You only want me for your lover!" Maggie pulled her robe together. "This will never work out between us Richard! You only want me for sex. I want you as mine, forever. Not to share with a wife, lonely and missing the man who promise to love her forever. Just you and me Richard, no other hot sexy inmate that gets puts under your care!" She looked up into his wandering eyes, taking in her curves. "Can you give all that up for me Richard or do I walk out of your life for good?"

"You, stupid girl, walk out of 'my' life? How far could you go Maggie, to your damn cell and hide there forever!" Maggie noticed a different look come to the once romantic man's eyes, now demanding and stern. "You are under my authority and I can and will do whatever I please with you!" He grabbed her wrist and

116

forced her to his bedroom, then pushed her on the bed after removing her robe and tossing it on the floor. "No little jailbird slut is going to give me orders! I am the head warden and I WILL HAVE YOU NOW!" as tears raced down Maggie's face, Richard Hackler raped her repeatedly until she fell unconscious.

CHAPTER 17

The following morning, Maggie woke up, beaten and swore, as she tried to crawl to the bathroom. When she saw her reflection in the mirror, she picked up Richard's hairdryer and threw it against the mirror, shattering it in a thousand pieces. She reached down and picked up the largest piece of sharp glass.

"If I see that bastard this morning, I swear, I will slit his throat!" Maggie ran water in the large tub, knowing from then on, life in the prison would be hell. There was no chance of parole so she had only one option left, suicide. Maggie made sure the bathroom door was locked before she laid the sharp glass on the tub before climbing in. Remembering her mama helping her say her prayers at bedtime, Maggie prayed, for the first time since her mama died.

"Lord, I have made a mess of my life. I killed a man because he raped me time and time again. I wanted him to die Lord, but I didn't want to be the one to kill him. Not until little Elsa woke up and saw him on me! Then he grabbed her to rape Lord, and she only five! I tried to take Elsa and run away but they caught us and he punished me by rapping me repeatedly, just like Richard did early this morning! All my bad memories returned to being raped as a child and I wanted to kill Richard too. I cannot stay here any longer without getting raped over and over by the man I love and thought loved me! I didn't know he was already married or I would have never given in to his needs. Lord, please forgive me for what I am about to do, but I cannot live like this anymore when the only one who ever loved me besides my dear mama has left me behind. Please watch over my friend Ella Mae and her family and just let her always be happy like the happiness she gave me for ten short years." Maggie picked up the sharp glass after cutting off the water and cut her wrist, then closed her eyes, waiting for death to stop all the pain and hurt.

RALEIGH GENERAL HOSPITAL

Maggie had been found by the two maids she had helped when Miss Rollins was the warden. The authorities had been called in and discovered that Mr. Hackler had been having an affair with the young inmate and his previous record for beating up inmates that didn't co-operate with his orders was brought up. Thinking this tough warden only beat up on the men when he was at the men's prison, they switched him to the women's prison, where reports from all the female inmates stated he was a perfect gentleman and treated the prisoners as ladies. After hearing from several staff members like Wanda Jones, the canning instructor, all the female inmates had the hots for their new warden and he supplied all their needs. They also told how the entire female inmates had it out for Miss Spillman because the warden preferred her. Richard J. Hackler was let go and was sent back to Guilford State Institution for men, where his family lived in Charlotte.

Maggie had been admitted just in time to save her but she was still in critical condition because of blood loss. The hospital had a shortage of blood and her blood type was completely out. The emergency staff were hot of the phones trying to reached blood donors with the rare blood type.

Maggie's friend in Sleepy Grove had been given the news about her friend's condition and Ella Mae got busy dialing every church in her community and have their congregations pray for Maggie. Thousands of prayers went up and reached heaven where the Lord had already prepared the way for the scared young girl who prayed her heart out to him before she tried to take her life. Jesus had other plans for Maggie Spillman and He was ready to lead her to the Sacred Garden to be healed.

Maggie lay quietly listening to the nurses working over her bed and she knew they were not aware she could hear their gossip. "They say the poor girl had been beaten to a pulp by her lover, the prison warden. When the maids, Mildred and Mae Baxter, found her, they said the bath water reminded them of Moses's rod being dipped into the Nile River when God turned water to blood. We all can testify to how white she was when they roll her in ER."

"Just when I was thinking what a horrible man that warden must have been to cause that girl so much pain she wanted to die, that I learned how upset and heartbroken he was when the news of her attempted suicide was reported to him while he was out making his rounds." The nurse gazed down on the anemic young woman. "How could someone be so angry one minute and completely broken up when he thought he had lost her?"

Joan Byrd

"Witnesses say Richard Hackler raced up to his quarters and pushed the guards away from her so he could carry her down to the arriving ambulance, and cried over her body all the way down repeating:

"Maggie, please darling, forgive me. I am so sorry my love. I felt trapped and my love for you couldn't let you go, because I need you in my life." Richard sobbed as he kissed her still cool lips. "Maggie, please don't die sweetheart! Come back to me! If you only knew why I can't marry you darling, at least not yet. It's not for my kid's sake that I stay with Cindy, they are grown up and gone off to college. My wife is dying my love, and I could never let her die alone. She only asked one request from me Maggie, to die in my arms." Richard had reached the paramedics and before handing the woman he loved in their waiting arms, Richard pulled her to his chest and whispered. "I love you Maggie. Come back to me."

Maggie closed her eyes and cried.

It had been several hours since Maggie had been brought in drained of blood and in desperate need of several pints. Night had fallen and the doctor on call when Maggie had arrived around eight a.m. stayed on, determined to help save the young woman who had fought so hard to stay alive after trying to take her own life.

"When we first saw this patient, she acted as though she didn't want to live but something happened while I was away making my rounds with the other patients that caused her to change." He spoke to the nurses that had been recalling what had happened after Maggie had been found unconscious in the bathtub, thinking their patient was asleep. "Ladies, was something said that could have made her decide she wanted to live? Perhaps something you said that triggered her reaction?"

"It might have been when Tracy and I were changing her fluids and having a quiet discussion about what had happened this morning." The stout nurse looked up sheepishly. "We both assumed she was still asleep sir. Her eyes were closed and she looked real peaceful like."

"Mrs. Daniels, you should know even patients that we assume are in a coma can hear the words we speak. Especially when you are standing directly over them." Doctor Gull checked the girls pulse after watching the heart monitor change rhythms. "Ladies, the patient's heartbeat is getting weaker, so go quickly down to the supply room and see if the new shipment of blood has arrived. If so, get as many of type B positive and get back pronto. I'll be out at the desk checking Miss Spillman's family records."

After the nurses left the room, the caring doctor lifted Maggie's weak hand and gave her a smile when she opened her eyes, trying to talk. "Maggie, save your strength darling. Help is on the way up." He walked to the window and whispered. "I hope." Doctor Gull lifted his eyes to the starlit night and lifted up his heart to the One who could help this young woman dying. "Lord Jesus, I will do whatever I can to save your beautiful servant, but, being human, I can only do so much. Please Lord, heal this brave young soul that has suffered far too long and by too many people. I must go out for a while, so I will leave her in your care Lord. When I returned, I believe with all my heart, she will be lifted up to new life in you." He glanced back at Maggie, now resting, eyes closed. "Amen."

Maggie had drifted off to sleep in the dark room and was suddenly awakened by a comforting voice beside her bed calling her name. Looking in the direction of the man's voice, Maggie could barely make out the empty bed next to her, but no sign of a male nurse or doctor. She was beginning to think she had only dreamed someone was calling her when the soft voice came again.

"Maggie, I have come to guide you to a special place of healing. Arise child, then we shall go." The voice was so peaceful, Maggie felt no fear. She even thought, she must have died due to the sudden light that formed where the voice came from.

"I would be more than happy to come with you sir if I had the strength to get up from this bed and follow." Maggie stared at the glowing light, wishing this being would appear. "I'm afraid it is impossible sir, I'm far too tired and weak."

"Maggie, for you alone, this thing I ask of you would most certainly be impossible because you have lost most of your faith in me, but with me, dear one, nothing is impossible." The sacred voice remained calm and loving. "Now sweet girl, rise and stand. I promise you Maggie, you shall not fall for I will have you in my arms, to carry you all the way."

Maggie had realized who was standing in this heavenly glow after he proclaimed, "You have lost most of your faith in me." Suddenly Maggie remembered her dying mother's last words to her and she heard herself telling them to the Lord. "My poor-sick mama found the strength to lift me up in her lap and cradle me against her chest as she tearfully told me goodbye. I was only five Lord, but I can still hear mama saying:"

"Maggie, my precious beautiful daughter, Mama wishes she could get better and see my baby girl grow up and find your prince charming, like in your favorite fairytale, but you know your mama won't be with you much longer. The same loving Jesus we pray to every night will come down from his home and take me to live with him. Heaven is a beautiful place, Maggie, and it is a very special place, where I can look down and watched my baby girl grow up and live out her life until Jesus escorts you up to live with us, where I'll give you lots of hugs and kisses to make up for all our missed years together. Maggie darling, there's one thing I want you to always remember. No matter how bad things may seem at times during your life, you are never alone. You must have the faith to believe in things you cannot see and although you cannot see the Lord, never doubt that Jesus is with you Maggie."

"Jesus, I'm sorry it took me so long to recognize you and if you say I can get out of this bed and stand, then I know it can be done with faith." Maggie sat up and moved slowly around until she was able to stand. White and peaked in the face, the weak girl smiled when she found herself laying in invisible arms. "Are you taking me to heaven now?"

"Not for some time Maggie. You still have a long life left on our earth and there is still undone work for you to do." The glowing light moved to the window, sealed shut due to being on the 10th floor of the hospital. Maggie looked over the situation and could only smile up into the invisible face smiling back, knowing only a superman could managed leaving this room by window, unless of course, it was the Almighty God's choice for exiting.

When the doctor and nurses finally returned with the blood, ready to start the blood fusions, they were surprised to find the room vacant. The nurses knew the patient could not have died since the bed was still used and the desk staff knew nothing about the girl's mysterious disappearance. On the other hand, Doctor Gull had made out what had happened since his prayer was lifted up to God's throne. The bed covers had carefully been turned back far enough for the girl to slowly turned around and stand up. There were two sets of footprints on the hospital carpet near the bed, one set belonging to the girl's bare feet and the other set a man's sandaled feet. But there were only the man's sandaled footprints walking across the room where they stopped at the window. Both Nurses had both stopped talking and were following the doctor's eyes, until they too noticed the unusual footprints and walked over to join him at the window.

"Doctor Gull, just how did this person get inside this room without anyone seeing him?" the stout nurse scratched her head, puzzled at their sudden disappearance.

"Bea's got a point sir and what about escaping from what appears to be this window and without even breaking it." The thin nurse pulled her glasses up from the chain hanging around her sniff collar. "And, unless the man can perform magic, how could they just disappear from the 10th floor of the hospital?"

"What has me flabbergasted is, why on earth was this man wearing sandals on his feet in the middle of winter?" Bea shook her head in confusion, while the doctor simply smiled. "Doctor Gull, do you know something we don't know?"

"It appears I do ladies. Perhaps you both are familiar with the moving poem about FOOTPRINTS IN THE SAND? Where two men are walking on the beach barefooted. How the one watching the footprints left behind them as they walk suddenly sees only one set of footprints instead of two. He turned to ask his companion where the other prints had gone and the man walking beside him said, You, grew weary, so I carried you on my back." This reminder of the poem about Jesus caused the women to reexamine the single set of sandaled prints and the doctor saw their tears as they knew who had made them. "If you guessed it was Jesus, our Lord that made these prints ladies, then you are correct, but instead of carrying our weak patient Maggie on His back, I see Him carrying Maggie in his loving arms. He can do what we could not."

THE SACRED GARDEN

Maggie found herself seated on a beautiful garden bench, the glowing light in front of her reflecting the green vista that surrounded them safely inside a cedar border. After looking around at the trees lining the garden, her attention returned to find the Savior standing in her mist, adorned by the light.

"Lord, what wonderous place is this? It feels so peaceful and even in the darkness, your light brightens it up."

"Maggie, the light you see is the love that radiates from my countenance, for I am love! That love I have will give you grace, fill your wounded body with healing, and lead you to the living waters of truth. The truth your young heart has been searching for, longing for."

"Lord Jesus, you speak of healing my wounded body, the wounds that I myself placed upon my body to take my life." Tears fell down her beautiful face. "I feel so ashamed Lord for hurting myself, but I felt all was lost. My very best friend leaving while I had to stay behind. Finally finding love only to learn the man I gave my heart to was married and wanted me just for sex." Maggie looked down, blushing. "Forgive my bold words Lord."

"Maggie, sex is not a bad word, we, the Father God, Holy Spirit and I created it as a beautiful act between a man and women who are husband and wife and made it pleasant, meant to be enjoyed between a married couple. I fear my old foe Lucifer has corrupted many beautiful things we created and now those who even say the word, made bad by my once beautiful Archangel, is considered foul language." Jesus held out His hands for Maggie to stand and take the nail-pierced hands. Without hesitation, Maggie rose up and laid her hands in the Lord's.

"Maggie, from this moment on you are healed, both in spirit and body. No more will you serve time in prison for a crime that was made by a frighten-young girl afraid for not just her own life but the life of sweet Elsa, who has grown into a strong woman of faith due to one brave girl that showed her so much love and protection." Jesus smiled down into Maggie's teary eyes. "Elsa never forgot the brave young girl who subjected herself to all the abuse from this drunken man who only pretended to be faithful to his beliefs in us, and made sure the scared little girl would never be touched again. Maggie, you had observed him watching the child as she grew older and when he thought he had sent you after a few groceries, you knew why he wanted you out of the house. You only pretended to leave. When the abuser made his move on Elsa, you were waiting for him behind the door with a knife."

"You saw everything Lord?" Maggie felt even more ashamed. "Then my mama saw what I did too. She must have been very disappointed in me."

"No child, your loving mama had seen all your sacrifice for

saving one of our children, Elsa. No one in heaven judges those still on earth Maggie. I am and will always be the final judge of all men, women and children. Those who believe in me, that I am the Son of God, and ask my forgiveness for their sins, will be forgiven."

"My sins are many, Jesus, but I know you will forgive me for all of them. I do believe in you, way before I seen you this day." Maggie fell at the feet of Jesus. "Jesus, please forgive me for everything!"

"Maggie, I already have child, this morning when you prayed in the tub, remember?"

"I remember every word, Lord!" Maggie recalled his words about no more prison time. She knew the Lord God could do anything, she just couldn't imagine how he could arrange her release after she got a life sentence.

"Maggie, you are wondering about my arrangements for getting you released." Jesus smiled when she looked up surprised that he knew her thoughts. "You recall your caring warden, Miss Hazel Rollins? I have placed it in her heart how to get you released and as of this morning, you are a free woman." The Lord gave a soft chuckle when Maggie brightened up with her own happy laugh. "There! That is the joy I have been waiting to see! Now, some more good news about your friend Ella Mae."

"Ella Mae?" Maggie almost jumped straight up. "Oh yes Lord, tell me all about my dear friend!"

"First, when Ella Mae learned about your accident, she called all the churches in her town and ask all the congregations to pray for her best friend Maggie Spillman. Respecting the most popular doctor in town, all her patients were delighted to lift up their prayers for Doctor Ella Mae Brown Stevens."

"A doctor?" Maggie giggle. "My little shy friend, the most popular doctor around town!" she paused, thinking. "What is the name of the town she lives in? Perhaps it's not too far to visit once I'm back on my feet with my own job!"

"Happy looks good on you Maggie!" Jesus squeezed her hands gently. "First things first. When I leave you, you will not be alone in the garden. My garden has a caretaker. His name is James, a kinsman. James will take you into his heart and home, much like a father figure. You will learn the man that takes care of the yard and garden, doing odd jobs around the cottage, will be like a brother.

His name is Simon. I believe your gift of cooking and canning will be appreciated by the family since, neither men can cook very well. Other kin will be arriving someday in the near future, and the wife will be glad not to be the one left cooking."

"Then, I would make a great addition to the family. I'm sure I will be able to help out with the cleaning and laundry as well." Maggie looked around for any sign of a father figure and saw no-one. "At lease, I'd be earning my stay."

"Maggie, you will be part of this family. No one here will expect you to do work for board. This home will be as much yours as it is my kinsman. Trust me child, neither James, nor Simon will be jealous or angry for sharing this home with one of my own." Jesus patted her smiling head. "Now, more good news, Ella Mae lives in the town of Sleepy Grove, just a few miles away. James will show you on the roadmap into two main towns where the crossroad is. But, you will not have to go to her Maggie, she will be coming here to see her best friend." Jesus grew serious. "There is one more person living in your heart Maggie and he is having a hard time now. I cannot tell you everything about our lost child Richard, but I needed you to know he feels the same way about you Maggie. Richard Hackler has been trapped in a loveless marriage for over twenty-years, at no fault of his own. One day you will know everything about the man you love, but until then, never give up the hope of a long-awaited reunion between you and Richard in the future." The Lord gave her a hug as His light grew brighter. "Sweet Peace Maggie." The Lord was gone and in his place, stood a robed man, whose arms were outstretched to welcome his new family member home.

CHAPTER 18

James sat at the table watching Maggie serve the coffee, his attention on her attire consisting of many layers. Watching her story, the day before and knowing it had only been almost two years since she arrived, he couldn't understand why she had appeared fat to him before he saw her with Richard. James had been very respectful to his job as caretaker and like his uncle, watched each story through the eyes of a heavenly being. So, any harsh language or personal nakedness did not effect, the caretakers physically. Never seeing Maggie in any other outfit, the younger James had assumed the woman was heavier than she appeared in the Miracle book story.

Sarah had been observing her husband's interest in Maggie, and knew it had something to do with what he had seen concerning the cheerful woman's story. She reached over and whispered in his ear.

"James, I have seen the way you are staring at Maggie. Do I have anything to worry about?" Sarah teased as he looked down at her helplessly, only to catch her beautiful smile. "You may have some explaining to do about why you were staring so closely at her. I wasn't the only one watching you darling. Your uncle has also been getting an eyeful."

"It's just the difference in her looks Sarah, that's all." James leaned over to whisper "I'll explain later and maybe you can in light me why she appears bigger than she was in the book. Too much of her own cooking?"

"James!" Sarah laughed and gave him a playful slap on the arm as she watched Uncle James get up and start around the table. "You had better prepare yourself sweetheart. Uncle James is heading this way."

"James, may I have a word while Maggie brings out the desert." The elder James gave Sarah a bright smile as he pulled his nephew's chair back. "Come along son. It won't take long." He led the way to the den and stopped at the warm fireplace. "Alright James, why are you staring at Maggie? You have not taken your eyes off that woman ever since we sat down to eat supper."

"I was just trying to figure out how she got so you know, larger than before." James turned red in the face when his uncle laughed out. "You must admit Maggie had a model's figure when she was with Richard and now, she appears well, homely."

"You didn't sleep through any of her story I see." Uncle James teased. "Maggie didn't have any clothes with her when the Lord brought her to the garden except a hospital gown. Now James, the girl could not very well prance around in front of her father figure and her brother Simon, now, could she?"

"Well, no! Everyone knows hospitals gowns are lacking a back." James twisted his lips, feeling irritated over being treated like a child. "So where did she get those unbecoming outfits that make her appear fat?"

"Blunt! You don't mind speaking your mind nephew when someone rattles your chain, do you?" the uncle patted his back. "If you must know, those clothes you see Maggie wearing belonged to your aunt, my precious wife, that died a stout but loving woman."

James suddenly wished he hadn't thrown off on the sloppy clothes Maggie wore. "I am truly sorry Uncle James. If I had known the clothes had been my sweet aunts, I wouldn't have referred to them as unbecoming outfits. I'm sure they looked better on you dear wife. You know, fit her curves better than a thinner woman."

"And you are right son but when Maggie first arrived that's all I had to give her, hoping to take her shopping after I slowed down, and buy her some more appropriate clothes." Uncle James looped his arm over his nephew's shoulders. "Perhaps Sarah can take her shopping tomorrow. Another lady taking her instead of me would prove far better. Now, let's go enjoy some of Maggie good apple pie topped with her homemade vanilla ice cream."

"Sounds great Uncle James and I'll keep my eyes on my beautiful wife while I indulge in the delightful dessert."

The family had managed to keep Sarah's mind off her anxious obsession over not being able to give her devoted husband a son. Since both James' agreed Sarah would be the best choice for taking Maggie into Sleepy Grove to shop for some new clothes. Then the girls could meet up with Maggie's best friend Ella Mae for lunch at the small town's popular café. True to His holy word, Ella Mae had made not only the first visit to her loyal friend, but at least one visit a month, since she arrived at Zion. After calling in advance of their arrival to Sleepy Grove, Ella Mae had made plans to take the day off and spend it with Maggie and Sarah.

James found himself seated back in the Sacred Garden, waiting to review the story about his uncle's friend and gardener. He watched the Miracle Book open and the blank-white page rise up into a large screen. Instantly, the younger caretaker heard the sound of hoes, striking through hard ground.

STORY: SIMON GRANGER LEARNS TO BELIEVE

"Sparky, I just don't understand why I always get stuck hoeing this no-count piece of land!" Eighteen-year-old Simon Granger lend on his hoe handle and stared down at the friendly old hound dog, wagging its tail. "That sorry brother of mine always finds a way to smooth-talk his way out of laboring in this damn sun all day while my words get wiped under the dirty rug!" Simon narrowed his eyes at the hoe, resting on the hard dirt. "I've got a notion to just toss this stinking hoe down and march right out of this place I used to love calling home!" Tired eyes lifted to the open sky, void of any clouds making the overhead sun shine down even hotter. "Things were different when mama was alive. She never compared me and Jason's abilities like our papa does. He thinks the sun rises on my twin brother and the moon falls over everything I do. Why the only thing that old man would miss if I left was having someone to do all his free labor!"

Hearing the backscreen door slam shut, Simon watched his favored brother make his way down to the sheep pasture, feed bucket in hand, to lure in the next sheep, to shear off his winter wool to take to Old Salem's Spinning Wheel display, where they died their own wool, then spin it into yarn as a demonstration for the many visitors who came to see the old 1700's German settlement.

Simon would watch this same theme carry out, spring after spring. Simon, the oldest twin, by thirty minutes, labored from sunup to sundown, seven days a week while Jason, the younger twin, got to tend the large herd of sheep along with two paid workers who did most of the work, while his brother merely sat back watching and pointed fingers. Jason took care of the shearing every spring due to the high pay he proudly received from the wealthy clients. Simon, on the other hand, got his meager allowance once a week for slaving in the fields, tending the garden with year-round crops, keeping the barns and stables swept out, the hay brought in and the corn silage blown into the large silo.

Now, thirty-eight, Simon had taken all he could and hatched a plan to get the farm for himself. He would bide his time, waiting for his old man to die from lung cancer, due to his heavy cigar habit. Never having attend the local Baptist church his dear departed mother had gone to while she lived, Simon only learned bits and pieces of the bible from her. Refusing to go with her for their son's sake, Wilber Granger thought preachers were only out to pick a hard-working man's pocket while the man behind the pulpit waving a bible and telling him he was going to hell if he weren't baptized in the town creek, never did an honest day's work in his life!

While his loving mother gathered her boys around her feet to hear her read from the holy book, Wilber would sit reared back in his worn-out chair, a cigar in one hand and a bottle of moonshine in his other, shaking his head and giving sarcastic laughs.

On one occasion, Sadie Granger was reading from the book of Genesis, the story about Adam and Eve's first two sons, Cain and Able. As she read how both brothers brought offerings to God, Cain, a keeper of the fields, brought of the fruit of the ground and Able, a keeper of sheep had brought the best sheep from his flock to give as an offering. Seeing Cain, the oldest, had brought only scraps of his grain while Able had brought his best. So, God was pleased with Able, but not Cain. Cain grew jealous over his brother and finding him alone in the fields, hit his head and killed him. Wilber Granger seeing the envy Simon showed his twin brother, the ungrateful father started calling his boys, Cain and Able, never knowing his oldest would one day try to carry out Cain's revenge.

Simon Granger lay in bed, his attention glued to the ceiling as he made final plans before becoming soul owner of Granger farms. Tomorrow, he and his twin brother would bury their father next to their mother. The following week would be the county fair and their last competition for having the best at the fair for either his perfect fall crop or his brother's prize-winning sheep. His father wouldn't be around this season to fix the winner by lining the judge's pockets with cold cash so his pet could take home the blue ribbon for the 34th consecutive year, since they were four years old. Simon gritted his teeth as he recalled his father's hurting remarks on the ride home with Jason, happily holding up his first-place reward while Simon always got second.

"Just face it Cain, you always come in second! Anywhere! Everywhere!" the rude father watched his oldest son from the rearview mirror, head turned, staring from the back window. "Even that pretty little neighbor you got a crush on will one day choose my boy Able!"

Anger over the one thing he had, Sue Marie Craver, who had given him her books to carry so she could hold his other hand while he walked her home. Setting straight up, ready to defend what was his, Simon called out. "I have taken about all I'm going to from you, old man! Let that pet of a brother anywhere near my girl and I will smash in his pretty face!" Simon set back seething while father and son in the front seat laughed.

Simon had never been saved and the lack of any more words from his mama's holy book, now thrown away inside her drawer, turned the young man into a heathen. His hate toward his brother had kindled from a burning ember into a blazing flame and watching Jason making over his new wife, Simon's own Sue Marie, only made his evil thoughts grow more dangerous. The Sabbath meant nothing to the revengeful man. His entire life had only known hard labor seven-days-a-week, so for Simon, Sunday was just another day on the calendar.

CHAPTER 19

Saturday came in with cloudy skies and a 90% chance of rain. Very appropriate Simon had stated to his grieving brother and sister-n-law, his old girlfriend, stolen by his brother. There were a few mourners at Mr. Granger's funeral, his old drinking buddies where he bought his white lighting, the men at the farm and seed, and a few ex-soldiers, friends from his army days, but there was only one person shedding tears for the death of the shifty old farmer who made a buck on anyone who gave him business.

Jason Granger had lost his biggest supporter and now he faced a revengeful brother who despised him. The younger twin knew one of them would have to go and he was already aware of what his loyal father left his favorite son, everything he owned. The other thing placed in Mr. Granger's will stated, his other son, Simon, could stay on and continued to work for his brother Jason, if he chose. If not, uproot to a new place and get off the property.

Simon stood back, staring down at the fresh grave of his un-loving father and the eldest son couldn't resist the smile that crept on his face. Standing near the grave, facing both sons, the Baptist minister reading a passage from the bible. He slowly closed the old bible and peered up over his glasses at the twin brothers, one crying and one smiling. His attention focused on the smiling brother.

"Simon, since you are the oldest, I thought you might like to share a word of remembrance about your dear departed father."

"I mean no disrespect Reverend Jennings since my mama thought the world of you, but I found absolutely nothing 'dear' about my old man." Simon felt everyone watching him as he kept his distance from his brother and the grave of his father. "The only memories I have of the hateful old goat are all bad. How he always treated my beloved mama, never showing her any respect or love! Father despised me from the moment I was born and gave all his devotion and love to my twin brother. In return, I hated the old man's guts!" he heard some woman catch her breath. "If you want someone to paint a pretty picture of the man, now, finally under me, just ask his favorite son. Jason will give you all the flattering words you want. After all, he was the only one the man ever loved or gave a damn about. As for me, I'm just glad the devil has finally met his own twin below!"

The minister had been listening to Simon's harsh words and noticed the only one who seemed concerned over his words was Jason's new wife, who had finally saw through her dead father-n-law, and why he had made sure she picked Jason over Simon, her first love.

A week later the will was read and Jason walked around like a proud peacock for inheriting all his father's estate, leaving his brother Simon nothing. After reading the will for herself, Sue Marie saw the cruelty over giving everything to her husband and sending his other son away penniless. Approaching Jason with all the deception and utter unfairness where his brother was concerned, being cheated out of half the inheritance, she would give her husband a choice, to give his brother half of the inheritance or give her a divorce.

"Jason, it must be one way or the other! So, if you want me to stay and remain your wife, then you must do the right thing by your brother!"

"Sue Marie, you are a woman, and have no knowledge of such things! Nor do you have any right to tell your husband, the man in our relationship, how to run his business!" Jason's eyes burned down on the brave girl. "You have one job woman and that is to please your husband! Understand?"

"I understand you sound exactly like your father right now!" Sue Marie was seeing this spoiled man clearly for the first time since their marriage and it wasn't a proud moment to learn the man she married wasn't as truthful or honest as he had pretended. "Jason, it appears I picked the wrong brother to wed!"

"Sue Marie, you must be kidding! Can't you see things clearly darling, we have it all! The house, the barns, fields, land and sheep, everything!" Jason took her hand. "You and I are soul owners of this large estate, 300 acres of the finest land around and tons of money!"

Sue slipped her hand free and stared up. "Is that all you think about Jason? Being the only heir to your father's vast fortune, after your twin brother worked his fingers to the bone, every single day, practically his whole life!"

"Sue Marie, you needn't feel sorry for Simon. We paid him well for his labor. He never went hungry and he always had a roof over his head and free board! The hired workers had to find shelter in the sheds." Jason tried to take his wife into his arms and she pulled away.

"Jason, you just don't get it, do you? You and your father treated Simon like one of your hired men, never part of your family, like it was when your mama was alive!" Sue Marie jerked away when he tried to pulled her over. "Simon is your brother! Your, twin brother!" She shook her head, opened her closet and took out her luggage, the began packing.

"Just what are you doing woman?" Jason walked over and grabbed Sue Marie's wrist, twisting it painfully. "You will not make a fool out of me Sue Marie! Do you hear! You are not going anywhere, understand?" in his rage, the younger twin slung his wife across the floor and she slammed into the dresser. The shouting and noise had not gone unnoticed by the moody man standing below the staircase listening to their conversation. "You will stay right here and not say a word of this to my brother or you will live to regret it!" Jason walked over and jerked her up, then lifted his hand back to strike her, when Jason felt a stronger hand grab it down, twisting it behind his back.

"Touch this girl one more time brother and I will kill you here and now, so you can join your daddy in hell!" Simon could see fear in his brother's eyes as he tried to pull his arm free, but Jason found his brother was too strong for him. "Tending fuzzy sheep has made you soft brother!" Simon sneered in his ear "My jobs over a lifetime have built my muscles to a strength you cannot match, little brother! Now I can take you down, little 'pet', then this entire place will be mine!"

"Why can't you brothers learn to get alone. There's only the two of you left in your family now." Sue Marie looked at the man who had been such a sweet, loving boy, walked her home after school, holding her hand, when they were high school sweethearts. The same shy young man that finally found the courage to tell her he loved her, before giving the long kiss she still dreamed about. "Simon, I know that young man I fell in love with when we were high school sweethearts, is still living somewhere inside that angry heart of yours." Sue Marie continued with her packing while Simon held on to his weaker brother, watching her closed the lid and pick it up. "I will be going now fellows and I will not cease praying for you. Mostly praying that you don't kill one another. I'm just glad your dear mama cannot see how her loving sons turned out. I sincerely wish you both well and remember Jason, I married you because your possessive father made me see Simon through his eyes, not my own. Simon, I knew after I married your brother how wrong your father had been about you. Never forget, you were always the Granger brother I was in love with." Seeing the anger in Jason's eyes, Sue Marie moved to the open door, not wanting to hear any more threating words from him. She looked back briefly to add "You will be hearing from my lawyer Jason." With those words, Sue Marie limped out, closed the door and left the brothers to fight it out.

Simon gave a winning laugh as he shoved his brother from his arms. "Looks like the privileged pet finally lost! The leading lady loves me Jason, not you!"

"Keep dreaming loser! Sue Marie would have never left with you Simon!" Jason gave a sarcastic laugh. "You are a loser big brother and you always have been!"

"Only because that sneaky cheat, we called papa, paid off every judge at the county fair so you could win a stupid blue ribbon!" Simon stormed out toward the door and slung it open, then slung around to face Jason. "Well little brother, the cheating stops here and now! The old man is dead and finally out of my hair, so I will fight for what is rightfully mine! I am the oldest, so I should be the one in charge of the farm, not you punk! You don't know anything about running a farm! All you have ever done is order the shepherds around while they did the work for you! I can and will take charge of doing it all!"

Like hell you will!" Jason pulled out a pistol from his pocket. "I won this place fair and square and I will gladly shoot any loser that tells me otherwise!"

Simon slammed the door back shut and took two steps back over toward his equally mad brother. "Look, you little jerk, I am sick and tired of daddy's boy calling me a loser! You are always so sure of yourself you're blinded by the truth! I have you know I'm worth as much as you are!" Simon had planned his time for revenge, but, by fate, it might come sooner than he thought. "What do you say to one more contest between us, Mr. perfect? Winner take all!"

Jason burst out laughing. "What can you possibly put up to equal the value of my property?"

"Correction brother, OUR property, not yours!" Simon returned with a big smile.

"Look, you, ignorant bastard, papa left me EVERYTHING! You, 'dear' brother got NOTHING!" Jason yelled and got even madder when his brother smiled even bigger. "Just what the shit have you got to smile about?"

"It appears 'dear' papa didn't share everything with his first-place winning pet!" Simon could see the confusion on Jason's face as he continued. "Then, buddy boy, let me fill you in. Papa paid me a salary every week, along with the hired help. There were some weekends the old geezer ran short of cash, so me being the only worker that was kin, he would pay me with parcels of his land, a $1/4^{th}$ acre at a time. To make it legal, I made him sign over a separate deed for each parcel until I received my full amount in one deed for all the acres written out to my name. Over all the years I worked, starting on my seventh birthday, I have saved a great substantial amount of money and have acquired over 150 acres of the best land for planting and pasture."

"I cannot believe papa would pay a worthless worker with our land!" Jason opened the top drawer and secured the will and opened it up, forgetting the gun was hanging limp in his left hand.

"Let me rephrase your rude statement 'brother'! Papa paid his hard-working SON with OUR land?" Simon had noticed the limp pistol and rushed over and knocked it from his hand, startling him. Simon pointed down at the will where the acreage was mentioned and heard his brother repeat the total he was to receive. "You can see, right there on the line, exactly how many you repeated, 100 acres of fine sheep pasture with a water fed pond, barns and stables, pigs, cows and chickens, smaller garden and the large farmhouse, plus all outbuildings."

"Just hold on there, Simon! We had 300 acres on this property! Papa showed me the deed many times, telling his favorite it would be mine someday! If this will, states only 100 acres and you have 150, that only comes to 250 acres. Do the math stupid! 50 acres are missing! They did not just disappear!" Jason grew sick in the stomach, seeing clearly, he wouldn't be the sole owner of his father's huge estate, nor could he be the one in charge, handing out orders, as long as his brother was still alive. "Did you steal the other 50 acres when papa was drinking Simon?"

"You would think that Jason, since that's the way your mind works! If you can't earn it by working, win it by cheating, you will steal the girl by lying, right along with the old man. You'd do anything to get high marks from papa, even make fun of your own playmate." Old memories still haunted Simon. "I sold my first 50 acres Jason because they were worthless for farming and papa knew it, and that's why he gave them to me for my wedges. But I figured land was land, and the new housing development was a Godsend, since they named it rolling hills, and my 50 acres boasts of lovely rolling hills and full-grown trees. I got a small fortune for that property and have made a lot of interest on it since putting it in the money market. With that substantial amount added to my life's savings, due to having no overhead for never having rent to pay or food to buy, I decided when I take over, I'm going to build myself a new home and burn this old one to the ground."

Simon noticed his brother had lost his cocky look as fresh tears collected in his eyes and slowly ran down his face. Jason tried to speak but his words came of shaky, from the first real tears he had shed since he was a small child. "Please Simon, tell me you're not serious about setting fire to our old homeplace?"

Still unsure of his brother's motives, Simon gave a soft laugh. "Why, too many memories of your papa spoiling you Jason?"

"It's not because of papa Simon." The usually outspoken man had grown melancholy, and Simon noticed a side of him he had not witnessed since they were small boys. "Simon, it's all we have left to remember our mama. How she would always be waiting by the back door, calling us inside from playing in the back yard all morning. Mama would stand there smiling, holding the screen door open, watching her two little boys she loved so much having fun together." Jason looked up at his brother. "Do you remember what our favorite game was?"

Simon loosened up his fist, the past flooding back like a sudden storm, only this one with a rainbow. "I remember Jason." Simon felt his own emotional tears falling, seeing his dear mama's face, looking down on her two small boys kissing them goodnight. "Mama had bought us both a little car to play in the dirt with."

Simon managed a real smile. "You had red and mine was blue. We made dirt roads around small weeds and rocks and occasionally switch cars with one another, because" Simon looked into his brother's sad eyes. "We loved each other and were the best of friends."

"Simon, we were happy as long as mama was alive. She put the happiness of the Lord inside us and taught us songs of praise." Jason recalled happier times. "Mama taught us how to pray, remember?"

"I do, brother, but I also recall papa telling us praying was a lot of nonsense and they were worthless. He would say, boys, no one will hear you anyway, cause this God is just a myth." Simon glanced over at his brother. "You know what I believe brother? I believe God is real and that He can hear our prayers."

"Why Simon, what reason can you have?" Jason sincerely needed to know the truth, once and for all.

"Because of mama. Not because she told us about Jesus and what He did for us all, which I also believe because it did come from my loving mama. I believe just by the way mama loved us, always sang praises while she worked, took us to church every Sunday until our devil of a papa put his foot down, telling her to go without us." Simon pulled out the old picture of his mama he had carried with him all his life since she died. "It was written on her angelic face and she glowed with the light of the Lord!"

Both brothers wondered down into the den, to reminisce their past happiness when Sadie Granger was still there, filling their small lives with her incredible love. Jason wondered over to the old piano, now closed and silent after so many years without their mother's playing it while she sang her favorite tunes and hymns. Both Jason and Simon felt as though they could almost hear their mother playing the old piano she had brought with her when she was a newlywed.

"Mother seemed to be so happy when we were with her." Jason lovingly touched the old piano. "What joy it would be to hear our mama sing again."

"We may have blown that chance Jason, for the way we have felt for one another since papa chose you to be his favorite." Simon picked up a framed picture of him and Jason standing with their mama. "Heaven don't permit heathen and haters inside those golden gates little brother." His eyes fell on the big portrait over the stone

138

massive brick fireplace. Just his father, the big man of the house, seated in his favorite easy chair wearing a fancy suit and smoking an expensive cigar, the weapon that took him to his grave. His dear mother had gone to her grave much too early and Simon would always blame his father for killing her.

"Look at the pompous jackass, sitting there like he's some kind of royal. A lord or a duke, but most likely a king, to rule his wife and sons the way he saw fit."

"Simon, why do you hate papa so much?" It seemed like an honest question, from the son that had never witnessed his father's mean streak.

"I can tell you the exact moment I started hating that evil man you adored." Simon fell into his mama's old rocking chair as the bad memory came back. "The day he treated me bad did not start the hate, it merely broke my young heart, as did my very best friend and twin." He noticed the new interest appearing on his brother's face as he too found a seat, his father's easy chair.

"Please Simon, go on and refresh my memory concerning papa's hurting you as well as I?"

"Like usual, we all gathered inside this den after having our evening meal to enjoy hearing mama sing along with her piano playing. Then you and I would gather around mama's feet so she could read a story from her old bible, now hid away, thanks to papa. I had been observing papa sitting apart from us and in my six-year-old eyes I felt sorry for him. He looks so lonely and left out of our family time. As mama read, I got up and walked over to papa, but he acted as though I were not there, so I climbed up on his lap and gave him a hug, then a kiss, before saying, Papa, I love you, please come and join us. Instead of returning my affection of love, he yelled for me to get off his lap and stop acting childish! Then he pushed me away, anger dripping off his viper mouth. "I never want you to tell me you love me again, mama's boy!" then he stormed out at her. "And put that ridiculous book up before you turned this sissy boy into a girl!" Simon looked at Jason, recalling his playmates behavior. "Then you jumped up and said, 'Yeh Simon, you've turned into a silly girl!' then your laughter continued as you said, 'Don't you know papa is a strong-powerful man brother! He doesn't need hugs and kisses from his boys, Papa respects a handshake, right papa?'" Simon recalled their father giving a laugh as he held out his hand for Jason to shake. "Papa felt fine then until you said, we would give our hugs and kisses to mama. That's when papa jumped up and grabbed your hand, saying he something he wanted to show his son, so he took you away to brainwash so he could possess you for his own."

"Simon are you just saying these things because papa didn't choose you to spoil? Suppose you were just an envious six-year-old, seeing poor papa's actions differ from mama's and you wanted to be the center of his attention."

"You are nowhere close Jason. He did hurt my feelings. I'll not deny that. I was just a kid! You betrayed me that day Jason and fell into papa's web of deceit. Without my playmate by my side, I had plenty of time to observe the things we had been missing while we were not with mama. All the hateful-hurtful words papa would hurl out to the good woman, his acts of betrayal and abuse, that always ended with mama getting hurt, both mentally and physically and was the one responsible for her death!"

"I cannot believe the man I admired and loved would treat any woman with disrespect!" Jason returned to his defense of the man he looked up to and had believed in.

"Papa molded you well Jason and he has you believing he is something he wasn't. A loud-mouth, wife beater, cigar smoking drunk that would end his night of rousing around with the 'boys' by paying a visit to Miss Mabel's whore house on the out skirts of town!"

Jason rose from the chair, dripping with anger. "That is a bald faced lie Cain!"

"Back to papa's favorite names for us buddy boy! The only liar living under this roof was our old man! He kept you in the dark so you wouldn't know about his seedy side!" Simon stood up to be equal with his brother. "If I am Cain, then this Able must have reversed rolls from the Cain and Abel in mama's bible! And this Cain and Abel's father is not named Adam, he is the serpent that tempted their mother to sin! Mama's only fault was loving an atheist who only loved himself. I told you earlier that devil put her in an early grave, so let me enlighten you just how. Mama stayed with him and his nightly abuse after we went to bed, because of us and she knew he would hunt her down if she took us away with her. Going to that whorehouse two nights a week finally caught up with the bastard. He caught a sexual disease by one of the prostitutes and since he wasn't allowed back, he would rape mama every night until she caught the disease."

"Simon. How on earth did a six-year-old boy learn all that grown up stuff! I am sure mama did not share any of this with you Simon." Jason was having hard time seeing his papa in another light. "Just be honest and tell me the truth instead of being so jealous over what I had with papa."

"Is that what you really think this is about brother? Me, being jealous over you?" Simon gave a sarcastic laugh. "Boy, you really are one-sided! It has always been papa who was jealous bother! Jealous because we loved our mama so much and hung by her all the time because he was either too cold toward us or gone off, where we assumed was at work. He saw it clearly the day I went over to ask him to join us, so papa decided to take one of us for himself, so mama couldn't have us both." Eyes cold on his brother once more, Simon would let him know how he found out everything. "I awoke one-night hearing papa's loud voice auguring with mama, so I slipped from my bed, now having my own room since papa moved you in with him, I knew no one would hear me. I peeked in the open crack and saw the old man slapping mama around. She tried to calm him down but in his drunk state he only grew madder and docked her across the floor so hard she slammed into the dresser and hit her head, causing her to go unconscious. Papa just walked over and laughed, giving mama a kick, before turning to stagger out the door. I hid behind the hall plant until the sorry devil went into his room, then raced in to check on mama. Calling her several times, I couldn't get a response, so I ran to the telephone and called Doc Mills. I watched from mama's window for the doctor's car, then raced downstairs to let him in, telling him about father's condition and why we should stay quiet. After Doctor Mills checked mama out, I could see concern on his face and he lifted her up and motioned for me to follow. He placed mama in the back seat of his big station wagon and ask me to ride along with them. On the way to the hospital, Doctor Mills filled me in on everything papa had been doing to mama and he was afraid this time the man had gone too far." With serious eyes, Simon concluded "After that 'fall' as papa called it, mama hemorrhaged inside her brain and died within minutes, never regaining consciousness. If you don't believe me

Jason, ask Doctor Mills. He was in the operation room when she took her final breath. We both knew papa was at fault but with the only witness being a small child, the case was dropped. Your beloved hero got by with the cold-blooded murder of our precious mama. The only thing in this stinking life worth living for!"

"If what you say was true Simon, why wasn't I ever informed?" Jason felt sick to his stomach again, learning this about the man he had looked up to and wanted to be like. He suddenly recalled acting exactly like his father when he hit his wife and knocked her across the floor. Maybe, he thought, he had already turned into his papa and now, he wasn't as sure that was the way he wanted to go.

"Everyone involved thought it best not to tell you Jason, since you were so close to the old man. They were afraid papa would find out I witnessed what he had done and then my life would be in danger. So, to protect us from papa's wrath, the sheriff dropped the case and said it was up to God now to put judgement on Mr. Granger."

"Then I guess I will only have your word on what happen Simon." Jason walked up to the large portrait of his father and found it hard to believe the man that gave him everything was so corrupt. "Well, Papa is gone now and it is up to God to give him judgement, not you brother! I will remain loyal to the man that saw the best in me and helped me grow into the man I am today."

"A selfish, arrogant bastard just like him, wanting everything for yourself!" Simon walked toward the door. "This will be settled once and for all brother in our final competition. You will get two options to choose from. The first is to do a day's work on the farm, alone, for one day. Starting at sunrise, to milk the two cows, then feed the hogs, chickens, and horses. After you have completed this, you will attend to the sheep, then break thirty-minutes for lunch. When you go back out, you will check the tractor over, making sure gas is filled, oil is full, blades are sharpened, then you will mow one of the large fields, your choice. They are the same size and grade. This should take you to five o'clock. Then you'll see that all the livestock is fed and bedded down in their stables for the night. I'll take the other day, repeating all the same work. The hired help will judge our work and the winner gets everything!"

"Simon, that is unfair and you know it! This is what you have done since you were seven, while I have attended the sheep only."

Jason raised his eyebrow. "There's no need for you to mention the help papa got me to help with the sheep, just fill me in on the second option, and it better be something we both are good at brother!"

"This should come easy for the favorite son of a murderer." Simon remained serious as Jason looked over in total surprise.

"Surely you are not referring to murdering each other, like Sue Marie was afraid we might do?"

"Even though we both have considered the possibility of killing one another over this land, that is not exactly what I had in mind." Simon fought his smile when he noticed his brother relax, looking relieved. "We will still have a duel with two witnesses. One to watch you and one to watch me, making sure neither of us turn around before the count has ended. We will both be given a pistol, containing one bullet, and the man who shoots the other man's leg, and causes him to fall, will be the sole owner of our entire estate!" Finally, Simon saw a sly grin on his cocky brother's face. "I wouldn't get to sure of your marksmanship brother. Sometimes the man who feels overconfident gets sloppy and makes mistakes."

"Simon, have you forgotten, I always win, while you come in second?" Jason laughed. "I have been taking target practicing for years and I never miss big brother."

"Then little brother, I must warn you about my years of target practice and I have never missed papa's cutout face ever!" Simon gave Jason a faux smile before adding. "I'll set it up tomorrow afternoon at two. Turner and Wesson will watch and judge us, so I wouldn't be tempted to bribe them with money little brother, because all the workers on the farm know me better than you or papa and we are all friends. Better lay off the booze tonight brother so you won't be shaking tomorrow afternoon." Simon left the house, knowing sleeping there tonight might prove fatal."

CHAPTER 20

Two o'clock rolled around quickly and the twin brothers stood facing each other in the east meadow while Frank Turner and Johnny Wesson prepared the pistols and gave them a final check before handing each man a gun. Turner, a history buff, had read many stories about famous men that had died while dueling, Alexander Hamilton being one, so he felt sure of the rules, minus the killing part. He knew today's law would not permit another man to take the life of someone else in a duel. In today's law, it would be considered premeditated murder and the shooter would get the maximum prison time. The brothers stared at each other while Johnny Wesson read the rules with the end results being changed.

"Gentlemen, I will ask you both to turn your backs away from one another then I will begin counting out starting with 10, then go down until I say fire, for the number 1. Like: 2 then fire! Do you both understand?" Both brothers nodded their heads and took the pistol from the man nearest them. "Your goal is to shoot your opponent in either leg, causing him to fall. The man left standing will be the soul owner of Granger Farms." Mr. Wesson looked from Simon to Jason. "Are you both willing to except the rules as they stand?"

Both brothers said loudly "Yes sir!"

"Very well, let's proceed." The judge held up both hands. "Gentlemen, I wish you both, good luck and may the best man win"

"I will guarantee the best man will be walking away with the prize again!" Jason gave the judges a cocky smile. "I have never lost, have I Cain?"

"Not until today favored son." Simon stood proudly, feeling confident this would be his first win against his brother. "The old man is not here to buy your victory little brother, so prepare to lose and see how it feels!"

"You both have spoken your mind. Now, the game will begin. Gentlemen, please turn and face away from your opponent. Raise your pistol up to shoulder height and prepare to step forward. One step for every number called. Turner and I will be watching all your moves and if any time we see one of you get out of line, we will call for the game to stop and give the opponent following the rules the win. On the count of ten, let the game start." Mr. Wesson began calling the numbers slowly backward. "10, 9, 8" as he counted each brother were having positive thoughts of winning.

Looking straight ahead, listening to the falling numbers, Jason felt more than sure he could take down his brother. "Soon, I will have it all and that loser will get lost for good!"

Just as sure, Simon kept his eyes on the distance forest, his thoughts on Jason finally losing to him without their old man around to buy his win. "The little pet will finally get what he deserves! Nothing!"

The count was coming down to the final outcome and as the brothers heard the 9 called, they braced themselves to get ready to shoot, knowing this time it wouldn't be just practice but the real thing. With a clear-calm voice, Mr. Wesson called out "FIRE!"

As soon as the brothers heard the word given to fire, they both swirled around, aimed their pistols and fired. While at the exact same moment, a brilliant light flashed around them and the twins froze in fear.

Afraid to move, Simon and Jason stood perfectly still, unable to see due to the flash of bright light. They waited for their vision to clear, then looked around at their unusual surroundings, sensing the flash of light had transported them to a strange new place. Instead of standing in their familiar open meadow where they had just shot at one another, the ground on which they stood was a beautiful green vista, surrounding by large cedar trees, that neither brother had ever seen growing in the state of North Carolina.

"Simon, what just happened to us? I recall myself turning then aiming my pistol on your leg, then firing the gun, only to see a burst of light." Jason could not understand his mixed feelings. The overwhelming fear of the unknown and the tranquil bliss of amazing peace. "Do you think we accidently killed each other like Sue Marie feared would happen and we are having an out-of-the-body experience?"

"Maybe the Lord saw what bad heathens we had become and struck us with His blinding light, just like he did Saul, from the holy book." Simon recalled the story of the Jewish soldier rounding up the new-found Christians for execution and how he had sat proudly

145

on his stallion to witness the Christian saint Stephen being stone to death. "Jesus stopped Saul on the road to Damascus and shined around him a light from heaven, so bright it blinded him, where he could not see, then led him to a man who took him to Peter."

"Now that you mention the story mama read, I recalled it and how the Lord change Saul's name to Paul." Jason looked around at the peaceful place. "If we did die, why do I feel the same? And, surely hell cannot be this nice."

"It's too beautiful and peaceful inside these, grove of cedars to be the dwelling place of Lucifer." Simon couldn't figure out what had happened to them any more than his brother could. The only real fact he knew was, they were not standing in the open meadow where they took shots at each other, out of greed and revenge. "I guess we will stay right here until someone or some being leads us onward."

"Yes Simon, you must wait until He leads you on, by the light." The all-familiar voice came softly, as both brothers first glanced at each other then in the direction of the invisible person who just spoke.

"Simon, that spirit that just spoke to us sounded familiar." Jason looked around, hoping to catch a glimpse of the spirit. "Did you recognize it?"

"I would never forget that beautiful voice brother, even though its been a long time since I heard her say my name." Tears filled the firstborn's eyes as he whispered "Mama, we need you."

Jason swallowed back the lump in his throat as tears filled his eyes as well, and softly her youngest repeated his brother's plea. "Simon is right mama. We need our mama to help us."

"Jason, Simon, my darling boys, you know just how much your mama has always loved you, but sons, there is One who's love for you is far greater than any love you have ever imagined. It is His light that has led you here to his secret garden and this is where the Lord will heal you both. From all the pain, hurt, selfish behavior, envy, over proudness, deception, your acts of falsely accusing your brother Jason, to put him down, Simon, for the terrible hate that has filled my loving boy's heart to the point your thoughts turned to murdering your only brother. My son, I cannot blame you for the disrespect you had for your ruthless papa. The way he always treated my precious boy was unworthy of being honored as a father.

The Lord knows your hearts and he will make you whole. Just follow his light, then sit and wait for his appearance."

The light once again appeared. This time it flowed gently down the wide vista and stopped over a smooth wooden bench. The brothers followed close behind and glanced at each other when they noticed just the one bench, waiting for them to come together. They knew the heavenly being waited within the light, but still having the same raw emotions of mistrust for one another, they considered the bench was too small for grown men their size. Once again, their mother intervened.

"Simon, Jason, must you act in such a hostel fashion toward one another in the presents of your Holy Creator? Do you not remember there is nothing impossible for our Lord to do? If you cannot show good control as adult men, then He can place you back inside your childhood, when you loved each other and were the very best of friends. Jason, why do you think your brother resorts back when he calls you buddy boy?"

Jason fought back his tears recalling just recently when Simon had called him the same name he had gave him when they were the best buddies in the world. "I'll take a seat with my brother. I'm sorry mama."

"And, I will sit beside my buddy boy mama. The Lord won't need to make these childish acting grown men back into the loving little boys we use to be."

"That sounds more like it my brothers." Hearing the words of the Lord, brought both brothers to attention as they looked to see the Lamb of God standing where the light had floated moments before. "You boys have suffered long enough and I need for you both to come home."

"Come home, Lord? Which home are you referring to, Jesus? Heaven or the Granger Farms?" Simon could see the incredible love flowing over the Christ. "Do we go there together?"

"Questions concerning being together Simon is a good beginning for healing." Jesus gave them a beautiful smile, that radiated around them. "Your heaven home will come later. Only one of you will dwell in your old homeplace while the other brother will find a new home and family to call his own. You shall never be far apart, my brothers, for families should always remain close, both in heart and in presence."

"Which one of us will have the homeplace Lord?" Jason had always felt close to the old place but now, he cared what happened to his brother and had thought if they worked out their differences, they could be equal partners.

"Your thoughts for your brother are far greater than they appeared earlier when you shot him in the leg." Jesus tried to keep a straight face when he noticed Jason perk up and glanced down at Simon's perfect leg.

"Lord, I see no wound on my brother's leg?"

"No, you would not, nor do you feel the one your brother hit you with, perfect aim, right in the kneecap. It would have sent you to the ground if I had not intervened." Now Jesus found it hard not to laugh at Simon's frantic searching. "Neither of you will find the shot wound since I healed your legs the moment they were injured. If I had not brought you here, things would not have ended well for the Granger twins. So, we must return to the night you both started to fall apart from one another. Look and you shall see everything more clearly. Jason, pay close attention. Your father was not the wonderful man he led his small son to believe he was." With a wave of his heavenly hand, the past came to life.

"Mama, what story are you going to read tonight?" Simon sat up on his knees below his mother's rocking chair. Her other son Jason, waited anxiously for her to begin reading.

"Tonight, I thought you boys might like to hear about Adam and Eve's first two sons." Sadie opened her bible to the front and smiled down at their excited faces. "You both remember how God created Adam, the first man, then he created Eve, the first woman."

"God created Adam out of the dust of the earth!" Jason answered, wide eyes. "I sure would have liked to see God do that magic! Did He make the dust into a ball of clay and mold it like me and Simon does with the clay we got for Christmas?"

"Boy, don't believe all that bible nonsense!" Wilber Granger picked up the moonshine jar and poured himself another full glass of the white lightning. "Use your brain, Jason! There ain't no way anyone can make a human being out of dust from the ground!" His angry eyes fell on his wife. "Stop filling these boy's heads with this garbage Sadie, or I'll send your ass packing!"

"Wilber, as long as I have breath in me, I will teach my sons about our heavenly Lord! With or without your approval!" Sadie

148

gave her frightened boys a bright smile. "Now boys, pay your papa no mind when it comes to this holy book. This book was given by the Almighty Himself and every word written here, is and will always be forever true." Her attention fell on Simon, who had been watching his father closely. "Darling, did you have something to add about the creation of Adam and Eve?"

He looked back at his mother, feeling nervous about his statement, afraid his papa would have something bad to say about his words, like he had his best buddy, his brother. "I remember the Lord put Adam to sleep and took a rib from his chest to make her. Mama, if the bible tells us how she was made, then I believe God's words."

"Thank you, Simon. You and Jason are exactly right so now we can learn about their first two little boys who grew up, competing for God's love."

"At least their story has some action in it." Wilber leaned over and made a dark face as he spoke in a deep-sinister voice. "There's even MURDER from one of the sons! Exciting, right?"

"Wilber, why can't you stop degrading the word of God? Do you not care where you will end up if you do not change your attitude and stop scaring our son's!"

"I will say anything I please woman, in my house, to my sons!" He pulled out a cigar and lit it. "Just quit filling their heads with all this junk! I'll teach my sons to be real men and how to not let women run over them!"

"If you have finished being a heathen, then smoke your stinking cigar and drink that wild brew while I put some hope and love inside our boy's minds and hearts." Bravely, Sadie began reading the story of Cain and Able as the grownup brothers watched tearfully.

Simon had sat listening to the envious brother killing his younger brother, and knowing he could never hate his twin brother, his best friend and playmate, he glanced down to hide his tears from the man watching his son's reactions to the story. Simon kept his eyes lowered on the blue truck in his hand while his mother went to get their bedtime snack of milk and cookies. As he sat eating the cookie, the six-year-old kept glancing up at his father, who now had his eyes closed, thinking, "Papa is just sad because he feels left out. Maybe if I showed him how much I loved him too, my papa would stop being so mean to my mama." Simon got up as his mother read another story for her sons while they enjoyed the milk and cookies. He walked over to his father and carefully climbed on his lap, causing the irate man to jump and yell out at the boy. "What do you think you're doing kid?" Simon nervously told his father that he loved him. "Papa, please come and have milk and cookies with us. I love you papa." When Simon hugged the harsh man, Wilber's large hands grabbed the small boy and knocked him off, calling him names and making fun of him.

Simon slowly backed away, just a small boy trying to show his papa love and in return, received hate. Then the small boy was really hurt when his very best friend and playmate hopped up laughing at him, while pointing a finger toward his tears. The words that came from Jason hurt him more than all the horrible things his papa had ever said to him, and Simon could feel his little heart breaking.

"Wilber!" Sadie was on her feet, drawing Simon in her arms. "Must you be so cruel to Simon! Have you no heart at all Wilber Granger?" Their sad mother reached for her other son. "And you Jason, saying such offal things to your brother!" her eyes fell on her husband. "Are you trying to spit these boys apart, knowing how much they care for one another?"

"Maybe, that is exactly what they need bitch!" Wilber stood up and pulled Jason free from his mother's grip. "Come along with me son. I have something to show you." Then Wilber Granger left with his young son, to change his life forever.

Jason had watched the horrible scene and couldn't help but noticed how his attention as the six-year-old Jason, was riveted on his father and not one time did he noticed his loving little brother's tears, as Simon had watched his brother betraying his best friend for his papa's attention. Suddenly Jason wished he could have done it all over again and chose his brother instead of the man that split them up and caused them to hate one another. Still staring down with regret, Jason spoke softly to his brother who had turned toward him when he said his name.

"Simon, I am so sorry." Jason felt his brother cover his shoulders with his arms as he heard Simon's answer.

"I forgive you buddy boy. Please, forgive me for the way I have acted towards you Jason." The hug from his tearful twin said it all and the Lord was pleased.

"Love is a powerful thing my brothers and to watch you unite again brings joy to your Savior's heart." The heavenly eyes fell on Jason once more. "The sins of your father were released on you son and just like the man you looked up to, you turned on your devoted wife and hit her, sending her across the floor, same as your papa did your devoted mama. Look and see how Wilson Granger really was, then you will know your brother's words about him are true."

The screen lifted once again and instantly the brothers recognized their parent's bedroom. Their mama had stayed with her boys until they fell asleep. Simon, now alone in the twin's room and Jason, in his father's big bed, alone. Wilber had made his nightly trip to Otis Cox's Still, to buy his usual quart of moonshine, 95% white lightning. Ever since the cheating husband got the sexual disease from one of the prostitutes, he had been asked to take his business else ware after beating up the whore that gave it to him. Desiring sex after the long night of heavy drinking, Sadie's drunk husband would stagger up the steps and walk inside the room she had taken after he ran her out of his, years before. Never a one to consider other people's privacy or wants, the demanding husband yanked off Sadie's covers, then her nightgown. Never a gentle man nor one of respect, all Wilber cared about was pleasing himself, so he would rape Sadie, until he released his urge. Even after affecting the good woman with his horrible disease, the arrogant man never cared how much it hurt her physically, much less mentally. The same abuse had continued for months, but Simon and Jason's mama never let on that there was anything wrong in their family. The two brothers would soon learn why their loving mama never said a word about the way their father treated her. It was the night that led up to her accident and when their mama was taken away from them.

After the heated husband had had his way with Sadie, he fell back, breathing heavy. His gruff voice filled her ears, while she lay weeping, her head turned away from the drunken smell.

"You did well tonight woman! Not one peep about the damn pain I was causing you." Wilber sat up, his head spinning, then lowered his head to her ear. "Marriage is for better or worse Sadie, remember that loudmouth preacher's words? The way I see it woman, if I get something worse, this damn disease, then as my wife, you must share the pain with me dear." Wilber tried to sit and fell back down laughing.

"Wilber, can't you be quieter? The boys are sleeping and in your drunken state, maybe you had just sleep it off here tonight, instead of in bed with our son." Sadie had kept her tone civil and soft, hoping it wouldn't rile up her trigger-temper husband. She gave a startled gasp when the big hand squeezed her throat.

"Look bitch, it was 'you' I told to be quiet after you would scream out every time I humped you! So, what if that damn disease was eating away and raw!" his fingers went tighter as Sadie tried to take in air. "Was I bragging on your staying still tonight for nothing woman? You know I meant what I said to you on the first night I came in here! If you do not let me have what I want, I will start killing a boy a night, starting with Simon!"

Tired of the treats about killing her little boys, Sadie had enough breath to reach for the bedside lamp and slam it over her husband's head, causing him to release her throat and fall off the bed. Sadie quickly rolled to the other side and jumped up, grabbing on her robe and a steel rod she had hid just for an occasion like this. Her heart beating in total fear, Sadie watched Wilber Granger slowly lift himself up from the floor, swaying back and forth, hand over his head.

"What the hell did you hit me on the head for woman? Are you trying to kill me?"

"You were trying to kill me, you devil! If you think I was just going to lay there and let you choke the life out of me, leaving my helpless little boys in your no-count care, you can think again!" Sadie suddenly felt the bravery of a mother's love and knew she had to take her sons and leave this bad heathen.

"Now, you listen to me woman!" in his drunken stage Wilber jumped when Sadie slammed the steel rod down on the iron woodstove.

"I am tired of listening to your big mouth Wilber! It is you who will listen to me for a change! This stops right now Wilber! All your mean threats about our innocent sons! All your sick abuse given to me! Your obvious intentions to break up our boys and the hopes to change Jason to be like you! God perished the thought!" The iron rod held steady in her hand, Sadie made her way passed Wilber, who had reluctantly moved out of her way, feeling her determination and wrath toward him. "If you are wise, you will remain in this room until morning and slecp off your drunken state. I will collect Jason from your room and sleep with our sons tonight in their room. You will find the door locked and bolted, should you attempt to storm the room to take revenge on me by harming our sons. What I have planned after that will be left in a letter to you. At lease you will have the only thing you have ever cared about Wilber. YOUR OWN SELF AND EVERYTHING YOU OWN!" Sadie backed to the door, not trusting the man she had married blindly ten years ago. "This is not goodnight, Wilber, this is goodbye!" Sadie opened the door and heard a small voice behind her.

CHAPTER 21

"Mama, is everything alright in here?" Jason stood there, staring up, wiping his sleepy eyes. "I woke up and papa wasn't in bed with me. I got real scared mama. I thought something had happened to my papa, then I heard your talking. Is everything o.k. mama?"

Before Sadie could say or do anything, Wilber had slipped up to grab her arms back, away so his son couldn't see what he was forcing her to drop.

"Everything is just fine Jason. Mama and I were just making plans about a little family vacation this summer. Would you like that pal?" Wilber gave his small boy a smile while he mashed Sadie's fingers, making it hard for her to keep a straight face.

"Yes papa, that sounds swell." Jason's little hand reached up and touched his mama's spare hand. "Mama, are you sick or something? You don't look like you feel good."

"Jason darling, mama will be alright, so please don't worry sweet baby boy." Sadie knew this may be the last time she saw either of her two little boys alive, so she managed to squat down to hug him and give him one last kiss. "Jason, never forget how much your mama loves you and Simon. Please be a sweet boy and love each other the way mama and Jesus, loves you."

"We will mama, I promise." Jason hugged her neck and gave a sweet kiss. "I love you mama." His young innocent eyes went up to his father. "I love you too papa."

"That's my boy! Now, run along and hop in bed. Papa will be in shortly son."

The young boy ran back to the end bedroom to wait for the man he believed, while Wilber Granger shut the door, and gave Sadie his evil smile. "Too bad you never learned, the man of the house always has the last say. You will never take my boys away from me, you, stupid woman. The only way you will leave 'my' house is in a body bag!" Wilber lifted the iron bar then slammed it across Sadie's head, then her back, knocking her across the floor where she slammed into the dresser, knocking her out cold. Now, it was the other small son watching from the open crack at what his papa had done to their loving mother.

Made by the Master's Hand

At this point, Jason was in tears, after years of being brainwashed by the man he had admired for so long, the incident witnessed by six-year-old Jason had long been forgotten. Seeing all that happened before she opened the door and recalling his mama surprised look when she saw him standing there, Jason realized he had given his papa the chance to take away her only defense for saving her and them from their father.

"It's all my fault! I stopped mama before she could escape from our evil papa! She was coming to save us and take us away!" Jason sniffed as he tried to speak. "Mama died because of me! Her last words to me, same as said she knew papa would kill her! Why did I get out of bed!"

"Jason, you were just a little boy. It wasn't your fault brother." Simon tried to comfort his brother, finally seeing everything clearly for the first time. "It was probably the arguing and fighting that woke you up too and you got scared because you were alone. I must have just missed you in the hall."

"Well, nevertheless Simon, I can see things clearly now." Jason looked up at the Lord, who had been listening to the brother's showing affection for each other instead of hate. "It is what you were referring to earlier Lord. You said, one of us would remain at the homeplace and the other brother would find a new home and family."

"Yes Jason, that is right. One of you will stay and the other will begin over." Jesus knew his next words, but he would let him speak to them. "What do you believe the choice will be Jason?"

"It's plain for me to see Lord. Since I am the one that done wrong, Simon shall keep the homeplace and the woman he has always loved, Sue Marie."

Simon looked up into the eyes of the Lord and saw a different answer. "May I Jesus." Getting a nod from his Savior, Simon reached for his brother hand. "Jason, I feel certain the Lord wants for you to have the homeplace, so you can raise your little son when Sue Marie comes back with the good news, she is with child."

"A baby? Me and Sue Marie?" Jason glanced up hopeful and Jesus gave him a bright smile. "My brothers, you shall know soon enough. For now, I send you back to the meadow where you were planning to decide the homeplace's owner by shooting at each other. The judges, Turner and Wesson have been suspended in time,

155

waiting your return. You will find yourselves walking away from each other, backs turned, and the count will be at number 9. Simon, Jason, make the right choice! You will know which one is correct!"

BACK AT THE GRANGER FARMS MEADOW.

Backs turned from their brother, both Simon and Jason heard Wesson called out the number 9, and knew the Lord had brought them back exactly where he had proclaimed, giving them another chance to change the outcome of their contest. On the final word, FIRE, the twins turned around slowly and guns still pointed in the open sky, shot off the pistol, dropped their weapons and commenced hugging one another, while laughing over at their judges' faces. Both Wesson and Turner walked over and stared at each man, angry with one another before the game began and now the best of friends.

"Excuse me Simon, would you and Jason care to explain what happened to you two? It just isn't normal to go from hate to "

"Love Wesson, the word is love." Simon laughed. "You might say, Jason and I just had an awakening! What Satan pulls apart, the Lord draws back together!"

"That is a beautiful way of putting what happen to you two." Sue Marie had gotten there just in time to hear Mr. Wesson call out fire and she was afraid she was too late to stop these brothers so she could share with them the good news she had brought. "I would defiantly say you had a miracle from the Lord. All those prayers I've been sending up really paid off!"

"I would have thought you wouldn't care what happened to me Sue Marie, after the way I've been acting." Jason could only see love written on her radiant face. "I guess that beautiful glow on your face is the love you are feeling for Simon. I admit, my brother is the best man between us."

"Nonsense, buddy boy, you have been a victim of papa same as I have." Simon looped his arm over his shoulders, like he had done when they were playmates. "I just bet the special glow on your beautiful wife's face is coming from something else. Perhaps, a little bundle from heaven?"

"Simon, how on earth would you know that I am pregnant!" Sue Marie blushed when both men chuckled. "And as for you Jason Granger, I will have you know, I do love you, very much." Her attention fell on Simon. "And yes, you will always be my first love, Simon Granger, the love of my youth. Now, I am a married woman, who happens to have fallen in love with the other Granger, and the father of my baby. The truth is, you Granger twins are easy to love when your conniving father isn't around to muddy your record."

"Sue Marie, are you saying you're coming back to me? And we are going to have a baby?" Jason didn't know happiness could feel this perfect and whether the baby was a girl or a boy, he would be one proud daddy. No more papa."

"Yes, Jason and I hope your son looks and acts just like his present daddy!" Knowing their papa had torn their family apart by sending their mama to an early grave, Sue Marie never wanted to hear their children call their father papa. "So, which one of you will be over the farm?"

"The owner Sue Marie." Simon actually was amazed at how great he felt giving everything he had worked for, as well as the rest of their homeplace to his only brother and wife. "You and Jason will be the happy homeowners of this 300-area farm, and my little nephew along with all his sisters and brothers, can grow up in a home filled with love and the beautiful memories of their Granma Sadie."

"Where will you go Simon?" Sue Marie walked between the men she loved. "There's plenty of room for you too. Maybe, it's time for the playmates to become farm partners and work side-by-side. You can meet a lovely lady, fall in love and fill the other half of our home with your kids."

"Sue Marie Granger, you have a beautiful heart and I truly thank you for the moving invitation, but the Lord Jesus has other plans for me. I will somehow, find my own family to love and they will take me into their heart and home."

"But you already have a family of your own Simon and we want you to be a part of our home, because you already live in our heart!" Sue Marie looked at her husband for help. "Jason, please darling, you ask your brother to stay."

"Darling, you know I would love nothing more, but Simon or I cannot go against the wishes of our Savior." Jason noticed the tall stranger walking their way and some how he felt familiar. He gazed over at his brother, who had also spotted the man, wearing some type of robe.

"Greetings Simon!" the stranger knew which twin was the man he was seeking. "My name is James. The Lord has sent me to take you to your new home. You will be happy to know, you have paid it a visit recently, when Jesus led you there through His light. The garden that holds the miracle bench is connected to our land. It is called, the Sacred Garden." The man named James gave the other twin a wink. "A son, you will make a wonderful 'daddy' Jason! Our heavenly Savior knows a home with a lot of little anxious children running about needs lots of room and love to grow up healthy and happy." James turned to the smiling young lady, the mother-to-be, glowing with happiness. "And Sue Marie, Simon will never be far away from his birth family, so he can visit whenever he chooses. I'm sure he is ready to start spoiling his new nephew when he comes into God's world." The man of pure faith laid a hand on both Jason and Sue Marie. "To make your joy fully complete, young ones, start attending church regularly, so when your new one arrives, he will be brought up in the Lord's word." James nodded to the two workers, who had been silently observing all that was done and said. "Gentlemen, you will find it a pleasure now working for Jason and Sue Marie. Love has a way of spilling over to everyone around." He walked back to Simon and looped his arm over his shoulder. "My brother, are you ready to see your new home? It will be where one day, you will find your true love. But, until then, we carry on with whatever duties you may enjoy."

"Simon is great at anything concerning the earth, sir?" Jason couldn't understand why he looked so familiar.

"I appear familiar to you Jason because I was in the garden when the Lord spoke to you. I am the caretaker of the Sacred Garden and it looks the way it does because I'm not responsible for its upkeep. The heavenly beings keep it in such a tranquil state." James chuckled. As for my gifts in attending the good ground, I'm afraid I fall short, but Jesus tells me my new brother has the perfect green-thumb and nothing fails to grow when he plants it."

"That is very true James." Jason pulled his wife into his arms. "You are welcome anytime whenever my brother pays us a visit. There's always room for more."

"Same at the cottage. If it appears too small, the heavenly builder just makes it more adequate for the growing family." James smiled at their confused faces. "Not to worry family, Simon is in good company. Good day all."

"I'm off for a new adventure Jason. Take care of that pretty little

wife and enjoy your life together. I know I will be enjoying mine."
He followed behind his new roommate "James, where did you leave
your car? Near the house?"

"Nowhere close." James walked on ahead, smiling to himself.
He knew his new-found brother would learn soon enough the
caretaker didn't need wheels when he had lightspeed.

CHAPTER 22

There had been a break in the lessons, as James' Uncle told his nephew the viewing lessons for training were completed and it was time for him to put his training to work as a caretaker. They would wait for the Lord to call them for the new person for healing, so having some free time, James took advantage of the time off to do things with his wife, who had been faithfully waiting.

After the loving couple discussed the things they would like to share together, their list grew and filled each day with some of their favorite entertainment. A day of sightseeing at Old Salem and relaxing at their favorite tavern for an enjoyable meal. A day spent strolling the streets of both small connecting towns, Sleepy Grove and Haven Brook, where they had lived. Another day was filled with morning bowling, then a lovely lunch at the Haven Brook Café before taken in the latest box-office hit. They had been invited to one of their friend's wedding and dinner after, so Sarah and James decided to spend their morning together at the cottage, reading and relaxing until they had to get dressed for the evening affair.

All the busy activities kept Sarah's mind off her misfortune for being barren and spending much needed time together had helped her attitude. As they were enjoying their quiet time, a soft knock came on their door and they heard Uncle James ask if it would be possible to have a word with James.

James opened the door smiling. "Uncle James, you may speak to me whenever you need. Sarah and I won't be leaving until around 5:00 this evening."

"Oh, that is right. Blake and Joyce are being married today at six. Lovely couple." James smiled over at Sarah. "I bet our Sarah will be as beautiful as the bride."

"She will be prettier, Uncle James, but I will restrain from any rude comments in front of the bride." He laughed when Sarah gave him a playful slap on the arm.

"Be serious darling. All brides look radiant on their wedding day, Joyce as well."

"They certainly go together. Both always smiling and cheerful.

Especially when there lots of food setting in front of them." The younger James really love his friends and even tried to help his buddy Blake, loose a few pounds for his wedding, but the happy-go-lucky bridegroom just laughed and remarked, he needed to stay big to match his bride. "Let's hope they don't sit the happy couple in front of the very-large wedding cake."

"James!" Sarah couldn't stop laughing. "Just go and see what our darling uncle needs to talk to you about." She gave him a kiss and one to the smiling uncle. "I'll go ahead and get my long shower so we won't have to argue who will go first. Ta-ta boys, have fun talking."

The uncle and nephew made their way to the backyard garden and could see Simon Granger busy dead-heading the roses. The elder James pointed to a corner bench and they walked over and took a seat.

"What's on your mind Uncle James? Has the Lord contacted us to prepare for the new person for the Miracle Bench?"

"Simon! Simon is on my mind, James." He stated it so bluntly, James stared over at his uncle, who's attention was planted on the gardener.

"Simon is on your mind? Is he ill or something?"

"Heavens no! Simon is as healthy as a horse on race day!" The elder James removed his fall cap and shook his head. "It's just that I have been wondering about something ever since I found out who the Lord would be healing next."

"Has someone in his family gotten sick? Perhaps his young nephew Mark?"

"The ones to be healed are not part of Simon's family James. At least not at the present." Uncle James jumped when his nephew gave him a pat on the back.

"The love interest you told Simon would be coming into his life! That's it, isn't it uncle?" He paused to reflexed on the situation, then looked down seriously. "Uncle James, you're not suggesting we have to play matchmaker once this lady is made well, are you?"

"Something like this has not remotely happened to me before, nor can I recall any of the old healings I have watched over the years, had it to happen." The elder James looked from Simon to his nephew. "When it's Richard Hackler's time to be healed, Maggie will already know her love interest. It is my hope that the Lord gives us His permission to let Simon sit in on the next healing."

"Uncle James, didn't you tell me just the caretakers are allowed inside the Sacred Garden at all times and we have the ability to be invisible to the one or ones being made whole by the Lord?" James was now observing the tall-muscular man working between the many different rose bushes.

"There are exceptions once and a while James. If a caretaker sees a need for the subject who will be involved with the one being made whole, should witness the person's reasons for needing the Lord's healing, the caretaker must put in a pray request for them to be present. To witness the one who will fill that void in your heart can make the transaction smoother for both involved."

"So, the one to be healed next is defiantly Simon's long-awaited love!" James glanced over at his uncle. "Should I put in a prayer as well?"

"It won't be necessary James. One prayer for the request is significant, where a caretaker is concerned." Uncle James glanced up toward heaven. "I put in my request as soon as I found out and have been pondering this ideal of Simon's coming in with us, ever since. I was thinking, by his getting to know her before they actually met, might move things along a little quicker."

"Is there some reason you want to move this romance forward so swiftly, Uncle James?" James had never saw his uncle this nervous before and he only wished to help calm down the elder James.

"I guess it just the waiting to hear from the Lord." Uncle James smiled over sheepishly. "And you were pretty close about the reason I am so flustered. I never had the gift of matchmaking any more than I did gardening. I'm gifted at being a caretaker and pastor, same as you son. Other than those very faithful skills, I'm pretty-much lost!"

"You will be fine uncle, because we both know the Lord will not give us more than we can handle and He certainly doesn't expect us to be the fiddler on the roof!" James laughed when his uncle looked over confused. "The musical Uncle James, where the Jewish father with lots of single daughters, would play his fiddle up on his roof. One of the featured songs reminded me of your dilemma. It goes: Matchmaker, matchmaker, make me a match! Quite the appropriate song for us."

"Well, at least one of us is staying calm over the pending

situation." The senior James laid his head in his hands. "All this will pass, young nephew, when the Lord speaks and puts all my insecure fears at rest."

"My delightful uncle, I really don't know why you worry yourself with this new arrangement." James laughed when his uncle narrowed his eyes at him.

"Then, I suppose you are perfectly alright over the knowledge we may be responsible for getting these two, very different people together."

"I feel totally at ease over the entire matter Uncle James and I owe it all to you." James gave him a winning smile.

"Why? You will stay calm because I am a wreak?" The elder James shook his head when his nephew laughed even harder. "Then nephew, please refresh me on how I made this irritating waiting easier on you, so I can recall it and relax like you obviously are."

"Because Uncle James, everything is in the Lord's hand. You said one prayer was significant for Him to hear a caretaker, so I have simply left the matter in God's most capable hands." James watched his uncle sat up smiling.

"James, my boy, that is a very wise and faithful thing to do!" the man suddenly felt relief. "Of course, you are right and I thank you for reminding me the Lord has our back and we need not ever worry about the outcome. If it must be us to introduce the happy couple, then the Lord will provide us with the knowhow and knowledge on how to be the perfect matchmakers."

"Great! So now we just wait! Wait for the Lord to call us to the Sacred Garden and wait to see if Simon will be accompanying us."

MEETING IN THE ROSE GARDEN

It came down to the morning of the healing, that would take place after dark that same day, when the Lord spoke to His caretakers and agreed that Simon should be allowed to watch his new chosen bride's struggle. Now, all Uncle James and his nephew had to do was convince the gardener to come, after filling him in on what would be happened to his physical body after he stepped through the tall hedge hiding the Sacred Garden.

"Simon, do you recall me telling you about meeting the woman you would share your life with?" The elder James could see raw emotions running through his friend and Christian brother's eyes. "I'm sorry to just spring it on you so suddenly son, but I only got permission this morning to let you join me and my nephew in the garden to witness her past and present. James and I felt it would be good for you to know her before you actually met her and after the Savior answered my prayer this morning, asking for His approval, Jesus also thought it would be good for you. The Lord said:

"Seeing the past come to life can reveal old memories and new images of things not known."

"The Lord always knows best brother James, as do you. What sort of change will happen to my physical body? Will I become like you and young James, a caretaker for one brief healing?" Simon looked down at his work clothes and commenced to brushing off the dirt. "I will have to take a good-long bath. These clothes look as if I haven't changed my clothes in weeks, and that's not far from the truth."

"Then, a good-strong bath is certainly a must Simon." The young James chuckled. "Not because it's your first appearance for her to see what you look like. That would come later, but in the same evening, so once she has been completely healed from her lost of faith and her little girl, healed and given a new physical heart., the Lord will make you visible to them. The precious child has never lost faith in her creator and her love runs beautifully to all she meets."

"This child will make me an instant daddy then. What became of the little girl's birth daddy?" Simon felt overwhelmed by all the sudden revelation. "What will cause me to be invisible and will I be able to see and hear with invisible eyes and ears?"

"So many questions Simon. Let me try to answer them in the order in which they came. Yes, you will become the daddy of a very sweet five-year-old girl, with incredible big-blue eyes. You will learn what become of her real daddy and as for being invisible, the only ones to see nothing, and hear nothing from you, is little Bella and her very pretty mother, Beth." James looked over at his uncle. "Care to add anything Uncle James?"

"Simon, although you appear invisible, same as me and my nephew James, we still have all our senses, feel, touch, smell, taste, see, hear and talk. And, although we can still communicate with each other, the mother or child cannot hear a single word we utter. They can only hear and see all that the Lord says and does."

"Then, I shall be ready to go in with you." Simon glanced

toward the tall hedge hiding the garden where he had seen and heard the Lord speaking to him and his brother Jason. "My bath will also be out of respect for my Savior, as well as you boys. We are family after all." Simon turned to go back in the cottage, smiled at a thought, then looked back, trying hard not to laugh. "Brother James, I guess this means I'll get some time away for a proper honeymoon and you boys can babysit my new little girl and tend my garden, until I return, happy and rested up."

"We both can tell you brother Simon, when you return from your proper honeymoon, you will be extremely happy but nowhere near rested up!" James gave his smiling uncle a wink "We can assure you from our happy experience, from morning till night and all the hours in between, the loving never stops! Just show your bride how much you love her Simon, while the four of us, Uncle James, Maggie, Sarah and myself, enjoy having sweet Bella with us."

NIGHT FALLS IN THE SACRED GARDEN

James and his uncle walked through the hedge with Simon, and the caretakers were suddenly robed in sacred vestments, Simon remained in his clean jeans and blue cotton sweater. The young farmer looked around at the familiar garden and spotted the bench, both James' referred to as the Miracle Bench. Simon smiled, his thoughts recalling setting in it with his twin brother and thinking, it truly is a miracle bench. Not knowing the men could read his mind, he jumped when they spoke in regard to his last thought.

"And soon your future family will be seated on the Miracle Bench, like you and Jason were." Both James' having the same gifts inside the garden, made it easy to speak the same words at the exact time. "We have prepared the Miracle Book to record this story of Beth and Bella Rogers. Now we wait for the Lord's guiding light to appear then we become invisible, like the angels who have put out our chairs and one for you, Simon."

Just like magic, three soft chairs appeared and all three men took a seat to wait on the Lord.

BELLA AND BETH ROGERS STORY FOR HEALING BOTH BODY AND SPIRIT.

Beth Rogers waited nervously by the telephone, waiting for the hospital operator to switch her to the doctor who had been trying to reach her. He had the operator put the call in for him and ask that she put her strait in to his office. The call was a matter of life-or-death situation and time was critical if the mother wanted the heart for her little daughter.

"Go ahead doctor. Mrs. Rogers is on the line." The operator had done her job, now it was up to the mother's quick responses.

"Beth Rogers, this is Doctor Randy Taylor at Wake Baptist Hospital in Winston-Salem. We were on your list for possible heart donors and we got one this evening and need for you to get here as quickly as possible. I can have an ambulance sent out but it will take twice as long for them to go out then get back in time for your daughter to receive the heart. I'm afraid you must bring her to make it on time. We have a short window to remove the patient's bad heart and replace it with the donor's good heart. I cannot give you any details to what happen to the young donor who has made your little girl have another chance at living." The doctor glanced through the window at the young boy waiting, also in need of a heart transplant. "Mrs. Rogers, your daughter was first on the list for getting the first available donor heart, but if you are not here in two-hours, that is by 8:00p.m., we must give the heart to the next patient in line, who is already in the hospital."

"I will get Bella ready quickly Doctor Taylor and have her there before 8:00. "We live just outside Sleepy Grove, so I will take the safer back roads into Winston. It shouldn't take me but a little over an hour and it's only six."

"Then hurry on, but drive with care." The doctor knew the mother was anxious over the time limit. "Just say a pray that the Lord will get you here on time with little Bella. Someone will be downstairs at the entrance to show you up to surgery. Godspeed!" the phone went dead.

Beth got Bella and everything waiting for the call by the front door and took off to her old reliable Chevy. Beth had hoped the call would come soon for her little girl was running out of time. She made sure the gas tank was always full and her car had never let her down. Checking to make sure she had her cell phone, Beth dashed out the door and down the road, passing through the small town of Sleepy Grove. At the crossroads, Beth knew to turn left to Winston-Salem and right to Greensboro, so after turning left, she had only thirty-more miles to go. The darkness came in fast and it made driving more difficult. She glanced beside her and saw Bella looking from the window.

"Bella, you mustn't let the darkness frighten you darling. This road goes straight to Winston and soon you and I will walk inside that big hospital, all lit up."

"I'm not afraid of the dark mommy. Jesus has sent me a guardian angel and she keeps me safe from harm." Bella gave her mother a big smile. "You don't need to be afraid either mommy. Your guardian angel has kept you safe all your life. He's really good at watching you."

"He?" Beth laughed, trying to picture her guardian being a man. "Well, I can tell you one thing Bella, I really must have kept my male angel very busy protecting me when I was growing up. I was a real Tom boy! Climbing trees, haylofts, riding, every horse I met, wild or not, jumping off a cliff into a murky river."

"Mommy, that is really cool! I bet when I get my new heart I can do all those things, just like you!" Bella giggled. "Mommy, where did that doctor find my new heart? Did he order it online or something?"

"Sweet baby, you don't need to know where that little heart came from. Just say a pray of thanks for the child that gave it away." Beth had mixed feeling over transplants, knowing someone had to die to make the organ available for the patient in need of whatever was broken inside them. Her thoughts went to Brandon and as always, the same hurtful feelings returned to the young woman who had suffered so much grief already. Now her baby was dying with heart disease. How much more must she suffer before the Lord stops all her punishment for what happened so many years ago. Bella had been observing her mother's mood change and the caring child reached over to touch her mother's sad face.

"Mommy, please don't be sad. We will make it in time, I know we will mommy. Jesus loves me mommy and he wants me to get all better. Mommy, I wish you could smile and be as happy as I am. I'm not afraid mommy because Jesus told me to be a brave girl for you. Jesus loves you too mommy, He told me so."

"Bella, when did you dream about Jesus speaking to you darling?" Beth checked the car dash clock and grew tense when she noticed 7:15p.m. "Surely that town will be coming into view. Why is it taking so long to get there?"

Joan Byrd

"Maybe Jesus wants to take us to the garden I saw mommy. It was real pretty. An open yard with green grass and the tallest evergreens I have ever seen!" Bella remembered her vision. "Jesus was there waiting for us and he was all lit up like a Christmas tree with white lights!" she giggled and stopped when the car jugged to a stop along the dark unfamiliar road.

In a panic, Beth tried to crank back up the motor and noticed the blinking light lightning up the panel in front of her. "Oh no! Please God, don't let this happen to me! If you can hear me God, START THIS STUPID CAR!" she cried, frantic with worry and upset by the blinking clock. Beth grabbed her bag and took out her cell phone. "Maybe the hospital is in short distance and they can send us an ambulance to get us there on time. After turning her cell phone on she panicked when she saw the NO SIGNAL on the face. "He is punishing me again! Please, just take me Lord and let my little girl have my heart!"

"Mommy, please don't say that! I don't want you to die!" Bella reached for her mother's trembling hand. "Please mommy, just have faith! Jesus will help us. He heard my prayers mommy and yours too."

"Bella, you are just a little girl and I do not want to have to tell you the truth about this Jesus you keep talking about!" Beth looked around and did not recognize anything by the side of the dark road. "What kind of mother am I anyway. To bring her sick child out in the dark and depend on this damn car that hates me too!"

"Mommy, who hates you? I love you mommy and so does Jesus." Bella sat back against the car door when her mother slammed her hand down on the dash.

"Bella, I do not want you to say another word about this Jesus! Do you see him helping us? Do you?" Beth was losing her control. "He cannot help us Bella because Jesus does not" she paused when a light shone clearly through the trees by the road. "We may find some help after all Bella, so just stay inside the car and lock the doors until mommy gets back."

"No mommy, let me come with you." Bella un-buckled her seatbelt and opened her car door. "That's Jesus' light mommy and He wants us to follow it to Him."

"Alright sweetheart, maybe you're right about coming with me." Beth took her daughter's small hand. "You can't be too careful

168

leaving little kids alone at night inside an abandoned old car. Some jerk might spot the old Chevy and haul it away. I'll lock it up, then we can follow that light. Most likely to someone's house."

"I seen this place before mommy and there won't be a house waiting just through these woods. It's something much better!"

Beth and Bella walked slowly through the woods, keeping the light in sight until they came to a tall thick hedge, causing the little girl to jump up and down laughing and clapping her hands with delight.

"We found it! Look mommy, it's the secret entrance to the big green field. Jesus said it was His special garden! Let's go in mommy! I know Jesus will be waiting inside near His wooden bench!"

"Bella, please stop carrying on so, before you pass out from too much un-necessary excitement." Beth looked down at her daughter's anxious face and kneeled down to brush her wet hair out of her eyes. "Sweet girl, you are burning up with fever and if we don't find the owner of this porch light, we'll never make it to the hospital on time!"

"Mommy, I won't have to go to the hospital now, Jesus will make me all better, you'll see! Then, that little boy at the hospital already waiting for a new heart, can be saved as well!" Bella gave her mother a big smile but it didn't cheer up the nervous mother who had stood back up looking all around them for the missing light.

"Bella, how would you know there's a little boy waiting for that heart?" Beth continued her searching. "I just don't get it! I know we came in the right direction! Maybe the owner cut his light out."

"Mommy, the light of our Lord never goes out! And, Jesus told me all about Tommy Daniels needing a heart and would be at the hospital waiting." Bella jumped when her mother said her name loudly.

"Bella Rogers, just stop all this nonsense and help me find that stupid house!" hearing a sniff, Beth glanced down to see her little five-year-old puckered up. "Now Bella, we must be realistic over our bad situation. This is not just another one of your made-up fairytales darling, this is real life!" Beth watched her daughter walked over to the hedge and she franticly yanked her away from it. "Young lady, you had better start listened to your mama and leave the thick hedge along! It could scratch you up! There is no way Jesus will be inside that very thick hedge any more than he would have a garden down on earth when he apparently lives in the most beautiful one there is!" Beth looked around into the darkness and mumbled. "If this is a dream we're both having, then it is a nightmare of the worse kind!"

"Mommy, if you're searching for Jesus' light, you're looking in the wrong place." Bella braced herself for another outburst when her mother whipped her head around and stared down into her big blue eyes. "Please mommy, you gotta believe me. Have I ever told you a lie mommy? The good book says we must never bear false witness, and that means we must never tell lies, right mommy?"

"Then, yes Bella, that is what it says and my sweet innocent little girl has never once lied to me about anything. Even when I asked you if you ate more than two cookies like I ask." Beth patted her small head. "Do you remember what you said?"

"Yes mommy. I stood straight and confessed that I had to have a third cookie because they tasted way too good for just two." Bella giggled. "I know where the light is mommy and if you want me to get better, you can ask me where to look for it."

"Well, it can't hurt." Beth mumbled and smiled down at her beaming daughter. "Then, please tell me where to look and find that missing light Bella." Beth looked down at her watch and gave a sigh. "We're too late to make the deadline anyway. I kind of hope there really is a garden behind that mean-looking hedge with green grass and surrounded by evergreens."

"And a beautiful bench setting at the end!" Bella grabbed her mother's hand. "Look up over the hedge mommy and you will see where the lord is waiting for us!" She giggled when her mother looked up and spotted the light, then shook her head in dismay. "Boy, Jesus is smart! He said you would be difficult to convince, and He was right, as always!"

Bella took her mother's hand and easily walked through the secret entrance to the Sacred Garden.

CHAPTER 23

"I cannot believe it!" Beth looked around in amazement at the exact copy of her daughter's description, down to the wooden bench waiting on the far end. "It is exactly like you described Bella."

"I told you I couldn't tell a lie mommy." Bella giggled and pointed to the bench that now glowed with its heavenly builder. "Look mommy, Jesus is waiting for us at his bench. Isn't it beautiful?"

Beth gazed out at the heavenly sight and wondered why the garden only had the one bench. "So, Bella you said this bench belongs to Jesus?"

"Oh yes mommy! Jesus made it a long time ago when he worked with his Father Joseph. The good man who raised Jesus as his own son." Bella almost sang it out. "We must go at once and have a seat mommy. Jesus is waiting to heal us."

"Heal us?" Beth noticed her little girl heading quickly toward the wooden bench and she followed quickly behind her. "Bella, slow down darling. We wouldn't want that bad heart to give way!"

"Jesus won't let nothing happen to me mommy, because He told me so!" Bella reached the bench and sit down. "Hurry mommy! This is the best seat I have ever been on!"

Beth reached the bench, somewhat out of breath. Her eyes moved along the beautiful bench and knew a lot of love and care went into making it. Looking closely, she could find no nails or screws. The builder had put the bench together with wooden pegs.

"Well, it could easily pass for an ancient artefact, but the newness of the wood only proves it hasn't been built too long." Beth still could not believe Jesus would actually appear to them, but she hoped for her little girl's sake, he would.

"And that is where you are also wrong Beth Marie Matthews Rogers." Beth fell down beside her daughter and stared up into the face of Jesus. "First, I did make the bench you now rest on, over 2,000-years-ago and it appears new to you because of the blessing I placed upon it. Second, I would never tell young Bella I would meet her here if it were not true, for I'm am the way, the truth, and the life! Your precious daughter finally convinced her head-strong mother to listen to her. Beth, do you not remember the quote: Out of the mouths of babes comes truth. I did bring you both here tonight to heal you." Jesus smiled down at the little girl, who was all smiles. "I will heal Bella's heart and she will be just like new! And you Beth, your life-long guilt over your grandfather's death has eaten away at your belief in me and all the bad things that have befallen you have been blamed on us, the Holy Trinity. I will heal you daughter, of your lost faith and bring you back into my fold."

"Lord, my heart is joyful with grateful thanksgiving for the healing of my precious little girl, Bella. As for me, I guess all my misfortunes have been sent on me because I was the one responsible for grandpapa's sudden death." Beth looked down, still finding it hard to believe she had not been judged for such a loving man's death.

"We shall heal all your doubts later Beth." Jesus put out his hands for the small child. She jumped up and took his loving hands, feeling all the love pour inside her little body. "Bella, no more will you have a heart that doesn't match the glow on your face, the beautiful caring of the lest of these, your brothers, like young Tommy Daniels, who's heart was quickly giving out. Your love for others has shown me just how much you love me. Never have I seen so much love in someone so small. Bella Renay Rogers, you are completely healed and from this day forward you will be a happy, healthy, beautiful young lady."

Bella wrapped her arms around the Lord while her mother looked on at the incredible moving scene as tears flooded down her face. The Lord lifted Bella up in his arms and kissed her cheek.

"How would you like to go with Jasmine, your guardian, and trim, like a Christmas tree, one of my big cedars?"

"Gee-willigers! That will be swell Lord! Which tree can we decorate?" Bella looked around for her angel and smiled when the pretty lady appeared with a long string of white lights.

"The Holy Creator has given us a choice, Bella." Jasmine took her hand. "You may pick one."

"I pick the one in the middle!" Bella pointed to the right side, center tree and instantly noticed a big bright star appear at the top. "Look mommy, my tree has already been topped with the star!" Bella smiled back at Beth. "Just listen to Jesus, Mommy, and don't

172

fuss back! Then you might receive something special too!" Bella laughed and dashed away, knowing the Lord had told her about Simon being present.

RELIVING BETH'S PAST

"Now Beth, the reason you have held on to this feeling that you are the one responsible for your grandfather's death can be easily erased by seeing the whole picture of what happened that hot summer afternoon. First, I want you to tell me what you remember and why you believe it was you fault."

"Like you stated, it was a very hot summer Saturday in August when it happened. I had just turned six-years-old and my grandparents had invited me over to spend my birthday with them. Mama and daddy had to go into town for some kind of a meeting. I always had a great time with my grandpapa and we usually went for long hikes on his big farm. After we had eaten our lunch, we made plans to go for our hike, but grandma ask me to wait outside for Grandpapa while she talked to him. I thought they were planning a big surprise for me when we got back, like birthday cake and ice-cream. Grandma always made the best and she would make the icing fancy with candles and my name. So, waiting was fine with me. Grandpapa finally came out carrying his walking cane, because he was getting on up in years I guessed. On that hike, we walked a little slower, but we had fun cracking jokes we had heard. Then I spotted the creek that ran through the farm and it looked mighty inviting to the active tomboy I was. I told grandpapa how hot I was and I thought just one dip in that old creek would cool me down. Well, he got real concerned, telling me I couldn't get in that old creek because it was infested with Cottonmouth water moccasins, some kind of venomous snake that can strike under water. Now, most children would have been too scared to dive into such a creek, but not me! I wasn't afraid of nothing and grandpapa could not stop me when I jumped in, feet first. After slashing the dirty water over my body I smiled up at his shocked face, and glanced over in the direction that had his attention. That's when I seen the big snake heading straight to me. I commence to screaming until grandpapa told be to stay still, then I kept my eyes glued on that snake until I heard two loud splashes behind me." Tears filled Beth's eyes as she recalled what she saw. "I saw grandpapa lying face down in the creek and I knew he had drowned, trying to save me! Stupid me!

Why didn't I just listen to him and he would have still been alive!"

"Beth, all these years you have been blaming yourself for something that was not your fault. Because you didn't hear your grandparent's conversation before the hike and because the snake had all your attention, another act of Satan to keep you depressed enough to lose your faith in me, you missed out on what really took your grandpapa's life." Jesus sat down beside Beth and took her hand. "Now you will see what really happened, then you can start healing."

BETH'S BIRTHDAY WITH HER GRANDPARENTS

"Thanks grandma! That was a super lunch! Your fried chicken with mash potatoes and gravy with biscuits!" Young six-year-old Beth had cleaned her plate to her grandmother's delight. "Can Grandpapa take me on our hike now?" the young Beth winked at her loving grandfather, who returned his own wink. "If we take a long walk grandpapa, then I just bet Grandma might let us have our desert after!"

"That sounds pretty fine to me dumpling!" the jolly man pushed his chair back and took in a deep breath.

"Well, if you two are going out for a hike after that big meal, you better pretend you're a couple turtles." Nellie Matthews gave her granddaughter a kiss and placed her ballcap on top her head. "Now keep that cap on young lady. That noonday sun can get pretty hot in August." She walked Beth to the back door. "You can rest on the back steps until I have a word with your favorite grandpapa."

After the child went out, a concern wife grabbed her husband's frail hand. "John, you know the doctor told you not to spend much time out in that hot sun! especially right after eating such a big meal. That old ticker is wearing out sweetie and I'm not quite ready to tell you goodbye."

"Now Nellie, you and I know, my old ticker can stop at any moment darling, and I don't wish to spend what precious time I have left seated in that old rocker." John Matthews attention fell on the back door. "That little girl is the only reason I'm still breathing. I just about left this old world for heaven two weeks ago, but I prayed to the Almighty and ask if I could just be with my little Beth Marie one more time before I changed addresses." He turned back to his wife of 75 years. "Nellie, you and I have had a good, many years together, and I wouldn't trade a single minute of that time for anything else. You know, after all these years, how much I love you. That love won't die here after I'm gone on, because you and I will be together forever in our heavenly home. But, if I must leave today, let it be enjoying my time with my sweet dumpling."

Nellie could only loop her arms around the only man she had ever loved, give him a kiss, then let him go, to enjoy his last day on the earth.

Grandfather and granddaughter walked along the old familiar path they had taken so often, cracking funny-silly jokes, each had learned since Beth's last visit. Although the shade from the trees gave the odd couple some relief from the afternoon sun, the day had proved hotter than even the six-year-old expected. Hearing the rippling water, Beth reached for her grandfather's hand and pulled him faster toward the farm's creek.

"My, how refreshing that water looks grandpapa!" Beth let go of his fingers and ran to the bank and glanced in the water. "I think the water is calling me grandpapa! Just one quick dip and I'll be good as new."

"Beth, you mustn't get in that creek sweetheart. It is infested with cottonmouth water moccasins. They've been known to bite under water and it can be deadly for someone your size." He motioned her back to the trail. "I'll set the water hose up when we get back and cool us both off. O.K. dumpling?"

"Come on grandpapa, it won't take me long!" Beth laughed and threw him her cap. "Hold my cap until I take a quick dip, then I promise to get right out." Feeling brave, the young girl jumped in and slashed water over her then looked up smiling and noticed her grandpapa staring out at the water. She turned and saw the snake, headed her way. Suddenly frighten, she let out a scream then heard her grandpapa tell her to stay still.

As a grownup Beth watched herself staring at the aggressive snake coming for her, her attention went to the man she had always loved and admired. He had his cane lifted in the air and seeing the snake dropped under the service, John Matthews hurried in the water and slammed the cane down in the water over the snake's head, knocking it out while his old heart finally gave out. Filled with pain, he gave her his little dumpling one last look, then fell into the water, while his soul was lifted up to heaven.

"Grandpapa didn't drown after all. It was his bad heart." Beth

Joan Byrd

looked out at her little girl, her bad heart made well by the Lord. "Now I know why my baby was born with a heart problem. It must have run in our family."

"Your grandpapa knew he didn't have long to live Beth, and he chose to spend his last moments with you." Jesus comforted the weeping young woman. "John prayed for more time to spend with his granddaughter, so we granted him his last wish. Your grandpapa is very happy now and your grandma has made his joy complete."

Simon had been watching all the tragic things going on in Beth Rogers' life and as he looked on, the single twin pondered where he had met this woman before. She seems so familiar but there was something different about her. Reading Simon's thoughts, the younger James acknowledged his knowing her.

"Beth seems different Simon because she has grown up since you last saw her at fifteen. Do you recall these statements: 'what you will see from the past will reveal old memories and new images of things not known?'"

"Now that you mention it James, I do remember being told that." Simon studied Beth's face until the image of a younger Beth came into his mind. "Now I recall seeing this girl, at the farmhouse right after spotting her at the county fair. Young Beth Matthews was only eight when I first met her. She was seated on the stands witnessing all the farm entries for the best in show and we all wished the blue ribbon with #1 would be ours."

"And, you could have won many times Simon. Never have I seen a better bowl of fresh vegetables." The elder James could still see the young Simon holding up his prize select bowl of perfect cucumbers, squash, peppers, green beans, spring onions, and plump-juices tomatoes. "The only way Jason won after holding out his over fluffed skinny lamb was Wilber Granger's fat wallet."

"I did win something the day Beth's father took over for Henry Mason, the head judge. Papa had three of the judges paid off and Henry Mason was always a shoo in, but bribery wouldn't work for Jessie Matthews. The father of Beth Matthews was the new Methodist Minister down at Bethlehem Methodist Church in the town of Sleepy Grove."

"You said you won something that day. Was it at the fair or later, at your home?" James remembered he saw Beth at the farmhouse.

176

"It was later that evening at the homeplace." Simon noticed the Lord still comforting Beth, so he would go on with how he knew her. "I was upstairs when I heard their truck drive up at the house. I peered out the window when I heard my old man talking. I instantly recognized the head judge and he was holding some kind of trophy. I then heard him say my name and that's when I noticed the young girl staring up at me standing in the window. She told her father and we spoke a while. I moved away and dashed down the steps and out the back door before papa could get his greedy paws on my trophy. Reverend Matthews saw me and waved me over, but papa blocked me. They presented me with a first-place trophy with #1 graved in the golden base. I must have been smiling from ear to ear, because I heard Beth sing out.

"See daddy! I told you Simon Granger had a good-as-gold smile!" Beth had glanced over shyly before adding. "Simon, Daddy and I weren't the only two that thought you had the best in show, all the people seated on the stands thought so too because the vote was unanimous!" then I recall her looking over at a sneering papa, but the smart kid just gave him a pretty little smile and added. "You don't have to feel so bad sir. I should think you would be proud as punch to have both your sons win both first place prizes."

But you could always depend on papa to be rude. He yelled out "Two first place prizes? Who in the name of well, who went and changed the fair rules so two kids could be number one?" Papa was real mad that my prize outweighed Jason's ribbon, but Beth's father being a preacher man, made papa very unconvertable so he just let it slide. At least for that year. The big bully hatched his way back to the top by paying off the fair planning board and the rules were reversed to the one place winner, but instead of a blue ribbon, he wanted the winner to receive a big trophy."

"Well Simon, while you and James were reminiscing over your first encounter with this lovely lady, the Lord has taken her back to that very first moment she laid her eyes on the man she had dreamed of marring when she first saw you at eight. Let's watch and see what you might learn."

THE COUNTY FAIR

"Daddy, do I have to sat through all those boring farm boys waiting in a mile-long line for their number one winning cow or goat, pig or chicken, turnip or cabbage, pumpkin or tomato, win them the number one prize?" Beth Matthews made a face. "All that laboring, just to get ready to win a stupid blue ribbon! I say it's dumb! Super boring!"

"Beth Marie, we have discussed this darling and you are too young to go prancing around in a large fair crowd, just to ride those fair rides and play those carnival games until your allowance has been spent." Jessie Matthews kept a firm grip of the active tomboy's hand. "You will be staying with me while I judge these farm produces and animal owners. If it makes you more excited over the winner's prizes, I have included a new number one prize, to give the viewing audience a chance to vote with me. This prize will be a golden trophy, to be delivered to the winner personally."

"Well, it may make me look closer at the entries if I can vote." Beth reached around her father in a big hug. "Since we're new in the area, at least it won't be the same obnoxious boys waiting to show off their rubbed down animals."

"Ladies and gentlemen, the boys will bring their entry on stage for you to see, so please mark your cards where it describes each category. The four judges have narrowed it down to the top six contestants. Jason Granger for the best lamb, Vance Johnson for his Jersey cow, Steve Stone for his pot belly pig, Frankie Smith for his big rooster, Conner Randle for his watermelons and cantaloupe, and Simon Granger for his large wooden bowl of a fine variety of fresh vegetables. Now, this reward will be a surprise and the young fellows who have made it this far, and not know the audience is voting for the second #1 prize, which will be this fine trophy." Reverend Matthews held it up, then placed it back inside his briefcase. Let us begin. Mr. Grimes, you may bring the six contestants back inside the barn and up on the stage with their entry.

The boys filed on stage with their lamb, cow, pig, rooster, watermelon and cantaloupe in a small wagon and Simon, carrying the old wooden bowl holding a bounty of fresh vegetables. They all lined up in front of the judges, whose table was directly in front of the large audience. After the judges past their decisions to Jessie Matthews, his suspicions for the men seated with him were actuate. They had been paid off to choose Jason Granger's weak entry to please their benefactor, Wilber Granger. After hearing about the money being given to buy their votes so his favorite kid could take first, the discussed minister decided on the second prize for a first-place trophy, so the best contestant could win the prize he deserved but always lost to his twin brother. Reverend Matthews had heard through some town gossips that Wilber Granger had never shown his family love and only chose Jason to hurt his wife, whom they had said, met with a terrible accident. Mr. Granger had blamed her fatal accident on a clumsy fall, but those who know the brut man say otherwise. So, the 1st place trophy would be voted on fairly by the people watching, many of them upset with the judge's decision to give the blue ribbon to the boy with the worse entry. After the preacher dismissed the boys and the other judges, he asked the group to vote, then pass their ballots up for counting. After counting the results, he smiled up at the community citizens.

"Ladies and gentlemen, as well as all the youth, I am pleased to announce that along with my own vote, the count is unanimous!" The happy father smiled when his daughter Beth sat up with anxious excitement. "The happy winner will be Simon Granger, for the best-vegetables I've seen since my wife Bessie placed her large cornucopia out for our Thanksgiving centerpiece." Jessie Matthews waited for the loud clapping to cease and his daughter's loud whistling to stop. "My daughter and I will run Simon's 1st place trophy out to him this afternoon. I'm sure this will brighten up his sad countenance. I wished I could have handed it out to him while he was here so he could get the recognition he rightfully deserves."

Out on the farm, the preacher and his daughter arrived to find Wilber and his son Jason, seated on the back porch swing admiring the big-blue ribbon stating: THE NUMBER 1 ENTRY. At first father and son didn't respond to their visitors getting out of their new white truck, bearing a front license plate stating: A FOLLOWER OF THE LAMB.

Beth could tell the rude boy was reading the license plate then both Wilber and Jason started laughing over something the eleven-year-old boy had said. Gritting her teeth at the obvious heathen, the young girl spoke softly to her father. "Those two are really in for a big surprise daddy. Let's see how long their smirk stays in place on their bragging faces!"

Jessie Matthews tried to hide his laugher and he took his daughter's hand and moved forward toward the porch.

Simon Granger had moved over to his upstairs window when he heard the truck drive up. Having his bedroom window up, Simon could hear his papa and brother making fun of the preacher's front license. Seeing an object in the preacher's hand, he moved up to the glass for a better view, not noticing the beautiful green eyes looking up in a dreamy manner. The forgotten twin froze when he heard the head judge mention his name and instantly Simon noticed both his papa and brother walked off the porch toward Reverend Matthews. Simon listened while the minister introduced himself then his eight-year-old daughter Beth Marie, and looked down to see her watching him. He saw the girl tugged at her father's sleeve and whisper something in his ear, causing the judge to look up and wave.

"Simon, you are the one I came to see! Can you come down son? Beth and I have brought something to give you."

"You brought something for me?" Simon avoided his father's angry warning look and kept his attention glued on the preacher, who had treated him with dignity when he displayed his entry for the judges to see. "I did notice the judges didn't hand out the 2nd prize ribbon this year sir. You need not have wasted your time for me sir. I have four already from my previous entrances."

"Son, I can assure you the thing I hold is not a red ribbon and I believe, if you race on down here, you might find its something far better." Jessie Matthews could tell, even though he was looking up at the other twin, Jason Granger had exchanged his great smile for an envious scowl. "Come on and get your reward Simon! You earned it lad."

"Yes Sir! Thank you, sir!" Simon raced out the back door and was blocked by his hateful father.

Reverend Matthews walked up between father and son, as though nothing had happened, his young tomboy right behind him, holding out her hands, to present the handsome boy his own 1st place prize. "My daughter Beth Marie has asked if she could do the honors. Beth, go ahead." He called her up and handed her the golden trophy with #1 winner of the head judge and audience in attendance.

"Simon Granger, it is truly an honor to hand you the number one prize trophy for the best in show! Congratulation Simon! I, for one, knew you had the very best entry in the entire show."

"Wait a minute red!" Jason walked up and stared down at the shiny-new trophy, outweighing his ribbon in strength and size. "What kind of judge are you anyway preacher man? Think you can just pop into our town and take over, changing the rules and doing things so your pick can win?"

"Look you oversize spoiled bully, stop speaking to my daddy this way! I'll tell you what kind of judge my daddy is, papa's pet! My father is a man of faith and integrity and he has never taken a bribe to fix a contest so the rich man's spoiled brat can always win the top prize even if his entry is the worst in show! Like the poor sick lamb, you drug in today." Beth had resorted to her non-afraid, tough as nails, tomboy image! "I can tell you and your papa the citizens of Sleepy Grove are delighted to have us move here so the tainted rules can be cleaned up letting innocent, hardworking youth finally have a chance to win fairly! If you ask me Jason Granger, I would be surprised if you ever got in the first ten entries and you would never reach the last six entries!"

"What does a kid with braces and freckles know about what a real winner looks like!" Jason narrowed his eyes but Beth would not be scared away by his threating stare. "Just take a closer look at me and you will find out!"

"I have had a close look at you Jason Granger and I can tell you honestly, without a doubt, the only real winner living on this farm is your handsome brother, Simon Granger!"

Simon held on to his trophy as he listened to the bravest girl he had ever seen and thought, if Beth were a little older she would be my girl.

Watching the scene in his invisible state, Simon was shocked to actually hear his own thoughts about the beautiful young women seated next to his Lord.

CHAPTER 24

"Beth, you never forgot the eleven-year-old farmer, did you?" Simon perked up with Jesus' question to the beautiful young woman with the long silk strawberry blonde hair and emerald green eyes.

"Lord, it is hard to forget the one you loved so deeply it hurt to see him with his girlfriend Sue Marie, holding her hand and giving her glances that were written with deep love." Beth stared out remembering. "Up until my high school years, I rarely ever saw Simon, since I had been home taught through my eighth grade. I begged to have a chance to go to high school with all the other youth my age so I could feel some type of school spirit when attending school games. Mama wasn't convinced that was the right thing for their Christian daughter, but daddy agreed that I needed to take part in the local high school. To my delight, I found out I would be riding to school on the same school bus as Simon. But my happiness was short lived when I found out about Simon and Sue Marie." Beth gave a disappointing sigh. "This very popular new girl had all the high school boys drooling like love-starve pups. Sue was beautiful, a cheerleader, a prom queen and Simon's true love. The only thing I had in common with the high school queen was we both shared the same middle name and our deep love for Simon."

"But I recall one special time you felt, there might be something between you and the young man your heart belonged to." Jesus gave her a beautiful smile. "Being a freshman, you could only dream about going to the big school dance meant for juniors and seniors. I can still see the stars reflecting in your joyful eyes when you were asked to go."

"I shall never forget being asked or attending such a romantic dance Lord. Next to being saved and washed in your blood for my sins, being finally noticed and asked to be Simon's date for the prom, was the happiest day in my life. It was the only thing from my past I never shared with my Brandon." Beth's eyes met those of Jesus. "Brandon came into my life when I needed someone to fill that broken place inside my heart, finally excepting the fact that Simon was deeply in love with Sue Marie and one day they would wed. Brandon was really good for me. We enjoyed doing the same things and he kept my mind off the past, the one I could never have."

"But, you did feel something from Simon, didn't you Beth. Something that seemed more than just a friendship between two old friends." Jesus knew what happened and He wanted her to remember that special moment as well as Simon. "It happened the night Simon took you home."

Beth gazed down smiling, she had never forgotten. "This one thing between me and Simon will dwell in my heart and mind forever Lord. Perhaps if we were not interrupted at the moment, our lives would have been different."

"Then tell me Beth and perhaps the heart of another needs to recall what almost happened that night after the prom." Jesus knew Simon had stood up to hear her words about them.

THE PROM NIGHT

"It started out as just another disappointing school week as the school bus stopped at the road that let off several students living down the long country road. The Granger Farm set near the end of Willow Creek Road, as did several houses scattered along the mile-long road. Our house set half-way down as did Sue Marie's, whose family's large three-floor mansion set on ten acres. I instantly noticed Simon and Sue had stopped in the middle of the road arguing about the dance. I couldn't help but frown at Jason Granger for waiting behind his brother's girlfriend, giving his arrogant smile. I stood back to give them room and waiting to defend my friend again from this bad brother.

"Why would you except Jason's invitation to go to the prom this Saturday night Sue Marie? It is a simple question for a boyfriend to ask his girl!" Simon had raised his voice, pleasing his brother. "I asked you weeks ago and you said you would."

"I changed my mind, Simon! Nothing personal! Jason belongs to the football team and you don't!" She spoke back loudly.

"It's kind a hard to play football when you have work waiting for you every evening when you get home Sue!" Simon stared over at his brother. "Unlike Jason, papa makes me actually work on the farm! You knew this is why I never went out for any kind of sport! I can't see why that would matter anyway Sue, if you really loved me!"

"Simon sweetheart, it has nothing to do with not loving you. I still love you and you will always be my boyfriend but you aren't capable of asking me as your queen date for the prom court!" Sue smiled back at Jason. "Just football players are the only ones. Everyone tells me I have a great chance to be elected this year's prom queen." Sue reached over to caress Simon's face. "I went with you last year, Simon, but this will be my last chance to be elected queen. Wouldn't you like to be known as the prom queen's boyfriend, sweetie?"

"I had rather be known as the boyfriend that didn't get turned down by his own girlfriend over some dumb title!" Simon held out her books. "I had rather have your devotion and love!" he shoved the books in his brother's hands. "Go ahead and have fun with my brother, but do not expect me to start applauding if you are crowned queen and enjoy dancing with all your admirers your highness! It might be short notice, but I can still ask a girl to be my date and I promise, my date will get all my dances and attention!" Simon's eyes came in contact with Beth, who had been listening to all the hurtful words from Sue Marie. "I see the young lady I want to ask, so Jason, just walk your queen to her castle, I've got my own Cinderella to walk home."

Turning back to see who Simon was asking, Sue Marie suddenly regretted her decision to choose another beauty title over her sweetheart's feelings.

"Beth, I'm sorry you had to witness all that arguing." Simon had walked over and smiled down into Beth's amazing green-eyes. "I only found out about her date with Jason on the ride here."

"I can't blame you for being upset Simon." Beth felt like a million butterflies had invaded her stomach, just from his finally giving her recognition. "If I were your girl, I would be proud to be seen with you anywhere, old friend." Beth enjoyed his laughter and took a deep breath when he took her books before taking her hand.

"May I walk you home, old friend?" Simon glanced down, giving her a wink. "Beth, I know this is the last minute and the dance is tomorrow night, but will you consider going to the prom with me? I promise to show you a good time and if you don't mind my clumsy dance steps, I'll dance with my pretty date all night."

"Well, if you don't mind that your dance partner is somewhat clumsy herself while dancing and you're sure a freshman can attend the junior and senior dance, then I would be delighted to be your date. Simon Granger." Beth said while thinking to herself, I would be the happiest girl in the entire world if I was yours forever Simon Granger. "What time should I be ready?"

"The dance starts at seven, so I will pick you up at six-thirty." Simon walked her up to the Matthews' front door. "I hate to be the first one there and if you're last, everyone is too busy mingling around to noticed."

"That sounds perfect with me Simon. I hate being the center of attention." Beth glanced down blushing. "I promise to turn into a swan for the dance, Simon, so you won't get ribbed for asking a tomboy to the dance after having Sue Marie on your arm."

"Beth, you are a lovely young woman and I would be proud to escort you anywhere." Simon handed her the schoolbooks, brushing her fingers with his own, giving her beautiful feelings. "I will see my Cinderella at six-thirty tomorrow evening." With one last smile, Simon skipped down the steps and walked quickly down Willow Creek.

Beth's excitement wore off on her mother as she took her happy daughter shopping and bought her a princess style white dress, trimmed in emerald ribbons to match the girl's beautiful eyes. Calling her hairdresser, Mrs. Matthews took her joyful daughter to have her long tresses made into a real fairytale princess. Then with the shops make-up artist busy at work, brought out all the glowing features in the beautiful girl's face.

When Simon finally arrived to collect his date, he was not prepared for the transformation of the young lady who always wore jeans and a large sweater, her strawberry-blonde hair usually done up in a ponytail. Instead, Simon Granger was blown away by the vision standing in the doorway. Beth had truly turned into his Cinderella, the most beautiful young lady he had ever laid eyes on. Beth noticed his silent stare, his perfect lips gapped slightly open.

"Do say something Simon. Have I overdone myself for the dance or should I have done more?"

"Done more?" Simon came out of his mystical trance over his date's incredible beauty. "On the contrary Beth Matthews, you are as enchanting as a princess and I feel unworthy of my appearance."

"Nonsense my friend, you looked as handsome as a prince to me and I feel very blessed that you even noticed me to ask in the first place." Beth felt wonderful, knowing her appearance please the young man she adored.

Suddenly Simon felt ashamed that he only had the old truck to drive his beautiful date to the prom in. "Beth, I hope you aren't embarrassed to ride in my old truck? It's the only transportation my old man allows me to use for personal reasons. Brother Jason always gets the old man's car for his dates."

"Simon Granger, like I told you before, I would be happy to be with you anywhere and that includes that adorable old red truck you drive." Beth smiled up shyly, making her even more attractive to the young farmer. "Every time I see this red truck pass by our house, I get goosebumps knowing you're driving by."

"Do you?" Simon smiled and gathered her hand in his. "Then my beautiful Beth, let's go and show our school mates just what a perfect couple looks like."

"It will be my pleasure, Simon Granger." Beth went to the prom and as promised, Simon treated her like a princess the entire night and elected to dance every dance with the beautiful young lady he had walked in with, drawing everyone's attention, including Sue Marie and Jason Granger. As Sue was pronounced the prom queen, Simon only had eyes for the strawberry-blonde dancing in his arms. He could hear some of the prom goers standing nearby whispering that Simon's date would have made the prettiest queen and overhearing his classmate's statements about the girl his eyes were on he spoke softly in her ear.

"I know my Beth would have won the prom queen title tonight, hands down."

"Simon, I can assure you that your Beth would have been much happier right where she is right now, in your loving arms." This time, Beth's eyes did not stray away from his, but sparkled with all the love she had been hiding inside her. "Sue can have the crown she desired so badly she gave up her date to get it and I can have this night, with the man I have adored for so many years and store all these beautiful memories away in my heart forever."

Simon heard her confession of love, both then and now, standing invisible in the Sacred Garden hearing her say it again. He felt the exact same way he had then and Simon knew something was happening inside his own heart. Was what he felt for Sue Marie only a crush? Not the forever kind of love, like Beth had just confessed to him. She didn't need to say love, because Simon could see the love written in her incredible alluring green eyes. Without another word spoken between the young couple, Simon took her hand lovingly and led her out the door and to the old truck. The need to get away and be along with this girl that had come flooding in his heart.

Simon walked Beth slowly up the walkway to the lighted front porch. He stopped on the dark walkway and turned her around, looking down into her eyes. Simon lifted her face up and lowered his tall frame to kiss her, his heart pounding with new love.

"Beth, something has changed inside me and it's because of you. I have never felt like this before. I thought I loved Sue Marie, but now, it doesn't feel the same."

"Simon, I have seen the way you look at Sue and I have seen the way you look into my eyes." Beth reached up and traced his handsome face and his full lips. "There are different kinds of love Simon. With Sue, you feel like you love her, but when you're with me, you know you are in love with me Simon, the same way that I have always loved you since I was eight."

"Alright, that should make choosing the right girl easy for me, darling Beth." Simon took her face in his hands, once again desiring a kiss from the girl he was in love with. "Beth, my beautiful Beth" his lips were inches away. "I" before Simon could finish his declaration of love, Sue Marie came running up in tears.

"Simon, my dearest darling, I am so sorry!" tears flooded down her cheeks. "I was wrong to go to the prom with your brother! I regretted it the moment I looked back and saw you speaking to Beth. Suddenly that dumb title didn't matter anymore! I knew I had just hurt the only man I love and I am begging you dearest Simon, please forgive me and take me back!" Sue wormed her way between the close couple and grabbed her boyfriend. "Simon, I know how much you love me because just yesterday you ask me to marry you after graduation. I will Simon, I will be your bride and never hurt you again!"

Simon felt torn but he knew now he cared about someone else, but he must break it to Sue gently. "Sue, please stop crying, I forgive you."

Beth suddenly felt as though her happy dream had suddenly vanished and feeling the anguish over losing Simon's almost love and what obviously looked like a reunion for the fame couple, Beth, grabbed her heart and dashed up to the door and ran inside, never to see Simon Granger again.

BACK AT THE SACRED GARDEN

"My parents had remained in Sleepy Grove because of my reluctance to leave Simon behind, but after that night, I told them I was ready to disappear out of his life." Beth had lovingly watched her and Simon almost becoming a couple until Sue Marie ruined everything for any hopes for a future together. "So, I got married when I was twenty to Brandon Rogers, a career army veteran. We were your average married couple expecting our first child, a baby girl and I had never seen Brandon so excited over his baby not due for three-more months. My loving husband never got to see his precious Bella. Brandon was killed on a dangerous mission a week before she was born."

"Yes, and your brave husband died saving ten orphan children from certain death." Jesus once again consoled her while Simon felt anxious recalling how Beth had mistaken his moves toward Sue and never heard what he had said after he forgave her.

"Simon, just be patient." The elder James had read his anxiety over Beth's getting hurt because of him. "She will hear what you said after she ran away. Just try and relax my friend. Soon, you can tell her yourself how you still feel about the beautiful young lady with strawberry blonde hair and enchanting emerald green eyes. Listen, the Lord speaks."

"Beth, the night of the prom could also have had a different path if you had not rushed to conclusions over Simon's reactions toward Sue Marie. After all, she did ask him to forgive her, so being a good man, he did just that. Simon had also asked Sue the day before what she thought about getting married after graduation and her response had been

"Married? Simon, we still have college and I'm not ready to settle down and become just a housewife."

The only reason the girl had a chance of heart was watching the two of you becoming closer on the dance floor and noticing that Simon was looking at you in a far different way than he ever did her." Jesus took her head and faced it forward. "Now Beth, look and see what you did not see or hear."

RETURN TO THE PROM NIGHT

Simon had let go of Sue and took a step forward to watch Beth running into the Matthew's house. He closed his eyes, then turned back to the girl he thought he loved. "Sue, I cannot do this any longer. The only reason you changed your mind about marring me is because you can see I am interested in another young woman. I don't want to hurt you Sue Marie, but, I cannot fight love, when it finally fills your heart."

"Simon Granger, are you telling me, Sue Marie, the prom queen, that you are in love with that freshman? Oh, I'd admit the little plain ducking turned into a beautiful swan tonight, but are you blind? Why would you choose a silly freshman over the most popular girl in old Sleepy Grove High?"

"Get over yourself Sue! Beth is anything but silly. She is very mature for her age and respects me. Beth knows what I need Sue. Some one to love me unconditionally and as much as I do her!"

"Then I can tell you why I said I wanted to wait when you asked me Simon. I have been spending a lot of time with Jason, after speaking to your father over dinner at the fancy café in Sleepy Grove. He explained the big differences between you and your twin, with Jason being the more outgoing and ambitious twin." Sue threw her head back with pride. "When you get over this little infatuation with Beth Matthews, it will be too late to fight for me. The sad truth for you Simon is, I have already excepted your brother's proposal and Jason and I already have your father's blessings."

"Then, you really deserve everything you will get Sue!" Simon looked back at the house, still lit up. "Just go and enjoy your life with Jason and my devil of a papa! I've got to make things right with Beth."

"You can't expect me to walk home in thc dark Simon Granger!" Sue narrowed her angry eyes. "Just take me home first then you can run back to this child!"

"Just wait right here if you plan to get a ride from me Sue! That is, if a poor man's truck won't spoil your prom queen dress!" Simon ran up to the door and waited until Beth's father opened it. "Please Mr. Matthews, may I have just one word with your daughter. Something happened out there and I believe she mistook my actions."

"Son, Beth has already gone to bed. I believe the girl has had enough trauma for one night. Try again tomorrow after church." Reverend Jessie Matthews closed the door, leaving the young man staring at the wooden door.

"Daddy never told me about Simon coming to the door. My parents had always sheltered me, especially after what happened with grandpapa." Beth now wondered about Simon and what had become of the young man she loved so deeply. Simon had read her thoughts, being in this special garden gave him the ability or maybe Jesus waited for him to respond to her thought.

Simon moved up in front of the bench and spoke, unsure if she could hear his words. "Beth, I waited all day Sunday for evening to roll around so I could come to see you and tell you" Simon paused when he noticed Beth looked up into his face, recognizing the man she had always loved. "And tell you that I am in love with you. I was about to tell you when Sue ran up ruining our life together."

"Then, you really did love me, Simon?" Beth felt the Lord help her up and she moved in reach of the one she had dreamed about so long. "Oh Simon, I have always loved you. I never got over my feelings for you and even though I love Brandon, remember I told you there was a difference in love. I was never in love with him. You held that title in my hidden heart and I have kept it safely stored away in hopes that one day we would find each other again."

"And we have Beth." Simon reached for the girl he loved and pulled her into a warm embrace. "You made it all come back to me darling. After I loss you I poured all my time into my work and obtained a great deal of papa's land in payment for my labors. My brother had no knowledge of what I owned until papa's will was read."

"What happened to Sue Marie? Did you marry her?" Beth needed to know everything about her missed years with Simon Granger.

"I could have never married a woman I wasn't in love with." Simon smiled down in her alluring green eyes. "How could I when you held that title Beth. I guess I stored you so far away in my troubled heart I had lost my way in finding it."

Simon felt a tug at his pant leg and looked down to see the beautiful blue-eyed five-year-old smiling up. "Hello Simon, I'm Bella. My mommy and I have been waiting for you to come into our lives! I hope you love little kids Simon, because if you want mommy, you have to take me as well."

Simon laughed and reached down and picked her up, giving her a hug and kiss. "Bella, I would be a very happy man to have both you and your beautiful mommy in my life forever. I promised to be a good second daddy for you sweetheart, because I will never try to replace your real daddy who never had the chance to hold you like I'm doing. I guess, I'll have to give you enough loving for the both of us. Do you suppose your daddy will mind?"

"I doubt it 'daddy'! She giggled. "But I bet Jesus can tell you exactly how daddy feels about you loving me twice just for him."

"Bella, your daddy said he couldn't be happier for you or your mommy and that he was very proud of such a brave and smart little girl." Jesus gave Simon His bright smile. "And Simon, Brandon says he could not have found a better second daddy for his little Bella if he had handpicked him for himself." Jesus circled the happy little family. "Wedding bells soon will ring and my children, your life-long happiness will begin as husband and wife, mommy and daddy for little Bella." The bright light of Jesus flashed and the group found themselves standing at the cottage door.

CHAPTER 25

It had been a beautiful afternoon in the rose garden on the day Simon Granger finally became a married man and all his big extended family watched happily as he kissed his new bride after the elder James pronounced them man and wife. Bella had been standing between Sarah and James during the ceremony and jumped with gleeful joy over her mommy obvious happiness. The small five-year-old dropped Sarah and James' hands to race up to give her mommy and new daddy a loving hug.

"This is a happy-happy day!" Bella giggled. "Now that I know mommy is finally happy, I can go to bed without hearing her soft sobs through by wall."

Simon lifter his new daughter up and gave her a kiss. "Bella, I promise to make you and your mommy very happy from now on." He looked around at those watching his tenderness toward the cute child and turned her to face them. "Sweet girl, we will always be surrounded with love from our big extended family. You and your mommy will love living among such loving-giving people." Simon's attention fell beside him where his brother had been his best man. "Your Uncle Jason and Aunt Sue Marie will also be near to shower my new family with their love."

Bella looped her chubby little arms tighter around Simon's neck. "This will be the best home mommy and I have ever lived in, daddy! And, you and mommy don't have to worry about me when you leave on your honeymoon. Just enjoy being together! I know I will be having a great time here with my new family! Sarah and Maggie have been planning some really cool stuff to keep me busy." Bella smiled out at her good friends. "And, don't worry none about your gardening daddy! The three of us are going to have fun weeding, mowing, and taking care of all your beautiful roses while you're away."

"Just as long as the grown ladies do the mowing sweetheart." Beth reached up to kiss her daughter's cheek, before looking out at the small group in the garden. "I cannot thank you enough for taking me and Bella into your home and hearts. To finally find Simon again

192

and become his wife has truly made me incredibly happy. It will be a delight working along beside my new-found sisters and praying with such a devoted and faith-filled group of Christians."

"Beth, we are delighted to have you and Bella become members of our family and we are overjoyed at the total happiness you have given to our brother Simon." The young James moved up to take the little girl. "Your car has been gassed up, your bags are inside with directions to the mountain lodge you both requested, so now, all you need to do is go and become one totally. Bella will be safe with us so just enjoy your time together."

With Sarah and Maggie keeping Bella busy, both James' felt the Spirit of the Lord moved them to the Sacred Garden for the new healing. As soon as they entered, robed in their caretaker's vestments, Uncle James and his nephew noticed the large book turning toward the back of the book and they both knew instantly Richard Hackler's story would be coming out.

Settled in their chairs, they listened, as though a narrator was telling them a story about the small boy on the screen.

RICHARD HACKLER'S STORY
Forty-years ago, Richard Hackler was born. Not by happy parents but by a single woman who never wanted him in the first place. Liberty Hackler was a cheap prostitute who had brought in her customers from the streets of Charlotte, North Carolina, the seedy side of town. When she came down with what she assumed was the flu, she was off the streets for almost a month before she could return to her business. The sickness had made her nauseous and caused her to lose ten pounds before returning to the streets. After having laid with several men, the hooker started feeling ill again and wondered if she might be pregnant. After discovering her worse fears, she asked where she could get an abortion. Learning she was already beyond the legal limit to have an abortion and two failed attempts to have it done illegally, she excepted her fate and had her baby boy in the hospital's welfare ward. The handsome little baby boy was taken home to her apartment on the east side of town, where a mixture of races lived.

The young baby was left with the owner of the apartments for free sex from it willing mother while she worked the streets. He knew her business kept her bills paid and having her free was a plus, whenever his wife was gone to her day job. As little Richie got older, the prostitute kept him at home, to fend for himself. Now, thirteen, Richie had not only heard his hooker mother making it with her customer, but had on occasion enjoyed the show from a small crack in his wall. After learning about her son's interest in her 'business', she started sending him outside while she entertained a client.

This is where Richard met Willy, the fifteen-year-old black boy who had also found the streets more home than his small room in apartment 12, when his old lady, as he called her, would bring a strange man in and offer him a drink before running Willy outside. The two new friends set on the apartment steps watching predestines stroll by and noticed the small group of young men wearing black bandana's around their head staring at them from across the street.

"What's up with those dudes, Willy?" Richard felt a little apprehensive over the way they kept observing them. "Are they fixing to start trouble or something?"

"No! I think they're just checking us out Richie. See if we belong to another gang." Willy kept his eyes on the group of rough looking boys. "That's the eastside gang. They don't like no other gangs getting in their space." Willy stopped speaking and sat up. "Oh shit, they're heading over here."

"I thought you said they wouldn't start any trouble Willy?" Richard had sat up too. "What should we do? If we go back inside and our old ladies find out, we'll have to get a licking from them?"

"Just stay put Richie and act brave. Maybe they're going to ask us to join their gang?" Willy had lowered his voice as they grew closer.

"What should we tell them if they invite us to join?" Richard had heard of the gang wars and he wasn't sure he wanted to belong to any gang.

"That would be a great honor, Richie! To be invited to become a brother in the gang from our neighborhood would be swell!" Willy looked up when the older boys stopped in front of them and stared down seriously. "You're the eastside gang, aren't you?" Willy asked bravely. "I've watched you boys in action and silently rooted you on."

"Smart thinking boy!" The older young man standing in the middle spoke up. "To show your support for one gang can cause their enemy to turn against you and not belonging to any gang, you would find yourself bleeding to death." the gang leader stared over at Richard. "How old are you boy?"

"I am thirteen but I'm strong for my age." Richard spoke up bravely, although inside he was scared. "I've never had the honor to witness you in action sir."

"Thirteen is a good age to start training to be part of our gang." The gang leader turned back to the black boy. "Tell me your age young man, and both your names."

"I am fifteen Black Shark, and my name is Willy Wilson. My friend is Richard Hackler." Both Willy and Richard noticed the tall black youth gazed up to the second-floor apartment and smile.

"So, you're Lib's kid! Your old lady can show a fellow one-hell of a time." Black Shark gazed down, trying to see any family resemblance. "You must take after your old man kid. Most men probably don't notice your sexy mama's face, too busy checking her out from the breast down, but the Black Shark checks out every part of a beautiful broad."

"I see you have given my old lady some business." Richard had wondered if the gang leader was checking him out to see if he would defend his mother. "I'm sure I would recognize you if you came in while I was still awake Black Shark. You must have come in late after she had done business with all her other customers."

"Smart kid! Did you learn a lot while you watched your old lady in action?" the gang leader gave Richard a knowing smile when he saw the young man blush over getting caught for the obvious. "I was always Lib's last and very best lay, kid, and she gives me everything I want for free because I know how to satisfy her needs as well." The leader glanced around at the smiling gang members. "Right fellows?"

"No one does it like our leader Hackler!" the gang surrounded the leader. "So, Shark, do we take these losers in and teach them to be winners?"

"What do you boys say?" the leader looked from Willy to Richard. "I need gang members that want to join. Are you boys in or out?"

"Count me in Shark!" Willy jumped up as the gang welcomed him, then all stared down at the lone boy, who had watched his new friend except without reservations.

"What about you kid? If you join, the gang will keep you safe on the streets." The dark eyes stared down seriously. "If you're left on your own, anything could happen to you boy, after the streets turn dark."

"The way I see it shark, if I join your gang, I'll be the only white boy among seven black gang brothers. How would I know if we get in a fight with another gang, you boys won't leave me behind if things get bad?" Richard had watched the gang leader's mood to see if he would grow angry but only received a smile.

"Richard, if you join our gang son, we will not look at the color of your skin because you will be one of our gang brothers." The black shark held out his hand. "The truth is, you are not safe here Richard. All the other gangs consist of blacks too and they don't hold any love for the white man. They will as soon kill you as they would a stray dog." His hand held out for him remained steady. "Come with us Richard, let us protect you and make you a brother."

Richard took the strong hand and felt the gang leader pulled him up. He looped his arm around the young boy's shoulders and the eastside gang walked away, knowing no one inside the apartment building would be out looking for their sons.

James looked over at his uncle. "No wonder Richard was into his sexual behavior, after growing up and living in the same apartment as his prostitute mother. I guess joining the eastside gang was thrown into his lap as well, after the uncaring mother sent him to the streets."

"Yes, Richard had a hard start in life and it didn't get any better after joining the street gang." Uncle James was getting all the information fed to him, same as it was to his nephew. "At first, when the gangs fought with one another, their two young recruits stayed back a safe distance and observed. Willy was let in first, being older, and became a good fighter. Richard was anxious to have his first fight when the eastside gang had a turn for the worse. Up until the fatal night, all the gangs fought each other separately and Richard's gang brothers had always won, sending their enemy fleeing. Never breaking the gang rule for only two gangs going against each other was permitted, the eastside gang wasn't prepared for the teaming up from the other three gangs coming after them at once. It was a blood bath, with all eight eastside members getting either wounded or kill."

Made by the Master's Hand

BATTLE FOR THE STREETS

After the surprise attack on the eastside gang by the westside, northside and southside gangs, the noise finally died away, leaving all the members laying bleeding with knife wounds. Richard had fought hard, but knew they were outnumbered three to one. He opened his eyes, feeling the pain in his side as he managed to sat up and look at his gang brothers, some moaning in pain and other lying silent, eyes staring up into the starry night. Richard searched for Willy and saw his eyes opened in cold death. Richard managed to get up and balance himself as tears stung his eyes. Then he saw their leader, hand still raised as if fighting his foe. The young boy finally made his way over to the Black Shark and saw him looking up, past him. Richard fell down beside his brave leader and took the weapon from his stiff fingers as tears fell on his cold face.

"Why? Why Shark? I finally found someone who cared about me!" the young teen fell across his brave leader and whelped. He jumped when he felt a hand on his back and closed his eyes in fear, thinking the gangs had returned to finish their job. "I guess you're going to kill me too!"

"No son, no-one is going to kill you." Richard opened his eyes after realizing this man didn't sound threating. "We're here to help the survivors. I am with the police. They were called in by a witness who had seen the other gangs ambush your gang. We arrived as soon as we could but I'm afraid we're too late for four of your members." The man speaking, glanced down at the young black man the younger white boy was weeping over. "Looks like the Shark didn't have a chance this time to win."

"No sir. Those other gangs saw to it! They cheated by hooking up together and now Shark is dead and my good friend Willy." Richard felt the pain in his side and rolled over clutching it. "It hurts real, bad sir."

"Son, you're bleeding badly! I never knew you were in this fight!" The stranger called over to one of the officers, "Moser, get a paramedic over here at once! We have a youth that's been cut in the side and he's bleeding quarts!"

Moser called out. "Billings, get the stretcher over by Reverend Raines now!" within minutes the paramedics had Richard in the ambulance, with one other gang members and the two-ambulances drove away blowing their sirens loudly.

After the surviving gang members got better the police were waiting to escort all four down to the local jail. The oldest three members were led away to the adult prison while Richard sit waiting for the juvenile van to pick him up. To Richard's surprise, the driver was the minister who had found him the night of the fight and had paid him daily visits while he was in the hospital. The young teen watched as Russel Raines checked him out then led him out to the white van, motioning the guard to close the back door when he opened the passenger door and motioned Richard in. The minister got behind the wheel and buckled up before smiling at the serious young man.

"Richard, please buckle up son and we'll be on our way."

"On our way were sir, some prison with bars?" Richard had grown hard since joining the gang and he didn't trust anyone outside his gang brothers. "Why wasn't I taken with my brothers?"

"Because son, they are older than you are. You just turned fourteen the day you almost got kill with those other brothers. Someone your age should not have been expected to fight with other grown men." Reverend Raines kept his eyes on the road.

"I chose to fight! Shark gave me the choice! He treated me like family and all the gang treated me like I was a brother! They didn't care if my skin was white!" Richard stared from the car window. "Those other gangs hated white people and my brothers were looking out for me! Cleo took a knife in his shoulder for me when the southside gang member tried to attack me. He jumped in front of me and took the hit and Shark took care of business."

"Killing is killing son, and no one is above the law, especially God's law." The minister pulled the van into a church parking lot and cut it off, then watched the young man look around.

"Hey man, what kind of jail is this? I never knew they had such high steeples and fancy colored windows."

"They don't Richard. Jails are solid plain buildings with no windows and a lot of bars and guards. I cannot believe you have never seen a church young man." Russel unfastened his seatbelt and reached over to unsnap Richard's. "How did you know that was called a steeple if you haven't seen a church?"

"Steeples rise above anything else when you're down on the streets sir and Shark always told us if we ever got separated to look for the highest steeple downtown and go there and wait."

"The truth is, I asked to bring you home with me son so I could help you straighten up your troubled life." The kind man stepped from the car and opened the door for the reluctant young man. "I can tell you got a bad start in life and all I'm asking is a chance to help you turn your life around Richard. I know all about your mother and how she never gave you the kind of love a child deserves. Just give me a chance to help you. If you find yourself unhappy after a time, I'll take you back home to your mother. The choice will be up to you Richard. I won't push you with your decision."

"Alright Reverend Raines, I'll give you some time to try and help me. Anything is better than going back to my old lady." Richard got out and followed the preacher into the church.

The caretakers watched the big book close and they knew within a short time the Lord would be leading Richard Hackler to the Sacred Garden for healing and make him whole. For now, uncle and nephew would return to the cottage and wait for the Lord's call.

CHAPTER 26

A week went by before the Lord called them back to the garden and He asked that they bring Maggie with them, to witness the struggles Richard had faced his entire life. The week-long wait had had a purpose for the Lord needed for Bella's parents to return before Richard could be healed. Jesus knew Maggie had almost given up hope in ever finding Richard again, so she needed to be free of helping watch the young girl. Sarah and Maggie had made plans to take Bella for a visit to her aunt and Uncle Granger's farm when Simon and Beth showed up a couple days earlier than expected.

Knowing the reason Maggie was keeping Bella busy was also the fact that Sarah was distracted from her troubles of feeling useless when she was helping entertain the lively child. James pulled Maggie away from the welcoming committee after they both had helped with the newlywed's luggage by carrying it into Simon's rooms.

"Maggie, since Bella has her heart on the visit to the Granger Farm, I really think Simon should be the one to take her since God brought them back early so you would be free tomorrow." James could tell by her facial expression that she was unsure over his words.

"Why James? Is there something the Lord needs me to do tomorrow?" Maggie's attention fell on James' wife. "And what about Sarah, I could not possibly leave her alone if you're not with her. Ever since Bella came, she has filled all our extra time and it's a joy to see Sarah so happy."

"Maggie, the Lord knows of Sarah's heartache and He is forever by her side, so she is never alone." James had spent many nights and mornings on his knees asking God to watch over his beloved when he could not and the young minister knew he could leave the matter in His Savior's hands. "The Lord has asked us to bring you with us tomorrow Maggie when we go to the Sacred Garden. The time has come for Richard's healing and for the two of you to join as one."

Maggie had never heard such beautiful words before and it was like music to her ears. The moment was broken when Bella ran over with her joyful news.

"Maggie, mommy and daddy are going with us to the farm! Daddy said he would show us around the big farm where he and his twin brother grew up!" The happy little girl jumped up and down. "Sarah is planning a big picnic lunch to pack and she is making enough for Aunt Sue Marie, Uncle Jason, Buddy and Sally to join us!"

"Then Sarah will be going with you!" Maggie felt relieved. "I won't be able to make it this time Bella, but I'll join the family fun another time, o.k.?"

"I know Maggie, Jasmine told me the Lord needed you to be here to meet an old friend and that mommy and daddy would be back to take me and Sarah." Bella beamed. "I wouldn't dream of leaving my friend Sarah home alone. I love her."

"We all love Sarah, Bella." Simon had walked over and overheard part of their conversation. He had also heard James tell Maggie that she was wanted inside the Sacred Garden to witnessed Richard's healing. Knowing his friend would be subjected to becoming invisible, Simon thought it best to prewarn her what she should expect once inside the miracle garden. Simon lovingly patted his little daughter's head and told her to run back to her mommy, then smiled as he watched her skipped back to Beth, whose arms waited to scoop the angelic child. Simon turned back to James and Maggie, who had been observing how patient and caring their quiet friend had become since marring Beth and gaining a sweet daughter.

"Simon, you have transformed into a wonderful husband and have fallen into being a father with tenderness and great love." James laid his hand on his soul brother's shoulder. "You are also a good brother to me and Sarah. Thank you, for watching over her for me while I'm unable."

"That's what families do for one-another, brother James." Simon's attention fell on Maggie, feeling the need to warn her, but unsure if it was his place to bring up being invisible and unheard by those you are watching. "Thank you, Maggie for looking after my rose garden and vegetable garden. You, Sarah and little Bella have done a terrific job and the winter crop looks like its got a great start without the weeds choking them out."

"I'm sure I can count on you Simon if I should be away a while."

Maggie couldn't resist her chuckle at his shocked face, assuming she meant to take over the cooking. "Relax friend. I believe your Beth and James' Sarah can take over my kitchen until I get back. I was referring to the grocery shopping and carrying up fruits and vegetables from the root cellar."

"Maggie, it will take all the family to fill in for you, but I'm sure the Lord will see us through." James knew his wife wasn't great at cooking, but he knew she had helped Maggie with the things she could do. James had read Simon's thoughts about warning Maggie about being invisible, so he spoke his name softly and Simon looked over. "Go ahead Simon, tell Maggie what will happen in the miracle garden once she is inside. It will save me and Uncle James the time of explaining her state."

Simon stared over at the religious man, never realizing he too could read thoughts like Mr. James. "Well, alright, I thought since it happened to me, I could prepare her for the state of being invisible."

"Invisible? I will be invisible?" Now it was Maggie with a shocked expression. "Can I see myself? Feel myself?"

"I'm afraid once you become invisible Maggie, even you cannot see any part of yourself." Simon thought back to the odd sensation. "It's a weird, strange kind of unusual feeling, knowing you can still touch any part of yourself and feel it, then look down and see only the grass below your feet. Both caretakers are also invisible and when you speak, they are the only ones, besides Jesus of course, who can hear you."

"All that will happen once the Lord arrives with, in your case, Richard. Richard cannot hear anything we say, nor can he see us, the reason for being invisible. We can witness what is being said and see Richard's past, leading up to his healing and finally finding you." James took Maggie's trembling hands. "Precious girl, you have nothing to fear. When the time is right, our Savior will reveal your presence to Richard and his healing will be complete."

"Then I can get past the beating and cruelty Richard gave me?" Maggie still had bad dreams reliving the horrible night the man she loved almost killed her and spoke such hurtful words. "I know the Lord said Richard had ran up to get me and carried my bloody body down to the ambulance, crying over me and begging for my forgiveness."

"Maggie, when you can see for yourself what made Richard become the man you knew, you might feel different." James had only witnessed his youthful days, but he was aware the man Maggie had given her heart to had been dealt many more unhappy years as he grew up and became a man. "The Lord is aware of your doubt and struggles, Maggie, and you must go in with an open mind and heart if you want to help save the man you know you still love." James looked deep into her eyes. "You do still love Richard, don't you Maggie?"

"Yes James, with all my heart." Maggie took both Simon and James' hands. "If I can help save the one I love, then I will go in with an open heart and mind, invisible and silent as the night."

INSIDE THE SACRED GARDEN

Uncle James and James had helped Maggie and Sarah pack away the large picnic basket in the back of Simon's new SUV and waited for the other travelers to come out, dressed for a day on the Granger Farm. Simon carried out a big cooler, filled with cold drinks while Beth tagged along behind balancing a large dote bag with a picnic spread and a thermos of hot coffee. Bella danced down the steps carrying her bag of outdoor games, to play with cousins.

After the long car was loaded up, the gang drove away, waving at the three waving from the porch. Uncle James smiled down at Maggie as he motioned her toward the large hedge. "Maggie, the Lord has called us to the garden. There is absolutely nothing for you to worry about. We may become invisible to each other and Richard when the Lord appears, but have no doubt, Jesus can see and hear us."

"Uncle James is right Maggie and even though we cannot see each other or our own body, we can still feel each other and speak to each other. Richard is the only one unable to see or hear us." James was at the hidden entrance. "Do you have any questions before we go inside the garden?"

"Since I have seen inside this beautiful garden before and remember the peace it brings, I will be fine. I'm just glad you both will be near me."

"You shall be seated between us Maggie." James' eyes lit up. "To be healed by the Master's touch is a blessing in itself, and to witness the one you love being healed can be also moving. To witness the big book open and their life being relived right in front of you, can take your breath away."

"Young James is right Maggie. Tis a beautiful experience to be able to witness the writing of yet another story and miracle healing." Uncle James nodded for his nephew to enter and they stepped in, robed, Maggie wearing her pretty new dress she chose to be reunited with Richard.

THE HEALING OF RICHARD HASKLER

Richard had buried his wife alone due to his sons refusing to come to her funeral. In their words, 'to watch their drunk father weaving over their selfish mother's coffin.' Once again, the ex-warden had paid the local bar a visit and sat staring down in his fifth beer mug, pouring his heart out to the only one who would listen, the bartender, Joe Black.

"Joe, where did I go wrong? I found the perfect woman and for the first time in my stinking life I was in love." Richard smiled up shaky when Joe took the empty glass and placed a full mug in his fist. "You're a good friend Joe. I haven't had many friends in my forty-wasted-years." A faraway look came to the once strong handsome eyes that looked down at Maggie Spillman. "I found my first friend when I was thirteen. Willy Wilson lived in the same rotten apartment building I did. He was black, like most of the people living downtown." Richard struggled to sat up. "Joe, did I ever tell you about belonging to the eastside gang?'

"I believe you said there were eight members and your gang leader, was name sharpie?" Joe mixed a drink for the man at the end of the bar and slid it down, never taking his eyes off the drunk.

"Shark, his name was the black shark." Tears swelled in Richard's eyes. "They killed my hero, Joe and my good friend Willy."

"Yeh buddy, I know life can be unfair sometimes." Joe genuinely like Richard Hackler and remembered when the man was sober and had the great warden job at the prison. "I'm sorry for your lost Richard."

"Those were sad times back when I was just a kid but Joe, my worse heartache came when I lost" Richard pushed the mug back and fell on his arms weeping. "Why? Why, in God's name did I have to hurt my Maggie! She was the only one that ever loved me back! I had her Joe! She wanted to marry me and Cindy was standing in my way! That cheating bitch wouldn't stop calling me!

Maggie overheard me talking to her and I grew angry! I hit her and said some terrible things to my darling Maggie, then I took her against her will because I thought, because she was a prisoner, I had the right!" Richard tried to pick up the beer and it slipped from his shaky hand. "Damn trimmers! Get me another beer Joe. I need to get plastered!"

"I'm sorry Richard, you've had enough buddy." Joe patted his drooping shoulders. "Just stay put, I'll call you a cab, cab fare on me." Before the tall man could step away, he heard Richard call out in pain and clutch his hips. He tried to stand, and doubled over in even sharper pains, collapsing on the barroom floor, unconscious.

Joe Black had rushed over to check on his long-time customer and after checking his pulse, he called up to his helper, Brandy Bennet, the barmaid. "Brandy, call 919 immediately! Tell them one of our customers was having sever pains in his sides and has passed out. I think he may be dying!" the bartender's voice grew anxious. "Tell them to hurry!"

The ambulance had made it to the local bar in record time and with the patient loaded inside on life support, the driver flipped the siren on, then the lights commenced blinking as the ambulance sped away into the busy afternoon streets of Charlotte.

The sky turned dark and the wind began to blow in strong gust, causing the driver to fight the stirring wheel to keep the top-heavy ambulance in the road. Adding to their problem was a very thick fog that creeped in quickly and made seeing almost impossible. As Gilbert Steel drove carefully at a snail pace, the other paramedic called in to give the hospital their location and road conditions.

"It has gotten very foggy downtown as well Elaine, so my advice is to find a safe place to pull over and wait for this storm to clear out." The man in charge gave his good advice, then added. "Check on your patient and make sure all his vitals are stable, then let him rest and wait it out up in the cab with Gilbert."

The storm came in with fury and neither attendant noticed the wind blowing the black door open or the stream of peaceful light that fell over the unconscious man, hooked up to the life-saving machine. Richard opened his eyes when he heard someone say his name. It was no ordinary voice that had called him and made him feel a sense of peace that he hadn't felt since leaving Reverend Raines and his gracious wife, Pasty when he went off to college.

Not exactly sure where he was, Richard sat up and instantly noticed he was hooked up to some kind of monitor that constantly peeped. As he sat wondering how he got in such a strange place, he reached for the wires, the need to jerk them off and flee this strange hell. Before Richard could touch a single wire, they simply fell away, as if by magic. His mind was twirling over many different answers concerning this magical place and he could hear his own pathetic voice croak just above a whisper.

"I must be having a bad dream." Richard managed a soft chuckle. "That's it! Good old Joe called a cab for me and I came home and collapse on my bed! I cannot remember shit, because I am drunk."

"Richard, you are not having a dream, nor were you taken home in a cab and now lying on your bed. You are lying in an ambulance, was hooked up to life support because both your kidneys failed you at the exact moment." Richard looked around for the invisible man and only saw hospital equipment tangling down from the large van's ceiling.

"Where are you? Why can't I see you? Are my eyes giving out too?"

"Richard, I am the One who has always loved you. I have watched you suffer, find hope with the good family that adopted you and taught you right from wrong. I have watched you care for the one who mistreated you and cheated on your marriage. I was there to witness how you finally found love. To love and to be loved in the same way is hard to find but a joy to receive. Then I saw how you took that precious gift and tried to destroy it, causing the one who loved you to almost succeed in taking her own life, when that is my job alone to do." Jesus knew Richard was speechless because he had never really felt God existed, even though the young man had made Russel Raines believe he excepted Christ as his Savior, just to please the man he admired and loved. "Richard, there is another truth you were told and chose not to believe either. You went in for a physical and your doctor had you take bloodwork and sonograms on your kidneys. Richard, why would you continue your heavy drinking when you had stage four kidney cancer?"

"Because, I wanted to die, that's why!" Richard hadn't noticed that he wasn't inside the ambulance anymore but standing alone on an abandon road. Hearing thunder in the distance, Richard looked toward the sound and could see city lights far away. Suddenly Richard felt a chill and he shivered as he looked around at the unfamiliar surroundings. "Where am I? How did I get here? I was laying on a stretcher inside an ambulance a few seconds ago! Please, don't leave me out here! It's growing dark and I must have left my coat inside Joe's."

"Follow the light son." Came the still small voice and a stream of light lit an opening in the woods beside the roadway. "You will find warmth inside the trial guided by my light."

"Yes, I see it Lord?" Richard finally questioned the one leading him for he knew no human could lead him and remain invisible nor would they know everything about his past, many of the memories he had chosen to forget.

Maggie had been witnessing everything inside the peaceful garden on a big screen that seemed to float up from the massive book in front of them. Never had the young woman felt such heartache over anything like she had witnessed her beloved Richard going through, past and present. Even though she could not see the tears that flowed down her face, she could feel them, as could both James'. The elder James reached over and comforted her.

"Maggie, we needed for you to see why Richard lost his patience with you the day he hurt you both mentally and physically. I can tell you truthfully child, the moment he stopped and rolled overhearing you weep, he tried to muffle his own tears. He kept telling himself, if he could start over and live his time with you again, this horrible thing he had done to the only woman he ever loved and loved him in return, would not have happened and he would have found a way to make you his forever."

"Uncle James, I can see how much Richard loves me and my poor darling thinks he has lost me forever." The caretakers could feel her anxiety as she said. "Can't I just appear and tell the man I love I still want to be his forever?"

"Maggie, you must have patience and let the Lord call you out when the time is right." James reached for her hand. "Sometimes waiting in the stillness and in invisible form, can make you overanxious, but Richard is completely covered with all kinds of sickness and the kidney cancer is just a part of it. The Lord must mend Richard's old hatred for his mother, the three gangs that robbed him of his gang brothers, and his deceased wife's constant cheating and lying, not to mention the fact she was the one standing in your and Richard's way from having a life together."

"Maggie, my nephew is correct on all matters." Uncle James' voice was soothing to Maggie's ears. "The Lord brought you here to re-united you and Richard after the man has been completely healed of all the things James spoke of. The biggest and most important hurdle for Richard to get past is learning to believe in Jesus, as the Christ, the Son of God. Believing that God does exist and He is good and the creator of everything made."

"I never dream Richard's life was so mixed-up, but I am beginning to understand why he felt trapped when I walked in on him talking to his wife on the telephone." Maggie thought back to that early morning when she woke up and found Richard missing from their bed. "I accused him of cheating on his wife, never knowing she was the one cheating on Richard but refused to divorce him."

"We shall know soon enough Maggie. The Lord is leading Richard to the hedge and the man you love will soon be stepping inside the Sacred Garden and have his seat on the miracle bench, made by the Master's hand. This is why we became invisible the moment Richard started up the path to the Sacred Garden."

CHAPTER 27

Richard Hackler looked around after stepping inside of the peaceful garden. Suddenly the darkness that had surrounded him on the outside had vanished and the place he stood was like the noonday. Even with the garden in daylight, Richard could see the bright beam that had led him through the tall hedge now waited near the edge of the garden, shedding its glow over a beautiful bench. Once again Richard heard the soft voice of God speaking.

"My son, soon the medicine you received inside the ambulance will wear off and your great pain will return, so I need you to walk to the bench and have a seat now."

Richard noticed the great distance to the bench and his movements had been slow and weaving, most likely from all the heavy drinking throughout the day and then the five beers. "It seems to be too far away to make it quickly on my unsure legs." He stopped to listen, swaying back and forth, causing Maggie to jump up, wanting to help him get there before his pain hit.

Maggie felt the caretakers take her arms and help her back on her chair as James whispered. "Stop worrying, he'll make it in time."

Uncle James chimed in. "Left up to Richard he would be doubled over in pain halfway there, but remember, with God, all things are possible."

"Of course, you're both right." Suddenly Maggie could see the Lord smiling at her. "Thank you, Lord, for helping my loved one find his way quickly."

"Richard, you are seeing the distance as man sees it. Surely it cannot be done by your unstable moves, but do you believe that I can overcome the distance and get you there in time Richard?" the Lord gave a nervous Maggie a wink, seeing her stare anxiously at Richard, wanting him to answer yes Lord.

"It is obvious you have already worked many wonders for me to witness Lord, so, even though it is impossible for me to go that far fast, I believe you can get me there in a blink of an eye." No more had Richard spoke those words and took one blink that he found himself in front of the bench. He laughed and sat down, instantly feeling different inside.

"Richard, I have brought you here to this miracle bench to heal everything that has built up inside your life and has made you do some things that you have recreated but could never erase." Jesus had become visible to Richard and for the first time the troubled man actually believed this God was truly real. "Jesus held out his hands to show Richard the scares where the nails had pierce through. "You, like my disciple Thomas, had to have proof before believing in me. But, unlike Thomas, who had been with me for three-years, watching me perform miracles and hearing me teach the word, you had no one to teach you until you met my servant Russel. Your mother never guided you down the right path and this led to your getting caught between a gang war. You hated your mother because she never showed you love. She treated you badly because she felt trap by having a child. So, Liberty only saw you as standing in her way and cramping up her lifestyle. You learned at an early age about sex and it affected your life years later when you found your wife cheating, it caused you to turn to other women. You finally felt cared for when you bonded with your gang brothers and the hate they felt toward the other gangs, rubbed off on you. Not once did you ever consider that those young men who you hated had been brought up and neglected by their mothers same as you had been."

"You are right Lord. I only saw them as the enemy, standing there with the weapons held high, anger and hate written on their faces." Richard had been staring at the nail holes, like some of the gang brother's pierce ears with capping round holes when their massive gold earrings weren't in.

"I see you are comparing my scares to man's choice to scare their own body for appearance. I tell you true, I paid a big price for the holes left by the Roman's giant nails. These scares are not for decorative appearance Richard, they tell you that I died up on the cross for your sins so you could live with me in heaven forever. We created the human man in our image, just as we did the holy angels who have lived among us and work below for us. This beautiful gift of creation should not be marked to designate a single person's character but remain without blemish to fit the temple it shall become." Jesus looked down on the swaying man. "There are many

210

kinds of destruction a man can make on his own body Richard. To try to cover your guilty emotions for destroying your chances with Maggie and lose your depression over an unfaithful wife, you began drinking heavy. Now this self-abuse had taken a toll on your once strong-muscular body, and without a healing miracle, you will die in short time and never have the chance to reunite with Maggie."

"Reunite with Maggie?" Richard managed to sit up and look into the eyes of the Lord. "Can I be so lucky to actually find her again? I have searched and searched for any word of Maggie's whereabouts, but it's as if she has fallen off the earth. If I knew there were a chance that I would see her again and beg her forgiveness, I would Lord. I love her so."

"Perhaps if you learn how to find her Richard, you will see its not so hard. It starts with believing." Jesus sat down next to Richard and touched his hand, bringing a sense of peace and love inside him. "Let's go back to the night you saw four of your gang brothers murdered, which included your friend Willy and the man you looked up to, Randle Woods who went by the Black Shark. I led my servant, Russel Raines to that dark street the night you were wounded in the side and he found you and took you into his home and heart. This was the first time you knew what it felt like to have parents who actually cared what you did and gave you love. The gang brothers showed you respect and protected you, but the Russel's adopted you and gave you a future, sending you to college after you graduated from high school. The warm-hearted minister led you to church and taught you all about me, how I was born, lived, went out to teach and do wonders. You led him to believe you were ready for baptism and this made Russel bcam with happiness." Jesus turned him to face him. "Richard, why was you so convinced that I did not exist that you would blatantly lie to the man who helped save you?"

"Reverend Russell was the first person to tell me about faith and believing in the one God, Father, Son, and Holy Spirit." Richard looked down, too ashamed to look at the One he had denied and cursed. "My start in life didn't help my untrusting heart Lord and the gang never uttered any words about religion and frown at those who did. A wild group from school pulled me easily into their circle and behind Christian's backs we would make fun of them believing in childish stories written long ago. The words just didn't fit into my modern world but my love for Russel made me lie about a lot of false beliefs. I guess I had learned to lie so well, the good man was easy to persuade I was a believer."

"But Russel's words stuck somewhere deep down inside you Richard and when you needed them, they revealed themselves and came out." Jesus looked deep into Richard's eyes when he looked back up at Him. "Your wife Cindy had been given the bad news that she only had a few days left to live and once again, she had called on you Richard, the only one she could depend on to be there with her."

"Cindy and I had gotten married right out of college after I landed a great job as the head warden at the Charlotte Prison for men. I never knew at the time she had gotten pregnant by another college friend, who was engaged to her best friend. Our son Albert was born eight-months later and she just pretended he had come early. I could see no family resemblance in our son but I just assumed it was a past relative until he grew older and looked exactly like my red-headed friend Bart. After begging my forgiveness, we returned to normal, I thought, until we had our next son and there was no doubt then that Ron was not my baby when the little tot had dark skin.

Cindy said she met Harold by accident when he showed up to clean the pool instead of Jeb, our usual pool boy. She had gone out to sunbathed while the pool was having a good clean and she couldn't take her eyes off the shapely young man in the tan slacks with no shirt, showing his manly chest. I found out later she had invited the 'hunk' in for a glass of lemonade and they ended up having wine and sex. This little affair went on for almost three-years while I was away at work, paying for their wine and pool time. The boys were in school, giving their dear mother seven-hours to fool around with her playboy!"

"Yet, you let her remain with you Richard, after all her cheating." Jesus knew all. "Again, Cindy begged you not to kick her out, just for the boys. They needed both parents in their lives and you could not be there for them like she could. You knew the love affair with Harold continued and even after both your sons went off to college, you put Cindy and Harold up in your guest house."

"By then, Cindy had gotten cancer and it would come and go. As long as Harold could have sex with her, he stayed on while I paid for everything." Richard recalled her last attack of the deadly disease. "I had started seeing a lot of different women just for sex and it became an obsession with me. Then after taking Cindy to the doctor for her results, she learned she didn't have long to live and it had gone into her female organs. Harold had slipped away in the night without even saying goodbye to the woman he had possessed for nearly twenty-four years and Cindy cried in my arms until there were no tears left. Both boys refused to come home to be with their mother after walking in on her and Harold in bed, so I put the booze away to stay sober for Cindy's final days on earth."

"Cindy was afraid of dying, wasn't she Richard and your good heart knew she needed some kind of assurance to believe." Jesus had witnessed this man's words and he needed him to say them again for Maggie's sake.

"You're right Lord. I had never seen Cindy so scared as she talked about going into a black hole to total darkness and there would be nothing!" Richard couldn't control the tears that pooled in his eyes. "My lips started moving and I could hear the words I was saying. Words that held comfort not words of getting even, like, now it's your time to suffer. I said, 'Cindy, you will never go into this darkness of forever if you believe in Jesus, the Son of God, who came down from heaven to save all who would believe in Him and that He died on that cross for our sins. Cindy, we never spoke about God or faith in this family and now our two sons have left and our chances for helping them know the truth is lost. But Cindy, there is still hope for you, pretty girl. Open up your heart to Jesus and ask Him to forgive you and take you home to heaven.' Then I remembered my adopted parents telling me how beautiful heaven was., so I shared it with Cindy. 'My parents told me all about heaven Cindy and its as real as you and I are. I know, because Russel told me and Russel would never tell me a lie like I did him.'"

"Then, you gave Cindy the hope she needed and your words brought back her life when she too went to church every Sunday with her parents and learned the things you reminded her of about me." Jesus touched Richard's face. "Richard, Cindy did ask me to forgive her and gave me her thanks for having you in her life, asking me to watch over you and help find Maggie to place back in your life. You stayed by her side, hugging her like she wanted until she closed her eyes in death and opened them up to feel my arms around her in everlasting life. Now Richard, its your turn. Is there anything you want to say before you rise in pain?"

"You're right Lord, Russel's words were embedded inside me and when I needed them the most, they reserviced." Richard felt his tears running down his face. "I felt the kind of love my adopted parents had for one-another in my Maggie. There was no longer the need for just sex with her. She made me come to life, to feel something I had never encountered before and just being with her gave me purpose and I knew without a doubt I needed Maggie in my life forever. A love that powerful could not just happen without a divine being behind it." Richard gazed up into the eyes of his Savior. "I knew I was right the moment you first touched me, Lord. I felt that same majestic love, fill my whole senses. I am ready to face my pains Lord and if its death that comes for me, then as long as I am in your loving arms my Savior, I will go gladly, knowing I shall see my Maggie one day in heaven. Please forgive me Lord for all my sins and even though I tried to hide you away, I am so glad you would not allow my dumb choices to win."

Jesus stood up and held out his arms for Richard, who rose up on steady legs, all pain completely swept away. "Son, you have been forgiven and made whole. Your kidneys have been restored to new. Now, before we go, have you anything else to say?"

"My first hope is that Maggie finds happiness with the one meant for her and my other question, although unusual is, when those paramedics looked back for the patient and I'm no longer there, what will they think happened? That the heavy winds blew their patient out the open door?" Richard paused when he not only heard the Lord laugh, but the sound of a young lady's laugh. "Lord, did I hear a lady laughing or are the angels laughing because old Richard Hackler finally came to the truth?"

"You most certainly heard a young lady laughing at your funny remark, but tis no angel you heard." Jesus gave Richard a beautiful smile. "As for the two in the ambulance, they were never aware you had ever been the patient lying in wait for them. Another customer from the bar had a light heart attack and the ambulance driver has already made it back to the hospital." Jesus smiled at the young lady who had become visible while Jesus had Richard's attention. "Now son, you have someone here to welcome you back into her heart."

Richard closed his eyes in thankful prayer and softly said her name. "Maggie, it was your laugh I heard." His eyes met hers and the love between them drew them together in a warm embrace. No words needed to be spoken, for the love that radiated from their faces said what their hearts were feeling. When they finally heard their names spoken by Uncle James, they noticed they were standing inside the cottage, surrounded by all the family. Soon wedding bells would once again ring out for Richard and Maggie.

CHAPTER 28

Maggie and Richard Hackler left on their honeymoon and two-weeks later came back with the joyful news that Maggie was expecting a baby. To the happy couple's delight, they learned they were not the only couple blessed with a new addition. Bella had met them first jumping up and down with joy over the news that she was going to get a little brother in nine months. Everyone was rejoicing with the good news, everyone but Sarah, who once again felt the sting of being barren. She slipped away unnoticed to be alone and once again ask the Lord to give her strength to get through their happy-ever-after life while she would never know the joy of having a baby of her own.

James had found his wife missing and excused himself to go and check on her, causing Maggie and Beth to pause and walk to the stairs and gaze up.

"Oh Beth, I let my joy override my compassion for Sarah. How can she be feeling right now, seeing you and me aglow with motherhood and her unable to have the son she wants so badly?"

"I knew everyone was trying to keep Sarah busy doing things, but I never dreamed she was having difficulty over not being able to have children." Beth draped her arm around her new friend. "Sometimes adopting a baby at childbirth is close to being your own. Surely someone with a heart as loving as Sarah could except an innocent unwanted baby."

"Beth, it's not that easy in Sarah and James's case." Uncle James had watched his nephew run up the steps, worried about his wife and he had overheard Maggie and Beth's conversation regarding his precious niece. "James, like me, has been chosen to be a caretaker of the Miracle Bench that sets safely inside the Sacred Garden, where you and Bella were led by the Lord. Ever since the first caretaker received the bench as a gift from his brother Jesus, James, the first-born son of Joseph and Mary, had a revelation that the caretakers that followed him must hold the name James and remain in the Jesu family until the Lord returns on his final entry."

"But, you are James's uncle so if you're saying Sarah and James must have a son to name James, could not another cousin or brother of James have the son, named James?" Beth didn't know anything about any of the family's extended family except for Simon's brother.

"If it were only that simple." Uncle James glanced up the quiet staircase. "My brother just had the one boy and knowing my beloved wife couldn't have children, I asked him to name his son James. The only cousins we can find are all female and the Jesu name has stopped with my young nephew. Now you see why Sarah is so upset over being barren. James needs a son and I believe with all my heart that our gracious loving Lord will grant him and Sarah the miracle they need to carry on the legacy of James."

"Forgive me if I'm overstepping what I need to know, but just how long has this tradition for the caretaker's job been going on Uncle James?" Beth had been a recipient of the miracle bench where Jesus healed her but she didn't know much about this beautiful secret place, hidden from most of the world. "If the Lord gave the bench to his brother James, then the bench had to be someplace in Israel. So, how on earth did it get here to America?"

"All perfectly reasonable questions Beth and as one of our newest family members I'll try to make it plain." Uncle James needed to assure Beth of things relating to heavenly power instead of man's way of thinking. The tradition for all caretakers to be named James started over two-thousand-years ago, just outside of Nazareth in the peaceful countryside. For many years it remained there, gathering in those lost souls in desperate need of healing. The very first being James himself. Not from any kind of illness but the constant battle that went on inside his mind and heart, trying to reason with his feeling just who his eldest brother really was. When the final truth was revealed to James, he set out making the Sacred Garden the place you see today, along with this beautiful old cottage we all call home."

"Are you saying Jesus's brother James actually built this stone cottage we are standing in, as well as creating the secret garden surrounded by incredible cedar trees?" Beth felt dumbfounded over James's revelation.

"He did, my dear and he trained his son James to take over for him as caretaker after his death." Uncle James glanced up and could hear voices upstairs and knew his nephew was comforting his wife.

217

"Long before James departed this earth, he had a revelation from God asking him to keep the job of caretaker in the family line and have every generation name one son James, to be trained for caretaker at the appointed time." The oldest James knew her last question regarding how a garden and now a cottage to boot, managed to make its way to America. "As the years past, things began to grow dangerous for the Jewish nation and many wars started and the holy lands became unstable. Then years later the biblical accounts describing what would happened became a reality when Israel became surrounded by their enemy and still are, to this day.

The last caretaker to live in Nazareth had also been a highly religious man who had studied the bible throughout his long life and knew it well. He remembered reading about a new land of freedom so with continued prayer, the ninety-seven-year-old James Jesu got his answer. The Almighty Jehovah would deliver the Sacred estate to a new home where many different nationalities would come to seek this new-found freedom." Uncle James closed his eyes in a prayer-like state as he concluded. "Then on July the 4th, 1776, the Lord performed his miracle and the Sacred Estate found its new home in the humble state of North Carolina."

"Then, we are living on hallowed ground." Richard had come looking for his new bride and heard Uncle James's statements. He looked around at the small group who all seemed to look with interest up the flight of stairs where James and Sarah stayed. "Is there something going on I should know? Did either Sarah or James get sick or something?"

"Richard, you too are new to our family, so you are unaware of Sarah's condition. She is feeling a lot of pressure right now because her doctor informed her about being unable to have children." James glance over at the latest member. "We are all concerned over her unstable emotions and learning both Maggie and Beth are expecting babies, she has gone back into her depression state. James is upstairs trying again to assure his beautiful-loving wife, that God knows their needs and He will supply a son for them."

"So, James is wanting a son and the poor-unfortunate young lady cannot deliver." Richard rubbed his head, somewhat puzzled. "There are other means to have children when a wife is incapable of getting pregnant. Surely James will understand so the poor darling can stop worrying."

"Like Beth, you are not aware that James and I are both caretakers of the Sacred Garden. The very spot where you were healed by Jesus. You sat on the very bench the Lord made in the carpenter's shop where he worked beside of Joseph, His earthly father."

"You don't say! Jesus made the bench I rested on and couldn't feel a single pain while on it!" Richard paused, still unsure of the couple's reasons for needing Sarah to have their baby. "So, you and your nephew are the caretakers of the Miracle Bench and both your names are James. Couldn't James and Sarah just adopt a baby boy and name him James?"

"Again, it's not that simple Richard. All caretakers must be blood kin and in the Jesu line, so this son name James must come from my nephew's seed."

Maggie lit up, an ideal springing into her head. "Maybe I can give them the baby they need Uncle James! I would have to get your permission first Richard, but I know it can be the solution they're after!"

"Maggie darling, this little baby you're carrying is from my seed darling, so even though I thought for one second I would let you give them our baby boy, which I would not, it could not work!" Richard had made his way beside his wife and held her in his arms. "James has to supply the seed, remember?"

"Richard, I am not referring to our little bundle of joy, he will be forever your baby boy. I am talking about after I have had our little Richie and had time to wend him. James can provide his seed to be embedded in me, then pray it's a boy!"

"Maggie" everyone stopped and looked up to see James and Sarah waiting on the steps. "That is about the most selfless gift any one has ever offer me." Sarah let James lead her down to hug the young woman who had already helped her in so many warm beautiful ways and now she was offering to carry a baby for them so Sarah could stop worrying and feeling like a failure. "Maggie, you have already showed me so much kindness and now this." Sarah noticed Richard was holding tight to his wife. "Richard, you have a very special young lady there to offer us such a wonderful answer to our prayers, but you are her husband Richard, and nothing can be done without your approval."

James pulled Sarah back into his arms and touched Maggie's

sweet face. "Maggie, Sarah is right about you having such a giving heart and I cannot thank you enough for the beautiful offer, but the Lord wants my son to be a part of my wife. Sarah is struggling right now and what she really needs from you Maggie" James looked around when Simon stepped up where he had been listening. "From all of you, dear family, is your many prayers, asking the Lord to watch after her until He blesses Sarah with a baby of her own."

CHAPTER 29

The months went by and the three wives grew close, helping one another with the various jobs that needed doing at the cottage. Uncle James and Sarah's husband, James, kept busy being caretakers as well as pastors. When uncle and nephew didn't have a healing by the Lord, they would carry on with their various church work, assisting local ministers and filling in when a minister needed to be away. Now that they were full-time caretakers of the Sacred Garden and Miracle Bench, they had to give up pastoring their own churches. Simon and Richard kept busy doing all the outdoor labor, along with any maintenance that needed doing both inside and outside the large cottage. There was never a shortage of labor, but the loving group made working together a pleasure and always felt blessed and rewarded whenever a job had been completely and well done.

Young Bella got all the attention she needed and with a house full of adoring playmates, no matter their age, her young life was always filled with rewarding surprises, like her big sixth surprised birthday party. Coming back from her long hike with her mama and daddy, the happy child screamed with delight when she came inside to find colored balloons floating from the ceiling and presents piled up on a nearby table. Bella was plum giddy when she saw her big birthday cake with her name and age in frosted colors on the top after the words, Happy Birthday!"

"Oh, happy day!" Bella giggled. "This is my 3rd best day ever!"

Beth had watched how excited the family had made her little girl and it warmed her heart. Then Bella's last remark made her pause. "Bella, what were your other two best days?"

"My number 1 best day mommy was when I saw Jesus and he made me and you all better!" The little girl beamed. "My 2nd best day was when Jesus brought Simon back in your life and gave me a daddy!"

Simon reached down and scooped her up into his arms. "Come here my little angel! That is the way my best days stack up too! My number 1 best day was when Jesus helped me and my brother Jason mend our troubled hearts and the 2nd best day was when I received my beautiful two girls, your mommy and you Bella. Being the birthday girl's daddy is truly a blessing."

"And your little Bella has brightened up many a day in all of our lives as well!" Uncle James stood behind the punchbowl smiling. "And when everyone is ready to sample my great new punch recipe, I'll be happy to pour you a cup."

"Mumm! I love punch Uncle James?" Bella wiggled down from Simon's arms after giving him a kiss, then ran to the punch bowl and picked up an empty cup to hold out. After everyone had their punch, Bella blew out her six candles after closing her eyes to inwardly make a wish, then blew them out in one big buff. Happily eating her cake, Bella heard someone in the group ask her what she had wished for.

"If I tell you my wish, then it might not come true" Bella glanced at Sarah, whose eyes had dropped down over everyone joyful celebration. "And, this is one wish I really want to happen, for someone I love very much."

James had been observing where the small girl was looking and it brought a sweet sense of assurance in his worried soul.

Things had gone fairly well for Sarah until Maggie and Beth started to show their baby bump and as the weeks turned into months, both expectant mothers knew their baby would be arriving any day. Sarah, with the help of all the men, when available, had to take over all the heavy housework and do most of the cooking. Like Maggie, Sarah began to learn the basics of preparing a hearty meal that could easily feed their big family. She knew after the babies were born, she would also be needed to help the new mothers care and feed their newborns.

The doctor had been called in to give both mothers home deliveries, so once again Sarah had been asked to assist her family doctor, Kelly Brandon, with both deliveries. Everyone had assumed if Sarah remained busy she wouldn't have time to get depressed over two new arrivals when she hadn't delivered one and never could.

Like a good trooper, Sarah worked diligently, trying to keep busy and not think of what she could never have, a baby like the sweet infants she was handing their grateful mothers. Sarah could only dwell on being in her beloved James's way and if she were out of his life, he could, in time, find someone else to love and have his family with.

Made by the Master's Hand

As Sarah stood at the laundry room sink washing out the cloths and towels she and Doctor Brandon had used, Sarah's thoughts once again turned to her plan to take her own life so James could move on. Sarah had planned it out to the last detail, so no one would find her missing until it was too late. She had everything she needed stored away ready to grab whenever the perfect opportunity came. Hearing the happy fathers making over their newborns only convinced the troubled young lady that she had delayed her plan long enough. She knew to leave the man she loved heart broken, would never come easy, so the sooner she got it over with, the better it would be for them both.

The perfect time did finally arrive. James and his uncle had to leave on a weekend trip to a church conference in a nearby town and Sarah had been observing how both new families went up to bed every evening earlier than usual, due to having small infants to care for. After bidding them all goodnight, Sarah walked quickly up to their quarters and locked her door. Now determined to go through with her plan, believing her chances for giving childbirth were over, Sarah took out a sheet of her stationary and sat down to write James a farewell letter.

"My darling James, even though I know my words will be difficult for you to read, they must be said so you can move on with your life. It would appear the hope I once held for receiving that miracle you and Uncle James spoke of so frequently has vanished from my heart and soul. Do not get me wrong dearest one, my belief in our loving Lord still remains in my troubled heart and soul. I only hope my Savior will take pity on me and forgive that thing which I must do to set you free to marry again and have that precious little boy you desire so much. It was never an easy choice for me to make my love, because to leave your side not having your arms to hold me or your lips to kiss me, breaks my heart into a trillion pieces. If the pieces of a broken heart could float up into space, then the very stars that fill up the universe would have to make room beside them for each broken piece. I pray God will comfort you James when I am gone from you and that He will guide you to that one special girl that can fill your broken heart with a new love. So, if I am forgiven, my beloved James, I shall see you again in heaven. So, this is not goodbye, its simply, I'll be seeing you beyond the clouds of earth. I love you James and I always will. Forever, your Sarah."

Joan Byrd

Sarah slipped down the dark steps and made her way quietly out the back door. Knowing she was now safe from prying eyes, Sarah switched on the flashlight in her hand and slowly started her journey down the garden path that led to the old pond. As she made her way slowly her thoughts turned to that morning in bed, before her beloved husband had to leave her for his conference. A soft smile graced her lips as she recalled how romantic he had been and the extra-long time they had made love before he finally had to get ready to leave. Had James somehow felt she needed him even more that morning because they would be apart for two-days or did he sense something was amiss concerning the woman he adored and loved with all his heart. Could his last words to her be a clue of his feelings? She thought.

THE MORNING BEFORE

"Sarah, I feel as though I should stay here, with you darling?" James had gotten ready in a fog, feeling there was something not quite right with his wife. The sudden calmness where she had been jumpy and anxious over every little thing. It looked like one minute she had a problem, then the next minute, all seemed settled and forgotten. "I'm sure Uncle James can make excuses for me."

"James darling, don't be silly. I will be fine. It's a sure thing I will not be along with four adults, two small babies and one precious little girl moving through the house." Sarah got up from her chair to give her husband a hug. "When I do finally get to myself, I'll have plenty of time to remember all that wonderful loving you and I had this morning." Her fingers played in his thick dark hair "My James was some 'hot lover' boy!"

James finally gave her a smile before kissing her. "it was very special this morning darling, not that it isn't always, with my hot lover girl next to me. It just felt different this morning. Exactly like it felt on our wedding night, only better." James reached for his suit coat and slipped in it. "Who knows Sarah, that special feeling could have been the moment we made our baby." Sarah recalled her husband's playful wink before he stepped out, and that was the last time she thought she would ever look into his handsome face again.

All the thoughts that had filled her head concerning James had suddenly led her to the pond, where she planned to slip off into it once she fell unconscious from the strong pills and vodka. Sarah moved carefully down the deep slope leading to the banks of the

224

deep pond and once there, she sat down, tears welling in her beautiful eyes.

"Forgive me Lord but I know I must give my life for James's sake so your tradition can carry on. It is the one thing I can give my beloved husband, so even though my heart breaks for departing from my darling James, I do it out of love. I cannot give him a son but I can set him free to marry again." Sarah opened the bag of pills after taking the vodka cap off, she took a distasteful sip. "For my beloved James freedom. Just live on James darling and be happy!" Sarah poured the pills in her mouth and swallowed down half the vodka before everything started spinning around in front of her. Sarah felt her eyelids growing very heavy and soon, she knew she would fall into a deep sleep where she could never come out. But, before Sarah's eyes shut tight, she heard a small voice nearby calling out.

"Mommy, don't go to sleep mommy! I need you! Please mommy, wake up!"

CHAPTER 30

Sarah tried to open her eyes wider, but found it hard. All she could see in front of her was a blur, but she knew the voice was very close-by. She forced her fingers to move since no sound could come from her unfeeling lips. Her mind turning around in circles with thoughts. "Am I hallucinating? Surely Bella didn't follow me here?"

"Mommy, I am your son, please believe me mommy! I have not been born yet mommy but if you die I will go back into heaven! Daddy will be sad mommy, to lose both of us!"

"My son?" Sarah realized she had spoken, even though it came out very weak. "What is your name son? Do you know yet?"

"In heaven where our little souls wait with God, we know everything mommy. My name will be James, after my father!" there was a hint of laughter in his small voice. "Jesus told me I would be working for Him when I grow up, beside my father James." Then Sarah heard a sniffle. "But, if you die mommy, I can never grow up. Please sat up mommy and make the bad medicine and strong drink go away!"

"My sweet little boy, it's too late, I have already swallowed the pills and I cannot change what I have done!" Sarah lifted her arms to her face and started weeping, pulling herself up into a crunched position. As she cried, she spoke through her tears, "James was right all alone! That beautiful feeling we had this morning really did create our baby boy! Please Lord, only you can save me now from my foolish actions! I should never have doubted you and your giving miracles!"

"Then arise, Sarah, and follow the light!" This time Sarah knew she had just heard the voice of the Lord, so she looked up and saw she was seated in the rose garden instead down by the deep pond. "You have learned a great lesson Sarah and if your faith is strong you can stand and walk, then follow my light to the Sacred Garden."

"The Sacred Garden?" Sarah had instantly stood when the Lord gave her His command and she knew going to the garden meant Jesus would be healing her without the caretakers being present.

"You are concern over James being present to witness your

healing." The voice was soft and filled with love. "It was for this reason I sent both James' away, Sarah. This is one healing that will remain between me and thee."

"There is none as wise and perfect as you are Jesus. I shall gladly follow you to your Miracle bench I have heard so many beautiful things about." Now it was Sarah speaking to her Lord with complete love. "All the people of your world can never thank you enough for everything you have done for us!"

"Sarah, you are a wise and beautiful woman of great faith and that is why I chose you for James Jesu." The loving voice of Jesus created a guiding light around him. "You have just been lost for a while but soon you may know happiness from the joyful news I will bring to you. Just follow me Sarah and I will lead you to the bench."

Walking in the light of Jesus was a special joy in itself as Sarah walked easily behind until she found herself standing in front of the bench. As she beheld the smooth inviting bench that waited in front of her, Sarah recalled James telling her how long ago, Jesus had built it in the carpenter's shop where He had worked beside his earthly Father Joseph. Suddenly she felt guilty for trying to take her own life and the very thought knowing just how close she came to dying if she had not heard the child's voice. Was he real or did she only imagine it being her little boy. Sarah felt so embarrassed she didn't feel she deserved to even touch the Lord's bench, much less sat down on it.

"Sarah, it would please me very much for you to have a seat on this bench I made, just for this purpose." Sarah looked around and gasp at the heavenly man standing tall over her. His whole appearance was glowing, seemingly by his incredible smile. His majestic blue-green eyes sparkled with the lights of heaven. With a trembling hand, Sarah reached back to feel the bench and took a seat, then immediately she began feeling a peaceful-loving feeling float up through her. She realized she no longer felt sluggish. Sarah sat up straight, alert and ready to be healed.

"Sarah, you felt guilty for your sinful act and this made you feel unworthy to touch something your Savior made. My beloved, do not you remember how I died on the cross for that sin, among other little ones, you may recall, but I cannot. The day you excepted me as your Savior and asked me to forgive you for all your sins, I took those sins away to myself and buried them, to never be seen again." The

Lord joined Sarah on the bench, moving her to lift up his nail-pierce hand and gently kiss it, as her grateful tears fell on Him. The loving Lord wrapped his arms around her as he spoke. "Yes Sarah, I can feel your thankful heart within me. Now, to answer your question about the small boy's voice being real. Yes Sarah, it was the soul spirit of your son James asking his mother to wake up and not die. You see, the sweet child was already planted inside you Sarah. Your beloved James did feel something special when you both made love this morning. Heaven's Dove delivered the soul of baby James from heaven just when James planted his seed into your revived womb."

Sarah could not control her tears as she wept for joy over the astounding news given by the Lord. "Jesus, my loving Lord, this was the joyful news you spoke of that would bring me happiness! Praises and Glory is thine, most gracious and generous King!" Sarah recalled the Lord telling her He deliberately sent James away. "Jesus, did you send my husband away because you didn't want him to be hurt by my bad choice?"

"This was not the reason for my not wishing either caretaker to be here Sarah." Jesus stood up. "You were chosen to be the mother of a caretaker, much like Sarah was chosen to be the mother of the heir to the Israelites and Elisabeth was chosen to be the mother of John the Baptist. Rachael was chosen to be the mother of Joseph, whose brothers sold him and he became great in Egypt and saved the nation of Israel. You four were all barren, unable to have children. But the Almighty God had chosen all of you for His purpose Sarah. Just like Abraham's wife, Zechariah's wife, Jacob's wife and now you Sarah, James's wife, all have been blessed by a divine miracle. Since this was a heavenly plan from the beginning, your story does not need to be written into this book. This was one reason the caretakers were not needed." Jesus gave Sarah another amazing smile. "The second reason I chose to tell you first was so you would be able to share this wonderful miracle yourself with your beloved. He should be coming inside the garden anytime now, for my messenger has returned to inform me of his arrival."

"James is coming inside here? But his meeting wasn't supposed to end until tomorrow night." Sarah had mixed emotions with James finding her inside the Sacred Garden with Jesus. Surely, he would guess what she had tried to do.

"Sarah, not tried to do." Sarah looked up, now with new

concern. "Yes child, you had taken enough drugs that turned lethal when mixed with alcohol and you did die." Jesus took her into his arms when she burst into tears. "I lifted you back up out of death and gave your son his words for you to wake up. Sarah, James knows everything but take comfort in knowing he was told by a caring spirit. Open your eyes Sarah and look upon my shoulder, the third part of us has led James here."

Sarah looked up and saw the white dove aglow on the glowing shoulders of her Lord and Savior. Then she heard the soft voice of the one she had given her heart to in marriage say her name.

"Sarah, my beautiful darling!" James grabbed her and held her tight. "Thank God you are alright! The heavenly Dove brought me your farewell letter and if it had not been for his power and tender guidance, I don't know what I would have done!" James looked up at two of the Holy Trinity. "My never-ending thanks Lord! You save my beloved and brought her back from death!"

"Sarah was lost for a while James, but she has come back to us and soon all this night will be forgotten except one beautiful revelation." Jesus held out his hands for Sarah, then he gave her one last hug. "I shall leave you now to share your joys with your husband sweet Sarah. Sweet Peace to you both." Jesus and the heavenly Dove were gone, leaving the flame of the Holy Spirit burning inside each Christian's soul living inside the stone cottage.

Sarah took James's hand and gave him a bright smile. "The Lord is right James darling. I have come back and I have never felt as happy as I do right now!" She couldn't resist her laughter. "James Jesu, you are about to become a father of a little son, to be born in nine months from this morning!"

"This morning!" James let out a shout for joy. "I knew it! Don't ask me how Sarah, but it just felt like something amazing happened this morning! And it did! Praise God, it did!" The young minister's eyes fell on the bench. "Sarah, I have seen some amazing stories that happened from lost-hurting souls and how our Lord Jesus healed them after He led them here, to this bench. This Miracle Bench that was made by the Master's hand!"

229

Joan Byrd

THE AUTHOR REFLEXS ON EVERYTHING THAT WAS MADE BY THE MASTER'S HAND

When Patrick informed me that we would be writing another book for the Lord, I felt overjoyed and waited for the title to be revealed. When he said MADE BY THE MASTER'S HAND, I immediately thought of Jesus's time working with His earthly Father Joseph in the carpenter's shop in Nazareth. Jesus probably started learning his carpenter skills at a very young age, around six-years-old. He would work there beside Joseph until his ministry started at the age of thirty so, that would mean our Lord labored building things for twenty-four-years. The last three-years of His short life was devoted to his ministry. His death on the Roman cross was the end of Jesus's human life on earth, but the Lord Jesus's resurrection on the first day of the week, our Holy Sabbath, revealed the risen Christ was in the same body, for He IS GOD!

Then being human and being God made everything Jesus touch immortal. It is a known fact that Jesus worked as a carpenter most of His human life. For twenty-four years our Lord MADE THINGS WITH HIS HANDS. All sorts of items, both big and small, from candle sticks to garden benches, wooden bowls, lampstands, decorative boxes, wooden chest, and many other various objects and furniture from the time period. So, these many things that have been touched by our Lord can and will be preserved forever, just like all the many other things our Creator has made, starting with the earth and everything in and around it.

An example of some items already found and are now preserved in safe keeping are remnants of the manger the baby Jesus was laid in, a board from the Roman cross where our Lord and Savior was nailed too, the actual wooden sign that Pilate ordered placed over Jesus's cross, a Roman nail, thought to belong to Jesus's cross, and the actual stairs that Jesus walked up three time to stand next to Pilate. Traces of blood was found on the steps, and was thought to be the blood of Jesus after Pilate order Him flogged with forty lashes. All of these items, that would have been touched by our Lord Jesus, have remained on earth for over two-thousand-years and they are all inside several of the church's that set inside the Vatican City.

The one-thousand, two-hundred-year-old St. Peters Basilica set on Vatican Hill in Rome until the Catholic Church built the new St. Peters Cathedral around it and the smaller chapels surrounding the Vatican City. All the found relics listed above are inside the Vatican and thousands of visitors come to witness the things that have been touched by the master.

If you are like me, you probably never considered all the beautiful treasures our Lord left behind until you read this. Once again, the Almighty Lord has revealed to me something that has stayed hidden for over two-thousand-years. Who knows if perhaps someone has found an old wooden candle holder with no markings, or had some un-known maker's beautiful wooden vase past down from one generation to the next. Whatever the Lord touches is eternal so wouldn't it be a blessing to find that miracle, that was MADE BY THE MASTER'S HAND!